W9-AHO-109

Nada

Carmen Laforet

N<u>ADA</u>

A new translation by Edith Grossman

Introduction by Mario Vargas Llosa

THE MODERN LIBRARY

NEW YORK

LIBRARY OF CONGRESS CATALOGING-IN-PUBLICATION DATA
Laforet, Carmen.
[Nada. English]
Nada: a novel/Carmen Laforet; translated from the Spanish
by Edith Grossman. — 1. ed.
p.   cm.
ISBN 978-0-679-64345-6
I. Grossman, Edith   II. Title.
PQ6621.A38N313 2007
863'.64—dc22   2006046656

3078

INTRODUCTION

TWO GIRLS

Mario Vargas Llosa

Until I came to Spain in 1958, I don't think I had read any contemporary Spanish writers living in the Iberian Peninsula because of a prejudice as widespread in the Latin America of those years as it was unjust: Everything published *over there* reeked of fustiness, sacristy, and Francoism. Which is why I didn't know until now the tender, asphyxiating story of Andrea, the small-town adolescent who arrives, full of hopes, in the grayish Barcelona of the early 1940s to study literature, a story that Carmen Laforet narrates in prose both exalted and icy, in which what is unspoken is more important than what is said, keeping the reader of the novel submerged in indescribable anguish from beginning to end. In this detailed autopsy of a girl imprisoned in a hungry, half-crazed family on Calle de Aribau, there is not the slightest political allusion except, perhaps, a passing reference to churches burned during the Civil War. And yet, politics weighs on the entire story like an ominous silence, like a spreading cancer that devours and destroys everything: the university purged of life and fresh air, the bourgeois families calcified in good manners and visceral putrefaction, the confused youngsters who don't know what to do or where to look to escape the rarefied atmosphere in which they languish from boredom, privations, prejudices, fears, provincialism, and a limitless confusion.

With admirable mastery, on the basis of sketchy anecdotal notes and very brief descriptive touches, an overwhelmingly depressing landscape emerges that appears to be a conspiracy of the entire universe to frustrate Andrea and keep her, and almost everyone around her, from being happy.

In the world of *Nada*—the unsurpassable title says everything about the novel and the city where it takes place—there are only the rich and the poor, and like a third-world country, the middle class is a thin, shrinking membrane and, like Andrea's family, has half its being sunk into that plebian jumble where workers, beggars, vagabonds, the unemployed, and the marginalized commingle, a world that horrifies the middle class and that it tries to keep at bay by means of fierce prejudices and delirious fantasies. Nothing exists beyond the small larval world that surrounds the characters; even the little bohemian enclave that Andrea sometimes visits, created in the old district by young painters who would like to be rebellious, insolent, and modern but don't know how, is parochial and something of a caricature.

But it is, above all, in the area of love and sex where the characters in *Nada* seem to live outside reality in a mysterious galaxy in which desires do not exist or have been repressed and channeled into compensatory activities. If in almost every aspect of life the world of the novel reveals an inhumanly prudish morality that alienates men and women and impoverishes them, it is in the area of sexuality that the distortion reaches incredible proportions and, in many cases, is surely the hidden explanation of the neuroses, the bitterness, the uneasiness, the vital disquiet of which almost all the characters are victims, including Ena, the vivacious and emancipated friend whom Andrea admires and envies.

Did Carmen Laforet, a girl in her twenties when she wrote this, her first novel, suspect that in it she portrayed, implacably and lucidly, a society brutalized by lack of freedom, censorship, prejudices, hypocrisy, and isolation, and that in the story of her poignant creation, Andrea, the ingenuous girl who is scandalized when "a kiss is stolen" from her, she exemplified a case of desperate, heroic resistance to oppression? Perhaps not—perhaps all of that was the result, as so often happens in good novels, of intuition, divination, and the authenticity with which she tried, as she wrote, to capture an elusive, dangerous truth that could be expressed only in the labyrinths and symbols of fiction. She achieved this, and half a century after it was published, her beautiful, terrible novel still lives.

—*translated by Edith Grossman*

TRANSLATOR'S NOTE

A few historical clarifications may be in order, since the period evoked by Carmen Laforet is now some seventy years in the past.

The war referred to throughout the novel is the Spanish Civil War (1936–39), often called a dress rehearsal for World War II, in part because it allowed Germany, Italy, and the USSR the opportunity to test and improve weapons and battle tactics.

The background to the conflict is, very briefly, this: King Alfonso XIII gave up the throne and a republic was voted into power in Spain in 1931. The liberal-left government provoked the enmity of the right, which included the Spanish Church (an especially reactionary institution within worldwide Roman Catholicism), monarchists, landowners, and supporters of the Falange, the Spanish Fascist party founded on the Italian model in 1933 by the charismatic José Antonio Primo de Rivera, son of Miguel Primo de Rivera, military dictator under the monarchy from 1923 to 1930. The republic was torn by factional strife among liberal republicans, socialists, communists (Stalinists and Trotskyists), and anarchists (a significant political movement in Spain, and particularly powerful in Barcelona).

In 1936, General Francisco Franco, commander of Spanish forces in Morocco, invaded Spain from Africa in collaboration with three other generals, in a military insurgency aimed at overthrowing the republic. The country divided, often on the basis of the loyalties of the local military commanders. The ensuing violence reached savage proportions and took on international ramifications when Franco's forces received assistance from Fascist Italy and Nazi Germany, and the Soviet Union used its aid to the republic to manipulate the domestic situation in favor of the Spanish Communist Party. With the exception of Mexico and France, which provided limited support to the Spanish Republic, the western powers maintained a deadly neutrality. Finally, in 1939, the last remnants of the republican forces were defeated, and Franco took power and held it until his death in 1975.

Supporters of the legitimate government were called Republicans, Loyalists, or Reds; supporters of Franco were called Nationalists, Rebels, Falangists, or Fascists. It has been claimed that a million Spaniards died in the Civil War. Vicious atrocities were committed against both civilians and combatants. The destruction of property, including the bombing of cities and other civilian targets by the Germans and Italians and the burning of churches on the ground by Loyalist soldiers, was catastrophic. Fighting and reprisals were notably ferocious in Barcelona, where Republican factions seemed to despise one another more passionately than they hated the enemy.

George Orwell wrote unforgettably about the conflict in Barcelona in *Homage to Catalonia*. Hugh Thomas's *The Spanish Civil War* is a fascinating, beautifully researched history of the war. Ernest Hemingway's fictional account, *For Whom the Bell Tolls*, has become an American classic.

EDITH GROSSMAN
New York, 2006

To my friends

Linka Babecka de Borrell

and

the painter Pedro Borrell

NADA

(fragment)

Sometimes a bitter taste,
A foul smell, a strange
Light, a discordant tone,
A disinterested touch
Come to our five senses
Like fixed realities
And they seem to us to be
The unsuspected truth . . .

JUAN RAMÓN JIMÉNEZ

PART ONE

I

Because of last-minute difficulties in buying tickets, I arrived in Barcelona at midnight on a train different from the one I had announced, and nobody was waiting for me.

It was the first time I had traveled alone, but I wasn't frightened; on the contrary, this profound freedom at night seemed like an agreeable and exciting adventure to me. Blood was beginning to circulate in my stiff legs after the long, tedious trip, and with an astonished smile I looked around at the huge Francia Station and the groups forming of those who were waiting for the express and those of us who had arrived three hours late.

The special smell, the loud noise of the crowd, the invariably sad lights, held great charm for me, since all my impressions were enveloped in the wonder of having come, at last, to a big city, adored in my daydreams because it was unknown.

I began to follow—a drop in the current—the human mass that, loaded down with suitcases, was hurrying toward the exit. My luggage consisted of a large bag, extremely heavy because it was packed full of books, which I carried myself with all the strength of my youth and eager anticipation.

An ocean breeze, heavy and cool, entered my lungs along with my first confused impression of the city: a mass of sleeping houses, of closed establishments, of streetlights like drunken sentinels of solitude. Heavy, labored breathing came with the whispering of dawn. Close by, behind me, facing the mysterious narrow streets that led to the Borne, above my excited heart, was the ocean.

I must have seemed a strange figure with my smiling face and my old coat blown by the wind and whipping around my legs as I guarded my suitcase, distrustful of the obsequious "porters."

I remember that in a very few minutes I was alone on the broad sidewalk because people ran to catch one of the few taxis or struggled to crowd onto the streetcar.

One of those old horse-drawn carriages that have reappeared since the war stopped in front of me, and I took it without thinking twice, arousing the envy of a desperate man who raced after it, waving his hat.

That night I rode in the dilapidated vehicle along wide deserted streets and crossed the heart of the city, full of light at all hours, just as I wanted it to be, on a trip that to me seemed short and charged with beauty.

The carriage circled the university plaza, and I remember that the beautiful building moved me as if it were a solemn gesture of welcome.

We rode down Calle de Aribau, where my relatives lived, its plane trees full of dense green that October, and its silence vivid with the respiration of a thousand souls behind darkened balconies. The carriage wheels raised a wake of noise that reverberated in my brain. Suddenly I felt the entire contraption creaking and swaying. Then it was motionless.

"Here it is," said the driver.

I looked up at the house where we had stopped. Rows of identical balconies with their dark wrought iron, keeping the secrets of the apartments. I looked at them and couldn't guess which ones I'd be looking out of from now on. With a somewhat tremulous hand I gave a few coins to the watchman, and when he closed the building door behind me, with a great rattling of wrought iron and glass, I began to climb the stairs very slowly, carrying my suitcase.

Everything felt unfamiliar in my imagination; the narrow, worn mosaic steps, lit by an electric light, found no place in my memory.

In front of the apartment door I was overcome by a sudden fear of waking those people, my relatives, who were, after all, like strangers to me, and I hesitated for a while before I gave the bell a timid ring that no one responded to. My heart began to beat faster, and I rang the bell again. I heard a quavering voice:

"Coming! Coming!"

Shuffling feet and clumsy hands sliding bolts open.

Then it all seemed like a nightmare.

In front of me was a foyer illuminated by the single weak light-bulb in one of the arms of the magnificent lamp, dirty with cobwebs, that hung from the ceiling. A dark background of articles of furniture piled one on top of the other as if the household were in the middle of moving. And in the foreground the black-white blotch of a decrepit little old woman in a nightgown, a shawl thrown around her shoulders. I wanted to believe I'd come to the wrong apartment, but the good-natured old woman wore a smile of such sweet kindness that I was certain she was my grandmother.

"Is that you, Gloria?" she said in a whisper.

I shook my head, incapable of speaking, but she couldn't see me in the gloom.

"Come in, come in, my child. What are you doing there? My God! I hope Angustias doesn't find out you've come home at this hour!"

Intrigued, I dragged in my suitcase and closed the door behind me. Then the poor old woman began to stammer something, disconcerted.

"Don't you know me, Grandmother? I'm Andrea."

"Andrea?"

She hesitated. She was making an effort to remember. It was pitiful.

"Yes, dear, your granddaughter.... I couldn't get here this morning the way I wrote I would."

The old woman still couldn't understand very much, and then through one of the doors to the foyer came a tall, skinny man in pajamas who took charge of the situation. This was Juan, one of my uncles. His face was full of hollows, like a skull in the light of the single bulb in the lamp.

As soon as he patted me on the shoulder and called me niece, my grandmother threw her arms around my neck, her light-colored eyes full of tears, and saying "poor thing" over and over again....

There was something agonizing in the entire scene, and in the apartment the heat was suffocating, as if the air were stagnant and rotting. When I looked up I saw that several ghostly women had appeared. I almost felt my skin crawl when I caught a glimpse of one of them in a black dress that had the look of a nightgown. Everything about that woman seemed awful, wretched, even the greenish teeth she showed when she smiled at me. A dog followed her, yawning noisily, and the animal was also black, like an extension of her mourning. They told me she was the maid, and no other creature has ever made a more disagreeable impression on me.

Behind Uncle Juan appeared another woman who was thin and young, her disheveled red hair falling over her sharp white face and over the languor that clung to the sheets, which increased the painful impression made by the group.

I was still standing, feeling my grandmother's head on my shoulder, held by her embrace, and all those figures seemed equally elongated and somber. Elongated, quiet, and sad, like the lights at a village wake.

"All right, that's enough, Mamá, that's enough," said a dry, resentful-sounding voice.

Then I realized there was yet another woman behind me. I felt a hand on my shoulder and another lifting my chin. I'm tall, but my Aunt Angustias was taller, and she obliged me to look at her like that. Her expression revealed a certain contempt. She had graying hair that fell to her shoulders and a certain beauty in her dark, narrow face.

"You really kept me waiting this morning, my girl! . . . How could I imagine that you'd arrive in the middle of the night?"

She'd let go of my chin and stood in front of me with all the height of her white nightgown and blue robe.

"Lord, Lord, how upsetting! A child like this, alone . . ."

I heard Juan grumble. "Now Angustias is ruining everything, the witch!"

Angustias appeared not to hear him.

"All right, you must be tired. Antonia"—and she turned to the woman enveloped in black—"you have to prepare a bed for the señorita."

I was tired, and besides, at that moment I felt horribly dirty. Those people moving around or looking at me in an atmosphere darkened by an accumulation of things crowded together seemed to have burdened me with all the trip's heat and soot that I'd forgotten about earlier. And I desperately wanted a breath of fresh air.

I observed that the disheveled woman, stupefied by sleep, smiled as she looked at me and also looked at my suitcase with the same smile. She obliged me to look in that direction, and my traveling companion seemed somewhat touching in its small-town helplessness. Drab and tied with rope, it sat beside me, at the center of that strange meeting.

Juan approached me:

"Andrea, don't you know my wife?"

And he pushed at the shoulders of the woman with uncombed hair.

"My name's Gloria," she said.

I saw that my grandmother was looking at us with a worried smile.

"Bah, bah! . . . What do you mean by shaking hands? You have to embrace, girls . . . that's right, that's right!"

Gloria whispered in my ear:

"Are you scared?"

And then I almost was, because I saw Juan making nervous faces, biting the inside of his cheeks. He was trying to smile.

Aunt Angustias came back, full of authority.

"Let's go! Everybody get to sleep—it's late."

"I wanted to wash up a little," I said.

"What? Talk louder! Wash up?"

Her eyes opened wide with astonishment. Angustias's eyes and everybody else's.

"There's no hot water here," Angustias said finally.

"It doesn't matter. . . ."

"You'd dare to take a shower this late?"

"Yes," I said. "Yes."

What a relief the icy water was on my body! What a relief to be away from the stares of those extraordinary beings! It felt as if in this house the bathroom was never used. In the tarnished mirror over the sink—what wan, greenish lights there were everywhere in the house!—was the reflection of the low ceiling covered with cobwebs, and of my own body in the brilliant threads of water, trying not to touch the dirty walls, standing on tiptoe in the grimy porcelain tub.

That bathroom seemed like a witches' house. The stained walls had traces of hook-shaped hands, of screams of despair. Everywhere the scaling walls opened their toothless mouths, oozing dampness. Over the mirror, because it didn't fit anywhere else, they'd hung a macabre still life of pale bream and onions against a black background. Madness smiled from the bent faucets.

I began to see strange things, like someone intoxicated. Abruptly I turned off the shower, that crystalline, protective magic spell, and was left alone in the midst of the filthiness of things.

I don't know how I managed to sleep that night. In the room they gave me was a grand piano, its keys uncovered. A number of gilt mirrors with candelabra attached—some of them very valuable—on the walls. A Chinese desk, paintings, ill-assorted furniture. It looked like the attic of an abandoned palace; it was, as I later found out, the living room.

In the center, like a grave mound surrounded by mourners—a double row of disemboweled easy chairs—was a divan covered by a black blanket, where I was to sleep. They had placed a candle on the piano because there were no lightbulbs in the large chandelier.

Angustias took her leave of me by making the sign of the cross on my forehead, and my grandmother embraced me tenderly. I felt her heart beating like a little animal against my chest.

"If you wake up and are afraid, call me, my child," she said in her tremulous little voice.

And then, in a mysterious whisper into my ear:

"I never sleep, child, I'm always doing something in the house at night. I never, ever sleep."

Finally they left, leaving me with the shadows of furniture that the candlelight exaggerated and filled with quivering, profound life. The stench noticeable throughout the house came into the room in a stronger gust. It was the stink of cat. I felt that I was strangling, and in a dangerous alpinist feat I climbed onto the back of a chair to open a door I could see between dusty velvet curtains. I accomplished my aim to the extent the furniture would allow and saw the door led to one of those open galleries that give so much light to houses in Barcelona. Three stars were trembling in the soft blackness overhead, and when I saw them I felt a sudden desire to cry, as if I were seeing old friends, encountered unexpectedly.

That illuminated twinkling of the stars brought back in a rush all my hopes regarding Barcelona until the moment I'd entered this atmosphere of perverse people and furniture. I was afraid to get into the bed that resembled a coffin. I think I was trembling with undefinable terrors when I put out the candle.

II

At dawn, the bedclothes were on the floor in a jumble. I was cold and pulled them up over my body.

The first streetcars were beginning to cross the city, and on one of them I could hear the clanging bell, muffled by the closed house, the way I could that summer when I was seven and had made my last visit to my grandparents. I immediately had a hazy perception, but one as vivid and fresh as if it had come to me with the scent of a recently cut fruit, of the Barcelona in my memory: this sound of the first streetcars, when Aunt Angustias would cross in front of my improvised little bed to close the blinds that were letting in too much light. Or at night, when the heat didn't let me sleep and the clatter came up the slope of Calle de Aribau, while the breeze carried in the scent of the branches of green, dusty plantains under the open balcony. And Barcelona was broad sidewalks damp after being washed down, and a great number of people drinking at a café. . . . All the rest, the large, brightly lit stores, the cars, the bustle, even the ride the day before from the station, which I'd added to my idea of the city, was something pale and false, constructed artificially, just as things that have been worked and handled too much lose their original freshness.

Without opening my eyes, I once again felt a warm wave of good fortune. I was in Barcelona. I had heaped too many dreams onto this concrete fact for that first sound of the city not to seem a miracle, telling me so clearly it was a reality as true as my body or the rough touch of the blanket against my cheek. I thought I'd had bad dreams, but now I was resting in this joy.

When I opened my eyes I saw my grandmother looking at me. Not the little old woman of the previous night, small and wasted, but a woman with an oval face behind the small tulle veil of a hat in the style of the previous century. She smiled very gently, and the blue silk of her dress had a tender palpitation. Next to her, in the shadows, my grandfather, very handsome, with his heavy chestnut-brown beard and blue eyes under straight eyebrows.

I'd never seen them together during that period in their life, and I was curious to know the name of the artist who had signed the paintings. That's how the two of them had looked when they came to Barcelona fifty years ago. There was the long, difficult history of their love—I couldn't remember exactly what it was . . . perhaps something connected to the loss of a fortune. But in those days the world was optimistic and they loved each other very much. They were the first tenants in this apartment on Calle de Aribau, which was just beginning to take shape then. There were still a good many empty lots, and perhaps the smell of earth brought memories to my grandmother of a garden somewhere else. I imagined her in the same blue dress, the same charming hat, walking for the first time into the empty apartment that still smelled of paint. *I'd like to live here,* she must have thought when she saw empty spaces through the windows. *It's almost in the outskirts, and it's so quiet! And the house is so clean, so new. . . .* Because they came to Barcelona with a hope contrary to the one that had brought me: They wanted rest, and secure, methodical work. The city I thought of as the great change in my life was their safe haven.

The apartment with its eight balconies was filled with curtains—lace, velvet, bows; the trunks spilled out their trinkets, some of them valuable. Ornate clocks gave the house its vital pulse, and a piano—how could there not be one?—its languid Cuban airs at twilight.

Though not very young, they had many children, like in stories. . . . In the meantime, Calle de Aribau was growing. Buildings as tall as this one and even taller formed its dense, broad blocks. The trees stretched their branches and the first electric streetcar added its peculiar characteristics. The building was aging, renovations were made, there were several changes in owners and porters, and they continued like an immutable institution in their first apartment.

When I was the only grandchild, I spent the most exciting times of my childhood there. The house was no longer quiet. It had been enclosed by the heart of the city. Lights, noises, the entire tide of life, broke against those balconies with their velvet curtains. Inside it was overflowing, too; there were too many people. For me the uproar was wonderful. All my aunts and uncles bought me candies and rewarded me for mischief I did to other people. By then my grandparents had white hair, but they were still strong and they laughed at all my tricks. Could all this be so distant?

I had a feeling of uncertainty about everything that had changed there, and this feeling intensified a good deal when I had to think about confronting the people I'd glimpsed the night before. *What are they like?* I was thinking. And I stayed in bed, hesitating, not daring to face them.

In the light of day the room had lost its horror, but not its awful disorder, its absolute abandonment. The portraits of my grandparents hung crooked and frameless on a dark-papered wall with damp stains, and a sunbeam was climbing up toward them.

It made me happy to think that the two of them had been dead for years. It made me happy to think that the young woman in the tulle veil had nothing to do with the little unrecognizable mummy who had opened the door for me. But the truth was that she was living, however lamentably, among the piles of useless furniture that had accumulated over time in her house.

Three years ago, when my grandfather died, the family had decided to keep only half the apartment. The old trinkets and excess furniture formed a veritable avalanche, which the workmen responsible for plastering over the connecting door had piled up at random. And the house had remained in the provisional disorder they'd left behind.

On the chair I had climbed the night before, I saw a cat with matted fur licking its paws in the sun. The creature looked ruinous, like everything surrounding it. The cat stared at me with large eyes, apparently endowed with their own individuality, something like brilliant green glasses placed above its snout and graying whiskers. I rubbed my eyes and looked again. The animal arched its back, and its spine was prominent in its skinny body. I couldn't help thinking that it bore a singular familial resemblance to the rest of the people in the house; like them, it had an eccentric appearance and seemed spiritualized, as if it had been consumed by long fasts, a lack of light, and perhaps periods of meditation. I smiled and began to dress.

When I opened the door of my room, I found myself in the gloomy, crowded foyer into which almost all the rooms in the house converged. Across from me I saw the dining room, its balcony open to the sun. On my way I stumbled over a bone, stripped clean, surely by the dog. No one was in the room except for a parrot, ruminating over private matters, almost laughing. I always believed that animal was crazy. At the most inopportune moments it would screech in a hair-raising way. There was a large table, an empty sugar bowl abandoned on top of it. On a chair, a faded rubber doll.

I was hungry, but there was nothing edible except for what was painted in the many still lifes that covered the walls, and I was looking at them when Aunt Angustias called to me.

My aunt's room connected with the dining room and had a balcony facing the street. She was sitting, her back to me, at a small desk. I stopped in astonishment when I saw the room, because it looked clean and orderly, as if it were a world apart from that house. A mirrored armoire and a large crucifix blocked another door that led to the foyer; beside the bed there was a telephone.

My aunt turned her head to observe my astonishment with a certain satisfaction.

We were silent for a while and from the door I initiated a friendly smile.

"Come, Andrea," she said. "Sit down."

I noticed that in the light of day Angustias seemed to have swelled, acquiring masses and forms under her green housecoat, and I smiled to myself, thinking that in first impressions my imagination had played bad tricks on me.

"My child, I don't know how you've been brought up. . . ."

(From the beginning, Angustias spoke as if preparing to make a speech).

I opened my mouth to respond, but she interrupted with a movement of her finger.

"I know you did part of your *bachillerato* in a secondary school run by nuns and stayed there during most of the war. That, for me, is a guarantee. But . . . those two years you spent with your cousin—your father's family has always been very strange—in a small town: What must that have been like? I won't deny, Andrea, that I've spent the night worried about you, and thinking. . . . The task that has fallen into my hands is very difficult. The task of looking after you, of molding you in obedience . . . Will I succeed? I think so. It's up to you to make that easier for me."

She didn't allow me to say anything and I swallowed her words in surprise, not understanding very well.

"Cities, my child, are hell. And in all of Spain no city resembles hell more than Barcelona. I'm concerned about your coming from the station alone last night. Something could have happened to you. People live on top of one another here; they ambush one another.

Total prudence in one's conduct is not enough, for the devil disguises himself in tempting ways.... A young girl in Barcelona must be like a fortress. Do you understand?"

"No, Aunt."

Angustias looked at me.

"You're not very intelligent, my girl."

Again we were silent.

"I'll say it another way: You're my niece; therefore, you're a girl of good family, well behaved, Christian, and innocent. If I don't concern myself with everything that has to do with you, you'll encounter a multitude of dangers in Barcelona. And so I want to tell you that I won't allow you to take a step without my permission. Do you understand now?"

"Yes."

"Good. Now let's move on to another issue. Why have you come?"

I answered quickly:

"To study."

(On the inside, my entire being was shaken by the question.)

"To study literature—is that it? ... Yes, I've already gotten a letter from your cousin Isabel. All right, I won't oppose that, but only as long as you know that you owe everything to us, your mother's family. And that thanks to our charity, you'll achieve your goals."

"I don't know if you know ..."

"Yes; you have an allowance of two hundred pesetas a month, which these days isn't enough to take care of even half your expenses.... Haven't you won a scholarship to the university?"

"No, but I have free matriculation."

"That isn't because you deserve it—it's because you're an orphan."

Once again I was confused, then Angustias resumed the conversation in a surprising way.

"I have to let you know a few things. If it didn't hurt me to speak ill of my brothers, I'd tell you that since the war they've been troubled by their nerves. ... Both of them suffered a great deal, my

child, and my heart suffered with them.... They repay me with in-
gratitude, but I forgive them and pray for them. Still, I have to put
you on your guard...."

She lowered her voice until she had reached a murmur that was
almost tender:

"Your uncle Juan has married an absolutely inappropriate
woman. A woman who is ruining his life. Andrea, if I find out one
day that you are her friend, you can be certain I'll be very dis-
pleased, and very sorry...."

I sat facing Angustias on a hard chair that dug into my thighs
under my skirt. I was desperate, too, because she'd said I couldn't
make a move without her permission. And without any compassion, I judged her to be not very bright, and authoritarian. I've made
so many bad judgments in my life that I still don't know if that one
was correct. What's certain is that when she became tender in order
to speak ill of Gloria, my aunt seemed very hateful to me. I thought
that perhaps it wouldn't be unpleasant to displease her a little, and
I began to observe her out of the corner of my eye. I saw that her
features, taken together, weren't ugly and her hands even had a
very beautiful shape. I looked for some repugnant detail in her as
she continued her monologue of commands and advice, and at last,
when she was about to let me go, I saw the dirty color of her teeth.

"Give me a kiss, Andrea," she said at that moment.

I brushed her hair with my lips and rushed to the dining room
before she could trap me and kiss me in turn.

By now people were in the dining room. I immediately saw Gloria, who, wrapped in an old kimono, was feeding spoonfuls of thick
pap to a baby. When she saw me, she smiled and said hello.

I felt oppressed, as if I were under a sky heavy with storms, but
apparently I wasn't the only one who had the dusty taste of nervous
tension in her throat.

A man on the other side of the table, with curly hair and an amiable, intelligent face, was busy oiling a pistol. I knew he was another

of my uncles: Román. He came over right away to embrace me with a great deal of affection. The black dog I'd seen behind the maid the night before followed his every step. He said the dog's name was Trueno and that it belonged to him; animals seemed to have an instinctive affection for him. Even I felt touched by a wave of pleasure at his affectionate exuberance. In my honor, he took the parrot from the cage and had it do a few tricks. The bird was still murmuring something as if talking to itself; then I realized they were curses. Román laughed, wearing a happy expression.

"The poor creature is very used to hearing them," he said. In the meantime, Gloria looked at us, enthralled, forgetting about her son's pap. Román then changed so brusquely that I was disconcerted.

"But have you seen how stupid that woman is?" he said, almost shouting, and not looking at her at all. "Have you seen how *that one* looks at me?"

I was astonished. A nervous Gloria shouted:

"I don't look at you at all, *chico.*"

"Do you see?" Román kept talking to me. "Now that piece of trash has the gall to talk to me."

I thought my uncle had gone mad, and I looked in terror toward the door. Juan had come in when he heard their voices.

"You're provoking me, Román!" he shouted.

"You—keep your shirt on and shut up!" said Román, turning toward him.

Juan approached, his face contorted, and the two of them assumed the posture, at once ridiculous and sinister, of fighting cocks.

"Go on, man, hit me if you dare!" said Román. "I'd like to see you try!"

"Hit you? I'll kill you! . . . I should have killed you a long time ago. . . ."

Juan was beside himself, the veins in his forehead bulging, but he didn't move forward. His fists were clenched.

Román looked at him calmly and began to smile.

"Here's my pistol," he said.

"Don't provoke me. Swine! . . . Don't provoke me or . . ."

"Juan!" Gloria shrieked. "Come here!"

The parrot began to scream, and I saw that Gloria was excited under the disheveled red hair. No one paid attention to her. Juan looked at her for a few seconds.

"Here's my pistol!" Román was saying, and Juan clenched his fists even tighter.

Gloria shrieked again:

"Juan! Juan!"

"Shut up, you bitch!"

"Come here, *chico*! Come on!"

"Shut up!"

Juan's rage swerved for an instant toward his wife, and he began to insult her. She shouted, too, and finally burst into tears.

Román watched them in amusement; then he turned toward me and said, to reassure me:

"Don't be frightened, little one. This happens here every day."

He put the gun in his pocket. I looked at it shining in his hands, black, carefully oiled. Román smiled at me and patted my cheeks; then he left calmly, while the argument between Gloria and Juan became more and more violent. In the doorway Román bumped into my grandmother, who was coming back from her daily Mass, and he caressed her as he passed. She came into the dining room at the very moment that Aunt Angustias, who was angry, too, came in to demand silence.

Juan picked up the little boy's dish of pap and threw it at her head. He had bad aim and the dish shattered against the door that Aunt Angustias had quickly closed. The baby was crying and drooling.

Then Juan began to calm down. Granny took off the black shawl that covered her head and sighed.

And the maid came in to set the table for breakfast. As she had done the night before, this woman drew all my attention. Her ugly face wore a defiant, almost triumphant expression, and she hummed provocatively as she spread the tattered tablecloth and began to set down cups as if, in this way, she were bringing the argument to a close.

III

"Did you have a good time, dear?" Angustias asked me when, still dazzled by the light, we walked into the apartment after being out.

As she asked the question, her right hand grasped my shoulder and pulled me toward her. When Angustias embraced me or called me by affectionate names, I had the feeling deep inside that there was something crooked and wrong in the way things were going. That it wasn't natural. Still, I should have been used to it because Angustias embraced me and used endearments with great frequency.

Sometimes I thought she was obsessed with me. She circled around me. She'd look for me if I took refuge in some corner. When she saw me laughing, or interested in the conversation of anybody else in the house, her words became humble. She'd sit beside me and force me to rest my head on her breast. My neck would hurt, but held down by her hand, I'd have to stay that way while she admonished me gently. When she thought I was sad or frightened, however, she'd become very happy and authoritarian again.

At other times I'd be secretly embarrassed when she obliged me to go out with her. I'd watch her firmly pull down a dark brown felt hat trimmed with a rooster feather, which gave her hard features a warlike air, and she'd oblige me to wear an old blue hat above my badly cut suit. At that time I couldn't conceive of any resistance other than a passive one. Held by her arm, I walked along the streets that seemed less brilliant and less fascinating than I had imagined.

"Don't turn your head," Angustias would say. "Don't look at people like that."

If I did forget that I was beside her, it was only for a few minutes. Sometimes I'd see a man, a woman, who had something interesting, indefinable in their appearance, and who carried my imagination away with them until I wanted to turn and follow them. Then I'd remember how I looked, and how Angustias looked, and I'd blush.

"You're very uncouth and very provincial, my child," Angustias would say with a certain satisfaction. "Surrounded by people, you're silent and awkward, always looking like you want to escape. Sometimes, when we're in a store and I turn to look at you, you make me laugh."

Those trips around Barcelona were sadder than anyone could imagine.

When it was time for supper, Román would detect the outing in my eyes and laugh. This was the prelude to a poisonous argument with Aunt Angustias in which Juan eventually became involved. I realized he always supported Román's arguments, though Román never accepted or thanked him for his help.

When something like this happened, Gloria would emerge from her usual placidity. She'd become nervous and almost shout:

"If you're capable of talking to your brother, don't talk to me!"

"Of course I'm capable! You must think I'm as rotten as you are, as he is!"

"Yes, my child," my grandmother would say, enfolding him in a look of adoration, "you're doing the right thing."

"Be quiet, Mamá, and don't make me curse at you! Don't make me curse!"

The poor woman shook her head and leaned toward me, mumbling into my ear:

"He's the best of them, my child, the best and the most unfortunate, a saint. . . ."

"Would you please not get involved, Mamá? Would you please not bother our niece's head with nonsense she doesn't care anything about?"

By now, having lost control of his nerves, his tone was harsh and disagreeable.

Román, involved in turning the fruit on his plate into a treat for the parrot, finished supper not paying attention to any of us. Aunt Angustias sobbed beside me, biting her handkerchief, because she not only saw herself as strong and capable of leading multitudes, but also as sweet, unfortunate, and persecuted. I don't really know which of the two roles she liked more. Gloria moved the baby's high chair away from the table, stood behind Juan, smiled at me, and raised her index finger to her temple.

Juan, withdrawn and silent, seemed agitated, ready to explode.

When Román finished his task, he patted my grandmother's shoulder a few times and left before anyone else. At the door he stopped to light a cigarette and fire off his final remarks:

"Even your imbecile of a wife makes fun of you now, Juan; be careful. . . ."

As usual, he hadn't looked at Gloria even once.

The result was not long in coming. A fist banging on the table and a string of insults directed at Román that didn't stop when the abrupt sound of the apartment door announced that Román had already left.

Gloria picked up the baby and was going to her room to put him to sleep. She looked at me for a moment and proposed:

"Coming, Andrea?"

Aunt Angustias's face was in her hands. I could feel her gaze through partially opened fingers. A distressed gaze, dry with much pleading. But I stood up.

"All right, yes."

And my reward was a tremulous smile from my grandmother. Then my aunt locked herself in her room, indignant and, I suspect, trembling with jealousy.

Gloria's room was something like the lair of a wild animal. It was an interior room almost entirely filled by a double bed and the baby's cradle. There was a special kind of stink, a mixture of the smells of an infant, of face powder, of clothing not well cared for. The walls were covered with photographs, and among them, in a prominent spot, a vividly colored postcard showing two kittens.

Gloria sat on the edge of the bed with the baby on her lap. The baby was good-looking and his little legs hung down, fat and dirty, as he dozed off.

When he was asleep, Gloria put him in the crib and stretched with pleasure, running her hands through her brilliant hair. Then, with her languid gestures, she lay down on the bed.

"What do you think of me?" she often asked me.

I liked talking to her because there was never any need to respond.

"Aren't I pretty and very young? Aren't I?" She had a foolish, ingenuous vanity that I never found unpleasant; besides, she actually was young and knew how to laugh madly as she told me about the things that went on in the house. When she talked about Antonia or Angustias, she was really amusing.

"You'll find out about these people; they're terrible, you'll see. . . . Nobody here is good except maybe Granny, and the poor thing's half crazy. . . . And Juan, Juan's very good, *chica*. Do you see how he yells so much and everything? Well he's very, very good. . . ."

She looked at me, and when she saw my reserved expression she began to laugh. . . .

"And I am, too, don't you think?" she concluded. "If I wasn't, Andreíta, how could I stand all of them?"

I watched her move and talk with inexplicable pleasure. In the heavy atmosphere of her room she lay on the bed like a rag doll whose red hair weighed too much. For the most part she'd tell me humorous lies mixed in with real events. I didn't think she was intelligent, or that her personal charm came from her spirit. I believe my fondness for her had begun on the day I saw her posing naked for Juan.

I'd never gone into the room where my uncle worked, because Juan inspired a certain wariness in me. One morning I went in to look for a pencil, on the advice of my grandmother, who told me I'd find one there.

The appearance of the large studio was very curious. It had been set up in my grandfather's old office. Following the tradition of the other rooms in the house, in it, with no order or arrangement, was an accumulation of books, papers, and plaster figures that served as models for Juan's students. The walls were covered with harsh still lifes painted by my uncle in strident colors. In one corner, inexplicably, an anatomy student's skeleton hung on its wire frame, and on the large rug stained with damp spots the baby crawled with the cat, which had come in for the golden sun from the balconies. The cat, with its flaccid tail, looked moribund, and feebly allowed itself to be tormented by the baby.

I saw all of this around Gloria, who sat naked and in an uncomfortable posture on a stool draped in curtain fabric.

Juan painted laboriously and without talent, attempting to reproduce, brush stroke by brush stroke, that slender, elastic body. It seemed like a useless task to me. What appeared on canvas was a cardboard doll as stupid as the expression on Gloria's face when she heard any conversation between Román and me. Gloria, in front of us, without her shabby dress, looked incredibly beautiful and white in the midst of all that ugliness, like a miracle of God. A spirit both sweet and malevolent quivered in the graceful form of her legs, her arms, her fine breasts. A subtle, diluted intelligence along the warm surface of her perfect skin. Something that never shone in her eyes.

This call of the spirit that attracts us in exceptional people, in works of art.

I had gone in only for a few seconds but stood there, fascinated. Juan seemed happy with my visit and spoke quickly about his pictorial projects. I didn't listen to him.

That night, almost without realizing it, I found myself starting a conversation with Gloria, and it was then that I went to her room for the first time. Her insubstantial chatter seemed like the sound of rain that one listens to lazily, with pleasure. I became accustomed to her, to her rapid unanswered questions, to her narrow, devious mind.

"Yes, yes, I'm good . . . don't laugh."

We were silent. Then she came closer to ask me:

"And Román? What do you think of Román?"

Then she made a special face to say:

"I know you think he's nice, don't you?"

I shrugged. After a moment she said:

"You think he's nicer than Juan, don't you?"

One day, unexpectedly, she began to cry. She cried in a strange way, disjointed and fast, wanting to get it over with quickly.

"Román's an evil man," she said. "You'll find out about him. He's done me terrible harm, Andrea." She dried her tears. "I won't tell you all the things he's done to me because there are too many of them; you'll find out in time. Now you're fascinated by him and won't even believe me."

To be honest, I didn't think I was fascinated by Román; almost the opposite—I often examined him coldly. But on the rare nights that Román became amiable after supper, which was always stormy, and asked me: "Are you coming, little one?" I felt happy. Román didn't sleep in the same apartment as the rest of us: He'd fixed up a room in the attic of the house, which turned out to be a comfortable refuge. He'd put in a fireplace made of old bricks and some low bookcases painted black. He had a divan, and beneath the small jalousied window a very pretty table covered with papers, and inkwells from different periods and in different shapes with quill pens inside them. A rudimentary telephone served, he said, to communicate with the maid's room. There was also a small ornate clock that struck the hour with a charming, distinctive chiming of bells. There were three clocks in the room, all of them old, rhythmically embellishing time. On the bookcases, coins, some of them very unusual; little Roman lamps from the late period; and an antique pistol with a mother-of-pearl handle.

The room had unexpected spaces between the shelves of the bookcases, and all of them held small curiosities that Román gradually showed to me. Despite the quantity of diminutive objects, everything was clean and in relatively good order.

"Things are comfortable here, or at least that's what I'm trying to achieve. . . . I like things," and he smiled. "Don't think I'm attempting to be original, but it's the truth. Downstairs they don't know how to treat them. It seems that the air is always filled with shouting . . . and the things are responsible for that, they're asphyxiated, grief-stricken, heavy with sadness. As for the rest of it, don't make up any novels about it: Our arguments and shouting don't have a cause, and they don't lead to any conclusion. . . . What have you begun to imagine about us?"

"I don't know."

"I know you're always dreaming up stories with us as characters."

"No."

Román, in the meantime, had plugged in the espresso coffeepot and brought out, from where I don't know, magic cups, glasses, and liquor; after that, cigarettes.

"I know you like to smoke."

"No; I don't like it."

"Why do you lie to me, too?"

Román's tone was always frankly curious where I was concerned.

"I know very well everything your cousin wrote to Angustias. . . . In fact, I read the letter, without any right to, of course, just out of curiosity."

"Well, I don't like smoking. In the village I did it just to annoy Isabel and for no other reason. To shock her, so she'd let me come to Barcelona because I was impossible."

Since I was flushed and annoyed, Román only half believed me, but what I told him was true. Finally I accepted a cigarette because his were always wonderful and I did like their aroma. I believe those were the times when I began to find pleasure in smoke. Román smiled.

I realized that he thought I was a different kind of person, much more cultivated, perhaps more intelligent, and of course hypocritical and filled with strange longings. I didn't want to disillusion him because I felt vaguely inferior, a little insipid, with my dreams and my burden of sentimentality, which I tried to hide from those people.

Román had enormous agility in his slender body. He spoke to me as he squatted beside the coffeepot, which was on the floor, and he seemed wound up, filled with springs beneath his dark muscles. Then, suddenly, he was on the divan, smoking, his features relaxed as if time had no meaning, as if he never had to get up. Almost as if he had lain down to die smoking.

Sometimes I looked at his hands, dark, like his face, full of life and nervous currents, slender, with fine knuckles. Hands that I liked very much.

Still, sitting on the only chair in the room, in front of his work-table, I felt very distant from him. The sense of being carried away by his likeability, which I had when he spoke to me the first time, never returned.

He prepared marvelous coffee, and the room would fill with warm fumes. I felt at ease there, as if it were a calm retreat from the life downstairs.

"It's like a sinking ship. We're the poor rats who don't know what to do when we see the water. . . . Your mother avoided the danger before anybody else by leaving. Two of your aunts married the first men who came along so they could get away. The only ones who stayed were your wretched Aunt Angustias and Juan and I, who are two reprobates. And you, a little rat gone astray but not as unfortunate as she appears, now you've come. . . . Tell me, don't you want to make some music today?"

Then Román opened the little cabinet at the end of the bookcases and took out the violin. At the back of the cabinet were a few rolled-up canvases.

"Can you paint, too?"

"I've done everything. Don't you know that I began studying medicine and left it, that I wanted to be an engineer and never applied for admission? I also began to paint as a hobby. . . . I was much better than Juan, I assure you."

I didn't doubt it: I thought I saw in Román an endless store of possibilities. At the moment when, standing next to the fireplace, he began to move the bow, I changed completely. My reservations, the light coating of hostility toward all of them that had been forming on me, disappeared. My soul, extended like my own hands, received the sound as if it were rain on dry ground. Román seemed a marvelous, unique artist. He wove in the music a joy so fine that it went beyond the limits of sadness. That nameless music. Román's music, which I've not heard again since that time.

The small window opened to the dark night sky. The light of the lamp made Román taller and more immobile, only breathing in his music. And it came to me in waves: first, innocent memories, dreams, struggles, my own vacillating present, and then, sharp joys, sorrows, despair, a significant contraction of life, a negation into nothing. My own death, the feeling of my total despair turned into beauty, an anguished harmony without light.

And suddenly an enormous silence and then Román's voice.

"You could be hypnotized. . . . What does the music say to you?"

Immediately my hands and soul closed up.

"Nothing, I don't know, I just like it. . . ."

"That's not true. Tell me what it says to you. What it says to you at the end."

"Nothing."

He looked at me for a moment, disappointed. Then, as he held the violin:

"That's not true."

He shone my way down with his flashlight because the stairs could be lit only from the porter's room, and I had to go down three floors to our apartment.

On the first day I had the impression that someone was going down ahead of me, in the dark. I thought it was childish and didn't say anything.

On another day the impression was even stronger. Suddenly, Román left me in the dark and focused the flashlight on the part of the stairs where something was moving. I saw a clear, fleeting glimpse of Gloria running downstairs toward the porter's room.

IV

So many unimportant days! The unimportant days that had gone by since my arrival weighed on me as I dragged my feet on the way back from the university. They weighed on me like a square gray stone on my brain.

The weather was wet and the morning smelled of clouds and damp tires. . . . Lifeless yellow leaves fell from the trees in a slow rain. An autumn morning in the city, just as I had dreamed for years that autumn in the city would be: beautiful, with nature entwined along the flat roofs of the houses and the trolley poles of the street-cars; and still, I was enveloped in sadness. I wanted to lean against a wall with my head on my arms, turn my back on everything, and close my eyes.

So many useless days! Days filled with stories, too many troubled stories. Incomplete stories, barely started and already swollen like an old piece of wood left outdoors. Stories too dark for me. Their smell, the rotting smell of my house, caused a kind of nausea in me. . . . And yet they had become the only interest in my life. Gradually, before my very eyes, I had begun to occupy a second plane of reality, my senses open only to the life seething in the apartment on

Calle de Aribau. I grew accustomed to forgetting about my appearance and my dreams. The smell of the months and visions of the future were losing their importance, while each of Gloria's expressions, each hidden word, each of Román's insinuations, grew to gigantic proportions. The result seemed to be this unexpected sadness.

When I walked into the house it began to rain behind me, and the porter shouted at me to wipe my feet on the mat.

The entire day had passed like a dream. After lunch I sat huddled in my chair, my feet in large felt slippers, next to my grandmother's brazier. I listened to the sound of the rain. With their force the streams of water were cleaning the dust from the windows to the balcony. At first they had formed a sticky layer of grime; now the drops slid freely along the shiny gray surface.

I didn't want to move or do anything, and for the first time I missed Román's cigarettes. Granny came to keep me company. I saw that she was trying to sew one of the baby's outfits with clumsy, trembling hands. Gloria came over a short while later and began to chat, her hands crossed at the back of her neck. Granny talked, too, as always, about the same topics. Recent events, like the war, and distant ones, from many years ago, when her children were little. In my head, which ached a little, their two voices combined in a ballad with a background of rain, and made me drowsy.

GRANDMOTHER: "There were never two brothers who loved each other more—are you listening, Andrea? There were never two brothers like Román and Juanito. . . . I've had six children. The other four were always up to something, the girls quarreled among themselves, but those two little boys were like two angels. . . . Juan was blond and Román very dark, and I always dressed them alike. On Sundays they went to Mass with me and your grandfather. . . . At school, if some boy fought with one of them, the other was always there to defend him. Román was more mischievous . . . but how they loved each other! All her children should be the same to a mother, but I cared for those two more than the others . . . since they were the youngest . . . since they were the unluckiest. . . . Especially Juan."

GLORIA: "Did you know that Juan wanted to be in the military, and when he failed the entrance exam for the Academy he went off to Africa, in the Foreign Legion, and was there for years?"

GRANDMOTHER: "When he came back he had a lot of pictures. . . . Your grandfather got angry when he said he wanted to be a painter, but I defended him and so did Román, because back then, my child, Román was a good man. . . . I always defended my children, tried to hide their mischief and their pranks. Your grandfather would get angry with me, but I couldn't stand it when he scolded them. . . . I'd think: 'You catch more flies with a spoonful of honey.' . . . I knew they went out carousing at night, that they didn't study. . . . I'd wait for them, shaking with fear that your grandfather would find out. . . . They'd tell me about their pranks, and nothing surprised me, my dear. . . . I had faith that gradually they'd find the good, urged on by their own hearts."

GLORIA: "Well, Román doesn't love you, Mamá; he says the way you acted ruined all of them."

GRANDMOTHER: "Román? . . . Ha, ha! Of course he loves me, I know he loves me . . . but he's more spiteful than Juan and he's jealous of you, Gloria; he says I love you more. . . ."

GLORIA: "Román says that?"

GRANDMOTHER: "Yes; the other night, when I was looking for my scissors—it was very late and all of you were sleeping—the door opened very slowly and there was Román. He was coming to give me a kiss. I told him: 'What you're doing with your brother's wife is wicked; it's a sin God won't be able to forgive. . . .' And then he left. . . . I told him: 'It's your fault the girl is miserable, and your brother's suffering, too, because of you. How can I love you the same as I did before?'"

GLORIA: "Román used to love me a lot. And this is a huge secret, Andrea, but he was in love with me."

GRANDMOTHER: "Child, child. How could Román be in love with a married woman? He loved you like a sister, that was all. . . ."

GLORIA: "He brought me to this house. . . . He did—and now he

won't talk to me; he brought me here in the middle of the war.... It
scared you the first time you came in here, didn't it, Andrea? Well it
was much worse for me.... Nobody loved me...."

GRANDMOTHER: "I loved you, we all loved you—why are you
so ungrateful when you talk?"

GLORIA: "Everybody hungry, as dirty as it is now, and a man
hiding because they were hunting him down to kill him: Angustias's
boss, Don Jerónimo; didn't anybody tell you about him? Angustias
gave him her bed and she slept where you are now.... They put
down a mattress for me in Granny's room. Nobody trusted me. Don
Jerónimo didn't want to talk to me because he said I was Juan's mistress and he found my presence intolerable...."

GRANDMOTHER: "Don Jerónimo was a strange man; imagine,
he wanted to kill the cat.... You see, the poor animal is very old and
it vomited in the corners, and he said he couldn't stand it. But naturally I defended it against everybody, the way I always do when
somebody's persecuted and sad...."

GLORIA: "I was just like that cat and Mamá protected me. Once
I hit that maid, Antonia, who's still in the house...."

GRANDMOTHER: "Hitting a servant is incomprehensible....
When I was young it wouldn't have occurred to anybody.... When
I was young we had a big garden that went all the way down to the
ocean.... Your grandfather once gave me a kiss.... I didn't forgive
him for many years. I..."

GLORIA: "When we came here I was very scared. Román would
say to me: 'Don't be afraid.' But he changed, too."

GRANDMOTHER: "He changed in the months he was in prison;
they tortured him there; when he came back we almost didn't recognize him. But Juan was even unluckier; that's why I understand
Juan better. Juan needs me more. And this girl needs me, too. If it
wasn't for me, what would have happened to her reputation?"

GLORIA: "Román changed earlier than that. At the moment we
drove into Barcelona in that official car. Do you know that Román
had an important job with the Reds? But he was a spy, a low, vicious

person who sold out the people who helped him. No matter why you do it, spying is for cowards. . . ."

GRANDMOTHER: "Cowards? Girl, in my house there are no cowards. . . . Román is good and brave and he risked his life for me, because I didn't want him to be with those people. When he was little . . ."

GLORIA: "I'm going to tell you a story, my story, Andrea, so you can see that it's like a real novel. . . . You know I was staying in a town in Tarragona; I had been evacuated. . . . Back then, during the war, we were always out of our houses. We'd grab the mattresses, some pots and pans, and run. Some people cried. I thought it was so much fun! . . . It was in January or February when I met Juan—you already know that. Juan fell in love with me right away and we got married in two days. . . . I followed him everywhere he went. . . . It was a marvelous life, Andrea. Juan was completely happy with me, I swear, and he was handsome then, not like now, now he looks like a crazy man. . . . There were lots of girls who followed their husbands and boyfriends everywhere. We always had nice friends. . . . I was never afraid of the bombs or the bullets. . . . But we didn't get too close to the dangerous places. I don't really know what Juan's job was, but it was important. I tell you I was happy. Spring was coming and we passed through some very pretty places. One day Juan told me: 'I'm going to introduce you to my brother.' Just like that, Andrea. At first I thought Román was nice. . . . Do you think he's handsomer than Juan? We spent some time with him, in that town. A town on the ocean. Every night Juan and Román closed the door and talked in a room that was next to the one where I was sleeping. I wanted to know what they were saying. Wouldn't the same thing have happened to you? There was a door between the two rooms. I thought they were talking about me. I was sure they were talking about me. One night I began to listen. I looked through the keyhole: They were both leaning over a map and Román was saying:

" 'I still have to go back to Barcelona. But you can pass over. It's very simple....' Slowly I began to understand that Román was urging Juan to pass over to the Nationalists.... Imagine, Andrea, that was when I began to feel that I was pregnant. I told Juan. He was thoughtful.... That night when I told him you can imagine how much I wanted to listen again at the door to Román's room. I was in my nightgown, barefoot; I still think I can feel that torment. Juan was saying: 'I've made up my mind. Nothing can stop me now.' I couldn't believe it. If I had, that was the moment I would have despised Juan....."

GRANDMOTHER: "Juan did the right thing. He sent you here, to me...."

GLORIA: "That night they didn't say anything about me, nothing. When Juan came to bed, he found me crying. I told him I'd had bad dreams. That he was leaving me alone with the baby. Then he caressed me and fell asleep without saying anything. I stayed awake, watching him sleep; I wanted to see what he was dreaming...."

GRANDMOTHER: "It's nice to watch people you love sleeping. Each child sleeps in a different way...."

GLORIA: "The next day, Juan asked Román, in front of me, to bring me to this house when he went to Barcelona. Román was surprised and said: 'I don't know if I can,' looking at Juan very seriously. That night they argued a lot. Juan said: 'It's the least I can do; as far as I know, she has no family.' Then Román said: 'And Paquita?' I'd never heard that name before and I was very interested. But Juan said it again: 'Take her home.' And that night they didn't talk about it anymore. But they did something interesting: Juan gave Román a lot of money and some other things that he's refused to give back. You know all about it, Mamá."

GRANDMOTHER: "Girl, you shouldn't listen through keyholes. My mother wouldn't have let me do it, but you're an orphan . . . that's why . . ."

GLORIA: "Since the ocean was so loud, I couldn't make out a lot of what they said. I couldn't find out who Paquita was, or anything else interesting. The next day I said good-bye to Juan and was very sad, but I consoled myself thinking I'd be going to his house. Román drove the car and I sat beside him. Román began joking with me.... Román's very nice when he wants to be, but at heart he's bad. We stopped a lot of times along the way. And in one village we stayed for four days in the castle.... A wonderful castle; inside it had been restored and had all the modern conveniences.... But some rooms were in ruins. The soldiers stayed on the ground floor. We were on the upper floors with the officers.... Román was very different with me then, *chica*. Very lovable. He tuned a piano and played things, like he does now for you. And he asked me to let him paint me nude, like Juan does now.... You know, I have a very nice body."

GRANDMOTHER: "Child! What are you saying? This naughty girl invents a lot of things.... Don't pay attention to her...."

GLORIA: "It's true. And I didn't want to, Mamá, because you know very well that even though Román has said so many things about me, I'm a very decent girl...."

GRANDMOTHER: "Of course, my dear, of course.... Your husband is wrong to paint you that way; if poor Juan had money for models, he wouldn't do it.... I know, my child, that you make the sacrifice for him; that's why I love you so much...."

GLORIA: "There were all these purple lilies on the castle grounds. Román wanted to paint me with purple lilies in my hair.... What do you think of that?"

GRANDMOTHER: "Purple lilies... they're so pretty! It's been so long since I've had any flowers for my Virgin!"

GLORIA: "Then we came to this house. You can imagine how unhappy I felt. I thought everybody here was crazy. Don Jerónimo and Angustias said my marriage was no good and that Juan wouldn't marry me when he got back, and that I was common, ignorant.... One day Don Jerónimo's wife came by, she visited sometimes, in secret, to see her husband and bring him nice things. When she found out that a so-called whore was in the house, she had a fit. Mamá sprinkled water in her face. . . . I asked Román to give me back the money Juan had given him because I wanted to leave here. That money was good, it was silver, from before the war. When Román found out I'd been listening to his conversations with Juan in that village, he became furious. He treated me worse than a dog. Worse than a rabid dog. . . ."

GRANDMOTHER: "But are you going to cry now, you silly thing? Román may have been a little angry. Men are like that, a little short-tempered. And listening behind doors isn't nice, I've always told you that. Once . . ."

GLORIA: "This was when they came for Román and took him to prison; they wanted him to talk and that's why they didn't shoot him. Antonia, the maid, who's in love with him, was like a wild animal. She testified in his favor. She said I was shameless, a bad woman, and when Juan came he'd throw me out the window. That I was the one who denounced Román. She said she'd slit my belly open with a knife; that was when I hit her. . . ."

GRANDMOTHER: "That woman's an animal. But thanks to her they didn't shoot Román. That's why we put up with her. . . . And she never sleeps; some nights, when I come out to look for my sewing basket, or the scissors—I'm always mislaying them—she comes to the door of her room and shouts at me: 'Why don't you go to bed, Señora? What are you doing up?' The other night she gave me such a start that I fell. . . ."

GLORIA: "I was hungry. Mamá, poor thing, saved some of her food for me. Angustias and Don Jerónimo had lots of things put away, but they were the only ones who tasted them. I watched their room. Every once in a while they'd give something to the maid, out of fear. . . ."

GRANDMOTHER: "Don Jerónimo was a coward. I don't like cowards, I don't. . . . They're the worst. When a militiaman came to search the house, I was very calm and showed him all my saints.

'But do you believe in all that God nonsense?' he said to me. 'Of course I do; don't you?' I answered. 'No, and I don't let anybody else believe it.' 'Then I'm more of a Republican than you are, because I don't care what other people think; I believe in freedom of ideas.' Then he scratched his head and said I was right. The next day he brought me a rosary as a present, one of the ones they'd confiscated. And I'll tell you, on that same day the upstairs neighbors, who only had a Saint Anthony over the bed, had their saint thrown out the window...."

GLORIA: "I don't want to tell you how much I suffered during those months. And it was worse at the end. My son was born when the Nationalists marched in. Angustias took me to a clinic and left me there.... It was a night of terrible bombing; the nurses left me alone. Then I had an infection. A very high fever for more than a month. I didn't know anybody. I don't know how the baby survived. When the war ended I was still in bed and spent my days in a stupor, without the strength to think or move. One morning the door opened and Juan came in. I didn't recognize him at first. He seemed very tall, very thin. He sat on the bed and put his arms around me. I leaned my head on his shoulder and began to cry, then he said: 'Forgive me, forgive me,' like that, very quiet. I began to touch his cheeks because I almost couldn't believe it was really Juan, and we stayed that way for a long time."

GRANDMOTHER: "Juan brought a lot of good things to eat, condensed milk and coffee and sugar.... I was happy for Gloria; I thought: 'I'll fix Gloria the kind of dessert we ate back home'... but Antonia, that wicked woman, doesn't let me in the kitchen...."

GLORIA: "We had our arms around each other for such a long time! How could I imagine what came afterward? It was like the end of a novel. Like the end of all sadness. How could I guess that the worst was yet to come? Román got out of prison and it was like another dead man had come back to life. He hurt me as much as he could with Juan. He didn't want him to marry me under any circumstances. He wanted him to kick me and the baby out. . . . I had to defend myself and say some things that were true. That's why Román can't stand me."

GRANDMOTHER: "Girl, secrets have to be kept and you should never say things to make men enemies. When I was very young, once . . . an afternoon in August, very blue, I remember that so well, and very hot, I saw something . . ."

GLORIA: "But I can't forget when I sat like this, with my arms around Juan, and how his heart was beating under the hard bones of his chest. . . . I remembered that Don Jerónimo and Angustias kept saying he had a fiancée who was beautiful and rich and that he'd marry her. I told him about it and he shook his head to tell me he wouldn't. And kissed my hair. . . . The awful thing was that then we had to live here again because we didn't have any money. Otherwise we'd have been a very happy couple and Juan wouldn't be so crazy. . . . That moment was like the end of a movie."

GRANDMOTHER: "I was the baby's godmother. . . . Andrea, are you asleep?"

GLORIA: "Are you asleep, Andrea?"

I wasn't asleep. And I think I remember these stories clearly. But my rising fever stupefied me. I had the shivers, and Angustias made me lie down. My bed was damp, the furniture in the grayish light sadder, more monstrous, blacker. I closed my eyes and saw a reddish darkness behind my eyelids. Then, the image of Gloria in the clinic, leaning, very white, against the shoulder of a Juan who was different, tender, without those gray shadows on his cheeks . . .

I had a fever for several days. I remember that one time Antonia came to see me with her peculiar odor of black clothes, and her face became part of my dreams, sharpening a long knife. I also saw Granny, young, dressed in blue, on an August afternoon by the sea. But especially Gloria, crying against Juan's shoulder, and his big hands caressing her hair. And Juan's eyes, which I knew as wild and restless, softened by an unknown light.

On the last afternoon that I was sick, Román came to see me. He had the parrot on his shoulder and the dog came in, too, impetuously, ready to lick my face.

"Why don't you play the piano for me? They say you play the piano very well. . . ."

"Yes, only as a hobby."

"And you've never composed anything for the piano?"

"Yes I have, sometimes—why do you ask?"

"I think you should have devoted yourself exclusively to music, Román. Play something that you composed for the piano."

"When you're sick you speak as if everything you say has a double meaning, I don't know why."

He ran his fingers over the keys for a while and then he said:

"This is really out of tune, but I'll play you Xochipilli's song. . . . Do you remember the little clay idol I have upstairs? . . . Don't think it's authentic. I made it myself. But it represents Xochipilli, the Aztec god of games and flowers. In his heyday this god received offerings of human hearts. . . . Many centuries later, in a fit of enthusiasm for him, I composed a little music. Poor Xochipilli is in decline, as you'll see. . . ."

He sat at the piano and played something happy, which was unusual for him. He played something that resembled the resurgence of life in the spring, with husky, piercing notes like an aroma that spreads and intoxicates.

"You're a great musician, Román," I said, and I really believed it.

"No. You don't know a thing about music, that's why you think so. But I'm flattered."

"Ah," he said when he was at the door, "you can believe I made a small sacrifice in your honor when I played that. Xochipilli always brings me bad luck."

That night I had a very clear dream in which an old, obsessive image reappeared: Gloria, leaning on Juan's shoulder and crying . . . Gradually, Juan underwent curious transformations. I saw him enormous and dark, with the enigmatic features of the god

Xochipilli. Gloria's pale face grew animated and began to revive; Xochipilli was smiling, too. Suddenly I recognized his smile: It was the white, somewhat savage smile of Román. It was Román embracing Gloria, and the two of them were laughing. They weren't in the clinic but in the country. In a field of purple lilies, and Gloria's hair was blowing in the wind.

I woke without a fever, and confused, as if I really had discovered some dark secret.

V

I don't know what caused that fever, which passed like a sorrowful gust of wind, disturbing the corners of my spirit, but also sweeping away its black clouds. The fact is it disappeared before anybody would have thought about calling the doctor, and when it was over it left me with a strange, feeble sensation of well-being. On the first day I could get up, I had the impression that when I pushed the blanket down toward my feet I was moving away the oppressive atmosphere that had hovered over me since I'd arrived at the house.

Angustias, examining my shoes, whose leather, as wrinkled as an expressive face, betrayed their age, pointed at the torn soles oozing dampness and said I caught a chill because I'd gotten my feet wet.

"Besides, my child, when one is poor and has to live on the charity of relatives, it's necessary to take better care of one's personal possessions. You have to walk less and step more carefully. . . . Don't look at me like that, because I'm telling you I know perfectly well what you do when I'm at the office. I know you go out and come back before I do, so I won't catch you. May I ask where you go?"

"Well, no place in particular. I like to see the streets. See the city . . ."

"But you like to go alone, my child, as if you were an urchin. Exposed to men's impertinence. Are you by any chance a maid? . . . At your age, they didn't even let me go down to the street door by myself. I'm telling you I understand that you need to go back and forth to the university . . . but that's very different from wandering around loose like a lost dog. . . . When you're alone in the world, do what you wish. But now you have a family, a home, a name. I knew that your cousin couldn't have taught you good habits in the village. Your father was a strange man. . . . It's not that your cousin isn't an excellent person, but she lacks refinement. In spite of everything, I hope you didn't run around the village streets."

"No."

"Well, you certainly can't do that here. Are you listening to me?"

I didn't insist—what could I say to her?

Suddenly she turned, her hair on end, when she was already on her way out.

"I hope you haven't gone down to the port along the Ramblas."

"Why not?"

"My child, there are some streets where if a young lady were to go even once, she'd lose her reputation forever. I'm referring to the Barrio Chino. . . . You don't know where it begins. . . ."

"Yes, I know perfectly well. I haven't gone into the Barrio Chino . . . but what's there?"

Angustias looked at me in a rage.

"Loose women, thieves, and the glitter of the devil—that's what's there."

(And at that instant, I imagined the Barrio Chino illuminated by a spark of beauty.)

The moment of my battle with Angustias was approaching, like an unavoidable storm. In my first conversation with her I knew we'd never get along. Afterward, the surprise and sadness of my first impressions had given a great advantage to my aunt. *But,* I thought in excitement after this conversation, *that period is coming to a close.* I saw myself embarking upon a new life in which I would dispose of my hours in freedom, and I gave Angustias a mocking smile.

When I resumed classes at the university, I seemed to be boiling inside with accumulated impressions. For the first time in my life I found myself being expansive and making friends. Without too much effort I established a relationship with a group of my class-mates. The truth is that what drew me to them was an indefinable eagerness that I can name now as a defensive instinct: Only these beings of my own generation and my own tastes could support me and protect me from the somewhat ghostly world of older people. And I sincerely believe I needed this assistance at the time.

I understood immediately that with these young people the mysterious, allusive tone of confidences, which girls usually love, the charm of analyzing one's soul, the light caress of sensibility stored up over the years, all that was impossible. . . . In my relation-ships with the group at the university, I found myself deep in a pro-fusion of discussions regarding problems I hadn't even dreamed of, and I felt off-center and happy at the same time.

One day Pons, the youngest boy in my group, said to me:

"How did you survive before, when you always avoided talking to people? I tell you, we thought you were pretty silly. Ena made fun of you and was very comical. She said you were ridiculous. What was wrong with you?"

I shrugged, a little hurt, because of all the young people I knew, Ena was the one I liked best.

Even in the days when I wasn't thinking about being her friend, I was fond of that girl and was sure the feeling was mutual. She had approached me a few times to talk very politely on some pretext or other. On the first day of class she asked if I was related to a famous violinist. I remember that the question seemed absurd and made me laugh.

I wasn't the only one who had a preference for Ena. She was

something like a magnetic center in our conversations, which she often presided over. Her mischievousness and intelligence were proverbial. I was certain that if she'd ever made me the target of her jokes, I really would have been the laughingstock of our entire class.

I watched her from a distance, with a certain rancor. Ena had a pleasant, sensual face in which a pair of terrible eyes glittered. The contrast between her gentle features, the youthful look of her body and her blond hair, and her large greenish eyes full of brilliance and irony, was fascinating.

While I was talking to Pons, she waved at me. Then she came over, making her way through the noisy groups waiting in the court-yard of the literature building for class to begin. When she reached my side, her cheeks were flushed and she seemed to be in an excellent mood.

"Leave us alone, Pons, okay?"

"With Pons," she said as she watched the boy's slim figure moving away, "you have to be careful. He's one of those people who take offense right away. Right now he believes I've insulted him by asking him to leave us alone . . . but I have to talk to you."

I was thinking that only a few minutes earlier I had been hurt, too, by jokes of hers that I hadn't known about before. But now I had been won over by her profound congeniality.

I liked walking with her through the stone cloisters of the university and listening to her talk, thinking that someday I'd have to tell her about the dark life in my house, which to my mind became filled with romanticism the moment it turned into a topic of discussion. I thought Ena would be very interested and understand the problems even better than I. So far, however, I hadn't told her anything about my life. I was becoming a friend of hers thanks to this new desire to talk; but talking and fantasizing were things that had always been difficult for me, and I preferred listening to her, with a feeling like expectation, which I found discouraging and interesting at the same time. And so, when Pons left us that afternoon, I couldn't imagine that the bittersweet tension between my vacillations and my longing to confide in her was coming to an end.

"I found out today that a violinist I mentioned to you a while ago . . . do you remember? . . . not only has your second last name, it's so strange, but lives on Calle de Aribau just like you. His name is Román. He's really not related to you?" she said.

"Yes, he's my uncle, but I had no idea he was really a musician. I was sure that except for his family nobody knew he played the violin."

"Well, you can see now that I knew him by reputation."

I began to feel a vague excitement at the thought that Ena might have some kind of contact with Calle de Aribau. At the same time I felt almost cheated.

"I want you to introduce me to your uncle."

"All right."

We fell silent. I was waiting for Ena to explain something to me, she, perhaps, for me to speak. But without knowing why, it seemed impossible now for me to discuss the world of Calle de Aribau with my friend. I thought it would be terribly painful for me to bring Ena to meet Román—"a famous violinist"—and witness the disillusionment and mockery in her eyes when she saw his negligent appearance. I had one of those moments of discouragement and shame so frequent in the young, when I felt badly dressed, reeking of bleach and harsh kitchen soap, next to Ena's well-cut dress and the soft perfume of her hair.

Ena looked at me. I remember thinking it was a great relief we had to go to class at that moment.

"Wait for me when we come out!" she shouted.

I always sat in the last seat, while her friends saved her a place on the first row. During the professor's entire lecture, my imagination wandered. I swore to myself I wouldn't mix those two worlds that were beginning to stand out so clearly in my life: my student friendships, with their easy cordiality, and my dirty, unwelcoming house. My desire to talk about Román's music, and Gloria's red hair, and my childish grandmother wandering through the night like a ghost, seemed idiotic. Aside from the charm of dressing all of it in fantastic hypotheses during long conversations, the only thing that remained was the miserable reality that had tormented me when I arrived and would be the one Ena might see if I ever introduced her to Román.

And so as soon as class was over that day, I slipped away from the university and hurried to my house as if I had done something wrong, running from the steady gaze of my friend.

But when I reached our apartment on Calle de Aribau, I wanted to find Román, because it was too strong a temptation to let him know I was privy to the secret—a secret he apparently guarded jealously—of his fame and past success. But that day I didn't see Román at dinner. This disappointed me, though it didn't surprise me, because Román frequently stayed away. Gloria, blowing her child's nose, seemed like an infinitely vulgar creature, and Angustias was unbearable.

The following day and for a few days after that, I avoided Ena until I could convince myself that she apparently had forgotten about her questions. Román was not to be seen in the house.

Gloria said to me:

"Don't you know that he goes away from time to time? He doesn't tell anybody and nobody knows where he goes except the cook."

(*Does Román know*—I thought—*that some people consider him a celebrity, that people still haven't forgotten him?*)

One afternoon I went to the kitchen.

"Tell me, Antonia, do you know when my uncle's coming back?"

The woman quickly twisted her awful smile at me.

"He'll come back. He always comes back. He leaves and he comes back. He comes back and he leaves.... But he never gets lost, right, Trueno? No need to worry."

She turned toward the dog that was, as usual, behind her, its red tongue hanging out.

"Right, Trueno, he never gets lost?"

The animal's eyes gleamed yellow as it looked at the woman and her eyes gleamed, too, small and dark, in the smoke of the fire she was beginning to light.

The two of them stood there a few seconds, unmoving, hypnotized. I was certain Antonia wouldn't add another word to her not-very-informative comments.

There was no way to find out anything about Román until he himself appeared one afternoon at dusk. I was alone with my grandmother and Angustias, and found myself in something like a correctional institution, because Angustias had caught me just as I was about to escape, going out on tiptoe. At a moment like that, Román's arrival caused an unexpected joy in me.

He looked darker, his forehead and nose burned by the sun, but emaciated, unshaven, and with a dirty shirt collar.

Angustias looked him up and down.

"I'd like to know where you've been!"

He returned the look, malevolent, while he took out the parrot to caress it.

"You can be sure I'm going to tell you. . . . Who took care of the parrot for me, Mamá?"

"I did, my child," said my grandmother, smiling at him, "I never forget. . . ."

"Thank you, Mamá."

He put his arm around her waist so that it looked as if he were going to pick her up, and kissed her hair.

"You couldn't have gone anywhere very good. I've been warned about your traveling, Román. I'm telling you that I know you're not the man you were before. . . . Your moral sense leaves quite a bit to be desired."

Román expanded his chest as if shaking off the exhaustion of his trip.

"Suppose I told you that perhaps in my traveling I've been able to find out something about my sister's moral sense?"

"Don't talk nonsense, you fool! Especially not in front of my niece."

"Our niece won't be shocked. And Mamá, even if she opens those little round eyes, won't be, either. . . ."

Angustias's cheekbones were yellow and red and it seemed odd to me that her chest heaved like that of any other agitated woman.

"I've been wandering a little around the Pyrenees," said Román, "and I stopped for a few days in Puigcerdá, which is a charming village, and naturally I went to visit a poor lady I knew in better days, whose husband has locked her away in his gloomy mansion, watched over by servants as if she were a criminal."

"If you're referring to the wife of Don Jerónimo, the head of my office, you know perfectly well the poor thing has lost her mind and rather than send her to an asylum he preferred . . ."

"Yes, I can see you're very familiar with your boss's affairs—I'm referring to poor Señora Sanz. . . . As for her being crazy, I don't doubt it. But whose fault is it that she's in that condition?"

"What are you trying to insinuate?" shouted Angustias, in such anguish (this time it was sincere) that I felt sorry for her.

"Nothing!" said Román with surprising lightness, while an astonished smile floated beneath his mustache.

I was left with my mouth open, cut short in the midst of my desire to talk with Román. I'd spent days excited by the prospect of talking to my uncle—so much news I thought he'd find interesting and pleasant and had saved up for him.

When I stood up to embrace him with more drive than I ordinarily put into these things, the happiness of the surprise I had prepared for him was dancing on the tip of my tongue. The scene that followed cut short my enthusiasm.

Out of the corner of my eye, while Román was talking to me, I saw Aunt Angustias leaning on the sideboard, very pensive, made ugly by a pained expression, but not crying, which for her was strange.

Román settled calmly into a chair and began to talk to me about the Pyrenees. He said those magnificent wrinkles on the earth that rise up between us—the Spaniards—and the rest of Europe were one of the truly splendid places on the globe. He talked to me about the snow, the deep valleys, the icy, brilliant sky.

"I don't know why I can't love nature, as terrible, as sullen and magnificent as it is at times. . . . I believe I've lost my taste for the colossal. The tick-tock of my clocks awakens my senses more than the wind in the narrow passes. . . . I'm closed off," he concluded.

When I heard him I decided it wasn't worth telling Román that a girl my age knew about his talent, since the fame of that talent didn't interest him. And since he also was voluntarily closed off to all external flattery.

As he spoke, Román caressed the dog's ears, and the animal rolled its eyes with pleasure. The maid watched them from the door; she dried her hands on her apron—those oafish hands with their black nails—not knowing what she was doing and looking, certain and insistent, at Román's hands on the dog's ears.

VI

I often found myself surprised, among the people on Calle de Aribau, by the tragic aspect that the most trivial events took on, even though all of them carried their own burden, a true obsession inside themselves, to which they rarely alluded directly.

On Christmas Day they involved me in one of their blowups; and perhaps because until that time I had tended to keep apart from them, this one made more of an impression on me than any other. Or it may have been the strange state of mind I was in because of my uncle Román, whom I couldn't help but begin to see in an extremely disagreeable light.

This time the argument had its hidden roots in my friendship with Ena. And much later, recalling it, I've thought that from the start a kind of predestination joined Ena to life on Calle de Aribau, so impervious to outside elements.

My friendship with Ena had followed the normal course of a relationship between two classmates who are extraordinarily fond of each other. I thought again about the charm of my secondary-school friendships, forgotten now because of her. And I was not unaware of the advantages of her affinity for me. The boys thought better of me. Surely they thought it would be easier to approach my good-looking friend through me.

But it was too expensive a luxury for me to share in Ena's customs. She dragged me every day to the bar—the only warm place, aside from the sun in the garden, that I remember at the stone university—and paid my bill, since we had made a pact not to allow the boys, all of them too young, and most of them lacking money, to pay for the girls. I didn't have money for a cup of coffee. And I didn't have enough for the streetcar—if I could ever get past Angustias's vigilance and go out with my friend—or to buy hot chestnuts in the afternoon. Ena provided everything. This chafed in a disagreeable way. All the happiness I enjoyed during this time seemed somehow diminished by my obsession with reciprocating her consideration. Until then no one I loved had shown me so much affection, and I felt gnawed by the need to give her something more than my company, the need felt by all people who are not very attractive to make material payment for what is, to them, extraordinary: someone's interest and affection.

I don't know if it was a beautiful or mean-spirited sentiment— and at the time it wouldn't have occurred to me to analyze it—that impelled me to open my suitcase and make an inventory of my treasures. I piled up my books, looking at them one by one. I had brought all of them from my father's library, which my cousin Isabel kept in the attic of her house, and they looked yellow and mildewed. My underwear and a little tin box completed the picture of everything I possessed in the world. In the box I found old photographs, my parents' wedding rings, and a silver medal with my date of birth. Beneath everything, wrapped in tissue paper, was a handkerchief of magnificent old lace that my grandmother had sent me on the day of my first communion. I hadn't remembered that it was so pretty, and the joy of being able to give it to Ena compensated for a good many sorrows. It compensated for how difficult it was becoming for me to be clean when I went to the university, and above all to look clean beside the comfortable appearance of my friends. The sorrow of mending my gloves, of washing my blouses in murky, freezing water in the washbasin in the gallery with the same piece of soap that Antonia used to scrub the pots and that in the morning scraped against my body under the cold shower. Being able to give Ena a gift so delicately beautiful compensated for all the wretchedness of my life. I remember taking it to the university on the last day of classes before Christmas vacation, and hiding this fact very carefully from my relatives; not because I thought it was wrong to make a gift of what was mine, but because that gift invaded the precincts of intimate things from which I had excluded all of them. By then I couldn't believe I'd ever thought of talking about Ena to Román, not even to tell him that someone admired his art.

Ena was moved and so happy when she found the pretty trifle in the package I gave her that her happiness brought me closer to her than all her previous displays of affection. She made me feel that I was everything I wasn't: rich and contented. And I could never forget that.

I recall that this incident put me in a good mood, and I began my vacation with more patience and sweetness toward everyone than I normally felt. I was pleasant even to Angustias. On Christmas Eve I dressed, ready to go to Midnight Mass with her although she hadn't asked me. To my great surprise, she became very nervous.

"I prefer to go alone tonight, dear. . . ."

She thought I was disappointed and caressed my face.

"You can go tomorrow and take communion with your granny. . . ."

I wasn't disappointed, I was surprised, because Angustias made me go with her to all religious ceremonies and liked to monitor and criticize my devotion.

I had slept a good many hours when a splendid Christmas morning dawned. I did, in fact, accompany my grandmother to Mass. In the strong sunlight the old woman, in her black coat, looked like a little wrinkled raisin. She was so happy as she walked beside me that I was tormented by dark remorse at not loving her more.

When we were on our way home, she told me she had offered up her communion to peace in the family.

"Let these brothers reconcile, my child, it's my only desire, and also for Angustias to understand how good Gloria is and how unlucky she's been."

As we climbed the stairs, we heard shouts coming from our apartment. Granny held my arm even tighter and sighed.

When we went in we found Gloria, Angustias, and Juan having a shouting argument in the dining room. Gloria was crying hysterically.

Juan was trying to hit Angustias on the head with a chair, and she had picked up another one to use as a shield and was making leaps to defend herself.

Since the excited parrot was shrieking and Antonia was singing in the kitchen, the scene was not lacking in a certain humor.

Granny immediately became involved in the quarrel, waving her arms and trying to hold Angustias, who became desperate.

Gloria ran to me.

"Andrea! You can say it isn't true!"

Juan put down the chair to look at me.

"What can Andrea say?" Angustias shouted. "I know very well you stole it. . . ."

"Angustias! If you keep insulting people, I'll split your head open, damn you!"

"All right, but what is it that I have to say?"

"Angustias says I took a lace handkerchief of yours. . . ."

I felt myself turning stupidly red, as if I had been accused of something. A wave of heat. A rush of boiling blood to my cheeks, my ears, the veins of my neck . . .

"I don't speak without proof!" Angustias said, her index finger pointing at Gloria. "Somebody saw you take that handkerchief out of the house to sell it. It was the only valuable thing my niece had in her suitcase, and you can't deny you've gone through that suitcase before to take something out of it. Twice I've found you wearing Andrea's underwear."

This was, in fact, true. A disagreeable habit of Gloria's, who was dirty and slovenly in everything and without too many scruples regarding other people's possessions.

"But it isn't true that she took the handkerchief," I said, oppressed by a childish anguish.

"See? You filthy witch! You'd be better off having some shame in your own affairs and not getting involved in other people's business."

This was Juan, naturally.

"It isn't true? It isn't true that somebody stole your first communion handkerchief? Where is it, then? Because this very morning I was looking in your suitcase and there's nothing there."

"I gave it to somebody," I said, controlling the pounding of my heart. "I gave it to somebody as a present."

Aunt Angustias came at me so quickly I closed my eyes in an instinctive gesture, as if she were trying to hit me. She stood so close that her breath bothered me.

"Tell me who you gave it to, right now! Your boyfriend? Do you have a boyfriend?"

I shook my head.

"Then it isn't true. You're telling a lie to defend Gloria. You don't care about making me look ridiculous as long as that whore comes out all right. . . ."

Usually Aunt Angustias was measured in her speech. This time she must have been infected by the general atmosphere. The rest happened very quickly: a slap from Juan, so brutal it made Angustias stagger and fall to the floor.

I bent down quickly and tried to help her up. Brusquely she pushed me away, crying. The scene had lost all its amusement for me.

"And listen, you witch!" Juan shouted. "I didn't say it before because I'm a hundred times better than you and the whole damn tribe in this house, but I don't care at all if everybody finds out that your boss's wife has good reason to insult you on the phone, which she does sometimes, and that last night you didn't go to Midnight Mass or anywhere near it. . . ."

It would be hard for me to forget how Angustias looked at that moment. With disheveled gray hair, eyes so wide open they frightened me, and the two fingers she used to wipe away a thread of blood at the corner of her mouth . . . she looked drunk.

"Swine! Swine! Madman!" she shouted.

Then she covered her face with her hands and ran to lock herself in her room. We heard the bed groan under her body, and then her weeping.

The dining room remained enveloped in an astonishing calm. I looked at Gloria and saw that she was smiling at me. I didn't know what to do. I tried a timid knock at Angustias's door and noted with relief that she didn't answer.

Juan went to the studio and from there he called Gloria. I heard them beginning a new argument that sounded muffled, like a storm moving away.

I went toward the balcony and leaned my forehead against the windows. On that Christmas Day the street looked like an immense golden pastry shop full of delicious things.

I heard Granny coming up behind me and then her narrow hand, always bluish with cold, began a feeble caress of my hand.

"Naughty girl," she said, "you naughty girl . . . you gave away my handkerchief."

I looked at her and saw that she was sad, with a childish distress in her eyes.

"Didn't you like my handkerchief? It belonged to my mother, but I wanted it to be for you. . . ."

I didn't know what to say and turned over her hand to kiss her palm, wrinkled and soft. Distress squeezed my throat, too, like a harsh rope. I thought that any joy in my life had to be paid for with something unpleasant. Perhaps this was a fatal law.

Antonia came in to set the table. In the center, as if it were flowers, she placed a large plate of nougat. Aunt Angustias refused to come out of her room to eat.

It was my grandmother, Gloria, Juan, Román, and me at that strange Christmas meal, sitting around a large table with its frayed checked tablecloth.

Juan rubbed his hands together happily.

"Wonderful! Wonderful!" he said, and uncorked a bottle.

Since it was Christmas Day, Juan felt very animated. Gloria began to eat pieces of nougat, using them like bread, beginning with the soup. Granny laughed with joy, her head unsteady after she drank some wine.

"There's no chicken or turkey, but a good rabbit's better than anything," said Juan.

Only Román, as usual, seemed distant from the meal. He took pieces of nougat, too, to give to the dog.

We resembled any calm, happy family, enfolded in simple poverty, not wishing for anything else.

A clock that was always slow sounded its untimely bells and the satisfied parrot fluffed up its feathers in the sun.

Suddenly it all seemed idiotic, comical, and laughable again. And, unable to help myself, I began to laugh when no one was speaking, when it was out of place, and I choked. They hit me on the back, and I, red in the face and coughing until tears came to my eyes, laughed; then I began to cry, seriously, in distress, sad, empty.

In the afternoon Aunt Angustias had me go to her room. She was in bed, placing cloths soaked in water and vinegar on her forehead. By now she was calm, and looked ill.

"Come here, dear, come here," she said. "I have to explain something to you. . . . I want you to know that your aunt is incapable of doing anything wicked or inappropriate."

"I know that. I've never doubted it."

"Thank you, child; you didn't believe Juan's slanders?"

"Ah . . . that you weren't at Midnight Mass last night?" I controlled my desire to smile. "No. Why wouldn't you be? Besides, I don't think it's important."

She moved uneasily.

"It's very difficult for me to explain it to you, but . . ."

Her voice was heavy with water, like clouds swollen with spring. I thought another scene would be unbearable, and I touched her arm with my fingertips.

"I don't want you to explain anything. I don't believe you have to account to me for your actions, Aunt. And if it's helpful to you, I'll tell you that I think anything immoral they might have said about you is impossible."

She looked at me, her brown eyes fluttering beneath the visor of damp cloth she wore on her head.

"I'm leaving this house very soon, dear," she said in a hesitant voice. "Much sooner than anybody imagines. Then my truth will shine."

I tried to imagine what life would be like without Aunt Angustias, the horizons that would open to me. . . . She wouldn't let me.

"Now, Andrea, listen to me." Her tone had changed. "If you've given away that handkerchief, you have to ask for it back."

"Why? It was mine."

"Because I'm ordering you to."

I smiled a little, thinking about the contradictions in that woman.

"I can't do that. I won't do anything so stupid."

Something hoarse rose in Angustias's throat, like pleasure in a cat. She sat up in bed, removing the damp handkerchief from her forehead.

"Do you swear you've given it away as a gift?"

"Of course I do! For God's sake!"

I was bored to despair with the matter.

"I gave it to a girl, a classmate at the university."

"Think about it if you're swearing falsely."

"Aunt, don't you realize that all of this is becoming ridiculous? I'm telling the truth. Where did you get the idea that Gloria took it?"

"Your uncle Román assured me she had, dear." She lay back again, weakly, on the pillow. "And may God forgive him if he told a lie. He said he'd seen Gloria selling your handkerchief in an antique store; that's why I went to look through your suitcase this morning."

I was perplexed, as if I had put my hands into something dirty, not knowing what to do or say.

I ended Christmas Day in my room, surrounded by that fantasy of furniture in the twilight. I was sitting on the divan, wrapped in the blanket, my head resting on my bent knees.

Outside, in the stores, streams of light would intertwine and people would be loaded down with packages. The crèches, with all their shepherds and sheep, would be lit. Candy, bouquets of flowers, decorated baskets, good wishes, presents, would be going back and forth across the streets.

Gloria and Juan had gone out with the baby. I thought their figures would be thinner, vaguer, lost among other people. Antonia had gone out, too, and I listened to the footsteps of Granny, as nervous and expectant as a mouse as she sniffed around the forbidden world of the kitchen, the domain of the terrible woman. She dragged over a chair to reach the closet door. When she found the sugar tin, I heard the nougat crunch between her false teeth.

The rest of us were in bed. Aunt Angustias and I, and upstairs, separated by the muffled layers of noise (sounds of the phonograph, dances, noisy conversations) on each floor, I could imagine Román lying down, too, smoking, smoking . . .

And the three of us thought about ourselves without going beyond the narrow limits of that life. Not even he, not even Román, with his false standoffish appearance. He, Román, more mean-spirited, more caught up than anybody in the minuscule roots of the everyday. His life sucked away, his faculties, his art, by the passion of the agitation in that house. He, Román, capable of prying into my suitcase and inventing lies and mischief against a person he pretended to despise to the point of affecting absolute ignorance of her existence.

This was how that Christmas Day ended for me as I froze in my room and thought about these things.

VII

Two days after the stormy scene I've recounted here, Angustias dusted off her suitcases and left without telling us where she was going or when she planned to come back.

But her trip didn't affect the character of silent escapade that Román gave to his travels. Angustias upset the house for two days with her orders and shouts. She was nervous, she contradicted herself. Sometimes she cried.

When the suitcases were closed and the taxi was waiting, she embraced my grandmother.

"Bless me, Mamá!"

"Yes, my child, yes, my child . . ."

"Remember what I told you."

"Yes, my child . . ."

Juan watched the scene with his hands in his pockets, impatient.

"You're crazier than a loon, Angustias!"

She didn't answer him. I saw her in her long dark coat, her eternal hat, leaning on her mother's shoulder, bending down until she touched that white head with her own, and I had the sensation that in front of me was one of the last autumn leaves, dead on the tree before the wind tears them away.

When she finally left, her echoes kept vibrating for some time. That same afternoon the doorbell rang and I opened to a stranger who had come to see her.

"Has she left already?" he said, agitated, as if he had been running.

"Yes."

"Then may I see your grandmother?"

I showed him into the dining room and he cast an uneasy glance at all that ruinous sorrow. He was tall and stout and had very gray, heavy eyebrows.

Granny appeared with the baby glued to her skirts, with her spectral, shabby dignity, smiling sweetly but not recognizing him.

"I don't know where . . ."

"I lived in this house for many months, Señora. I'm Jerónimo Sanz."

I looked at Angustias's boss with impertinent curiosity. He looked like a man with a bad temper that he controlled with difficulty. He was very well dressed. His dark eyes, almost without whites, recalled those of the pigs Isabel raised in the village.

"Jesus! Dear Jesus!" said Granny, trembling. "Of course. . . . Sit down. Do you know Andrea?"

"Yes, Señora. I saw her the last time she was here. She's changed very little . . . she looks like her mother around the eyes and in how tall and slim she is. In fact, Andrea bears a great resemblance to your family."

"She's just like my son Román; if she had black eyes she'd look like my son Román," said my grandmother unexpectedly.

Don Jerónimo breathed heavily in his armchair. He had as little interest in the conversation about me as I did. He turned to my grandmother and saw that she had forgotten about him and was busy playing with the baby.

"Señora. I'd like Angustias's address. . . . This is a favor I'm asking of you. You know ... there are some matters at the office that only she can take care of, and ... she didn't remember that ... and ..."

"Yes, yes," said my grandmother. "She didn't remember. ... Angustias forgot to say where she was going. Isn't that so, Andrea?"

She smiled at Don Jerónimo, her small eyes light and sweet.

"She forgot to give her address to anybody," she concluded. "Maybe she'll write. ... My daughter is a little unusual. Imagine, she insists on saying that her sister-in-law, my daughter-in-law, Gloria, isn't perfect. ..."

Don Jerónimo, red-faced above his stiff white collar, looked for the right moment to take his leave. From the door he gave me a look of singular hatred. I had the impulse to run after him, to grab him by the lapels and scream at him in a fury:

"Why are you looking at me like that? What do I have to do with you?" But of course I smiled at him and carefully closed the door. When I turned around, there was Granny's childish face against my chest.

"I'm happy, my dear. I'm happy, but I think this time I'll have to make a confession. Still, I'm sure it can't be a very big sin. But anyway ... since I want to take communion tomorrow ..."

"Did you tell Don Jerónimo a lie?"

"Yes, yes," said my grandmother with a laugh.

"Where is Angustias, Grandmother?"

"I can't tell you, either, you naughty girl. ... And I'd like to, because your uncles believe a lot of foolish things about poor Angustias that aren't true, and you might believe them, too. The only thing wrong with my poor daughter is that she has a very bad temper ... but you mustn't pay attention to her. ..."

Gloria and Juan came in.

"So Angustias didn't run off with Don Jerónimo?" Juan said brutally.

"Quiet! Quiet! ... You know very well your sister's incapable of that."

"Well, Mamá, we saw her on Christmas Eve coming home almost at dawn with Don Jerónimo. Juan and I hid in the shadows to watch them. Under the streetlight at the entrance they said good-bye, Don Jerónimo kissed her hand, and she cried. . . ."

"Child," said my grandmother, shaking her head, "things are not always what they seem."

A little while later we saw her leave, defying the icy darkness of the evening to make her confession in a nearby church.

I went into Angustias's room, and the soft stripped mattress gave me the idea of sleeping there while she was away. Without consulting anyone, I moved my sheets to that bed, not without a certain uneasiness, since the entire room was saturated with the smell of naphthalene and incense that emanated from its mistress, and the arrangement of the timid chairs still seemed to obey her voice. The room was as hard as Angustias's body, but cleaner and more independent than any other in the house. Instinctively it repelled me and at the same time called on my desire for comfort.

Hours later, when the house was in nocturnal peace—a short, obligatory truce—and it was almost dawn, the electric light shining in my eyes woke me.

I sat up with a start in bed and saw Román.

"Ah!" he said, his brow wrinkled in a frown, but with the outline of a smile. "You're taking advantage of Angustias's absence to sleep in her room. . . . Aren't you afraid she'll strangle you when she finds out?"

I didn't answer but gave him a questioning look.

"Nothing," he said, "nothing . . . nothing I wanted here." Brusquely he turned off the light and went out. Then I heard him leaving the house.

In the days that followed I had the impression that this appearance of Román in the middle of the night had been a dream, but later I still remembered it vividly.

It was an afternoon when the light was very sad. I grew tired of looking at the old pictures that my grandmother was showing me in her bedroom. She had a large box full of photographs in the most awful disorder, some of them gnawed on by mice.

"Is this you, Grandmother?"

"Yes . . ."

"Is this Granddad?"

"Yes, that's your father."

"My father?"

"Yes, my husband."

"Then he isn't my father, he's my grandfather. . . ."

"Ah, yes! . . . Yes."

"Who's this fat little girl?"

"I don't know."

But on the back of the photograph was a long-ago date and a name: AMALIA.

"This is my mother when she was little, Grandmother."

"I think you're wrong."

"No, Grandmother."

She remembered all the old friends of her youth.

"This is my brother. . . . This is a cousin who was in America. . . ."

Finally I grew tired and went to Angustias's room. I wanted to be alone in the dark for a while. *If I feel like it,* I thought with the slight discomfort that always assailed me when I considered this, *I'll study for a while.* I pushed the door gently and suddenly I stepped back, startled: Next to the balcony, taking advantage of the afternoon's last light, was Román, holding a letter in his hand.

He turned impatiently, but when he saw me, he forced a smile.

"Ah! . . . Is that you, little one? . . . All right, don't run away from me now, please."

I stood still and saw that with great serenity and skill he folded the letter and placed it on top of a small packet of letters that was on the small desk (I looked at his agile hands, dark and very clever). He opened one of Angustias's drawers. Then he took a key ring from his pocket, immediately found the little key he was looking for, and, after placing the letters inside, locked the drawer silently.

He spoke to me as he carried out these operations:

"Actually I wanted very much to have a chat with you this afternoon, little one. I have some very good coffee upstairs, and I wanted to invite you to have a cup. And I have cigarettes and some candies I bought yesterday, thinking of you. . . . And . . . well?" he said when he finished, seeing that I didn't answer.

He was leaning against Angustias's desk and the last light from the balcony fell on his back. I was in front of him.

"Your gray eyes are shining like a cat's," he said.

I shook off my stupefaction and tension in something resembling a sigh.

"All right, what's your answer?"

"No, Román, thank you. I want to study this afternoon." Román struck a match to light his cigarette; for an instant, in the shadows, I saw his face illuminated by a reddish light, his singular smile, then the golden strands burning. Immediately after that a red dot and again the gray-violet light of dusk surrounding us.

"It isn't true that you want to study, Andrea. . . . Come on!" he said, approaching rapidly and seizing my arm. "Let's go!"

I felt rigid and gently began to loosen his fingers from my arm.

"Not today . . . thanks."

He let go of me right away, but we were very close and didn't move.

The streetlights went on, and a yellowish streak reflected on Angustias's chair and ran along the floor tiles.

"You can do whatever you want, Andrea," he said at last. "It isn't a matter of life or death for me."

His voice sounded deep and had a new tone.

He's desperate, I thought, not knowing exactly why I found desperation in his voice. He left quickly and, as always, slammed the door when he left the apartment. I was stirred in a disagreeable way.

I felt an immediate desire to follow him, but when I reached the foyer I stopped again. For days I'd been avoiding Román's affection; it seemed impossible to be his friend again after the unpleasant episode of the handkerchief. But he still inspired more interest in me than all the other people in the house put together. "He's mean-spirited, he's a dishonorable person," I thought aloud, there in the tranquil darkness of the house.

Still, I decided to open the door and climb the stairs. Feeling for the first time, even without understanding it, that the interest and esteem a person may inspire are two things that aren't always connected.

On the way I was thinking that on the first night I slept in Angustias's room, after Román appeared and then I heard the door slam when he left and his footsteps on the stairs, I heard Gloria leave the house. Angustias's room directly received noises from the stairs. It was like a huge ear in the house. Whispers, doors slamming, voices, all of it resonated there. I'd closed my eyes to hear better; it seemed I could see Gloria, with her white, triangular face, pacing the landing, undecided. She took a few steps and then stopped, hesitating; then she started to walk and then stopped again. My heart began to pound with excitement because I was certain she wouldn't be able to resist the desire to climb the steps that separated our apartment from Román's room. Perhaps she couldn't resist the temptation to spy on him. But Gloria's footsteps reached a decision, abruptly, when she ran down the stairs to the street. All of this was so startling that it played a part in my attributing it to disturbances in my half-waking imagination.

Now I was the one climbing slowly, my heart pounding, to Román's room. In reality it seemed to me he really needed me, that he really needed to talk, as he had said. Perhaps he wanted to confess to me, repent before me, justify himself. When I reached his room I found him lying down, stroking the dog's head.

"Do you think you've done a great thing by coming?"

"No. . . . But you wanted me to come."

Román sat up, looking at me with curiosity in his brilliant eyes.

"I wanted to know to what extent I could count on you, to what extent you can love me. . . . Do you love me, Andrea?"

"Yes, it's natural. . . ." I said, feeling self-conscious. "I don't know how much ordinary nieces love their uncles. . . ."

Román burst into laughter.

"Ordinary nieces? Do you actually consider yourself an extraordinary niece? . . . Come on, Andrea! Look at me! . . . Idiot! Nieces of every kind usually don't care at all about their uncles. . . ."

"Yes, sometimes I think friends are better than families. At times you can be closer to a stranger than to your own blood. . . ."

The image of Ena, erased for all that time, made its appearance in my imagination with a vague profile. Hounded by this idea, I asked Román:

"Don't you have friends?"

"No." Román was observing me. "I'm not a man with friends. No one in this house needs friends. We're all we need here. One day you'll believe that. . . ."

"I don't think so. I'm not so sure about that. . . . You'd be better off talking to a man your own age than to me. . . ."

Ideas tightened my throat and I couldn't express them.

Román's tone was irritated, though he was smiling.

"If I needed friends I'd have them; I've had them and I've dropped them. You'll get sick of it all, too. . . . What person in this miserable, beautiful world is interesting enough to put up with? Soon you'll be telling people to go to hell, too, when you get over your schoolgirl's romanticism about friends."

"But you, Román, you're going to hell, too, behind those people you dismiss. . . . I've never paid as much attention to people as you do, and I've never had as much curiosity about their private affairs. . . . I don't go through your drawers, and I don't care what other people have in their suitcases."

I blushed and was sorry I had, because the light was on and a fire burned brightly in the fireplace. When I realized that, a new rush of blood rose to my face, but I dared to look in my uncle's face.

Román raised an eyebrow.

"Ah! So, that's the reason for your running away from me these last few days?"

"Yes."

"Look, woman"—he changed his tone—"don't meddle in what you can't understand. . . . You couldn't make sense of it if I explained my actions. As for the rest, I never dreamed of explaining my behavior to you."

"I'm not asking for that."

"Yes. . . . But I feel like talking. . . . I feel like telling you some things."

That afternoon Román seemed disturbed. For the first time I sensed the same mental imbalance in him that always made it so unpleasant to be near Juan. In the course of our conversation there were moments when his entire face lit up with mischievous good humor, and other times when he looked at me with a frown, his eyes intense, as if what he was telling me were really passionately important to him. As if it were the most important thing in his life.

At first it seemed he didn't know how to begin. He busied himself with the coffeepot. He turned out the light, and the only illumination for drinking our coffee more comfortably came from the fireplace. I sat on the straw mat on the floor, next to the fire, and he squatted beside me for a while, smoking. Then he stood up.

Shall I ask him to play a little music, the way I always do? I thought when I saw that the silence was lengthening. It seemed we had reestablished our normal atmosphere. Suddenly I was startled by his voice.

"Look, I wanted to talk to you, but it's impossible. You're a baby . . . 'what's good,' 'what's bad,' 'what I like,' 'what I feel like doing' . . . that's what you have in your head, as clearly as a child. Sometimes I think you resemble me, that you understand me, that you understand my music, the music of this house. . . . The first time

I played the violin for you, I was trembling inside with hope, with a terrible joy when your eyes changed with the music. . . . I thought, little one, that you'd understand me even without words; that you were my audience, the audience I needed. . . . And you haven't even realized that I have to know—that in fact I do know—everything, absolutely everything, that goes on downstairs. Everything Gloria feels, all of Angustias's ridiculous stories, everything Juan suffers. . . . Haven't you realized that I manage all of them, that I arrange their nerves, their thoughts? . . . If I could only explain to you that sometimes I'm on the verge of driving Juan crazy! . . . But haven't you seen that yourself? I pull at his comprehension, his mind, until it almost breaks. . . . Sometimes, when he shouts with his eyes open, he even moves me. If you'd ever felt this emotion, so dense and strange, drying your tongue, you'd understand me! I think that with a single word I could calm him, make him serene, make him mine, make him smile. . . . You know that, don't you? You know very well how much Juan belongs to me, how much he trails after me, how much I mistreat him. Don't tell me you haven't realized. . . . And I don't want to make him happy. And that's why I let him sink down by himself. . . . And the others. . . . And all the life in this house, as dirty as a muddy river. . . . When you've lived here longer, this house and its smell and its old things, if you're like me, they'll seize the life in you. And you're like me. . . . Aren't you like me? Tell me, don't you resemble me a little?"

There we were; I was on the mat on the floor and he was standing. I didn't know if he enjoyed frightening me or if he really was crazy. He'd finished talking almost in a whisper when he asked me that last question. I was quiet, wanting to escape, nervous.

He brushed my head with his fingertips and I jumped up, stifling a scream.

Then he really burst out laughing, enthused, childish, charming as always.

"What a fright! Isn't that right, Andrea?"

"Why have you told me so much nonsense, Román?"

"Nonsense?" But he was laughing. "I'm not so sure it is. . . . Haven't I told you the story of the god Xochipilli, my little idol accustomed to receiving human hearts? One day you'll be tired of my weak offerings of music and then . . ."

"Román, you're not frightening me anymore, but I'm nervous. . . . Can't you talk in another tone? If you can't, I'm leaving. . . ."

"And then"—Román laughed even more, his teeth white beneath his little black mustache—"then I'll offer Juan up to Xochipilli, I'll offer him Juan's brain and Gloria's heart. . . ."

He sighed.

"Miserable offerings, in spite of everything. Maybe your beautiful, ordered brain would be better. . . ."

I ran down the stairs to the apartment, pursued by Román's amused laughter. Because the fact is I escaped. I escaped and the steps flew under my feet. Román's laughter reached me, like the bony hand of a devil snatching at the hem of my skirt. . . .

I avoided supper so I wouldn't see Román. Not because I was afraid of him; one minute after it was over, the conversation seemed absurd, but it had disturbed me, I felt enervated and had no desire to meet his eyes. Now, and not when I saw him snooping so meanly, not respecting the lives of others, now, and not all those previous days when I ran from him, thinking I had contempt for him, now was when I began to feel an indefinable revulsion for Román.

I went to bed and couldn't sleep. The light from the dining room made a brilliant line under the door to the room; I heard voices. Román's eyes were on mine: "You won't need anything when the things in the house seize your senses." . . . This continual rumination on the ideas he had suggested had seemed terrifying to me. I was alone and lost under my blankets. For the first time I felt a real longing for human company. For the first time I felt in my palms the yearning for another hand to soothe me. . . . Then the telephone, there at the head of the bed, began to ring. I'd forgotten that this thing even existed in the house, because only Angustias used it. I picked up the mouthpiece, still shuddering with the impact of its piercing sound, and into my ears came a joy so great (because it was like a response to my state of mind) that at first I didn't hear her.

It was Ena, who had found the number in the telephone book and was calling me.

VIII

Angustias came back on a midnight train and ran into Gloria on the stairs. The sound of their voices woke me. I quickly realized I was sleeping in a room that wasn't mine and that its mistress was going to reclaim it.

I jumped out of bed, pierced by cold and drowsiness. So frightened that I felt I couldn't move, although, in fact, that was all I did: In a few seconds I pulled the bedclothes from the bed and wrapped them around me. I tossed the pillow onto a chair in the dining room as I walked past, and reached the foyer wrapped in a blanket, barefoot on the freezing tiles, at the very moment Angustias came in from the street, followed by the driver with her bags, and leading Gloria by her arm. Granny appeared, too, confused and stammering when she saw Gloria.

"Come, child, come. . . . Run to my room!" she said.

But Angustias didn't let go of Gloria's arm.

"No, Mamá. No, absolutely not."

The driver observed the scene from the corner of his eye. Angustias paid him and closed the door. Immediately she turned to Gloria.

"Hussy! Tell me, what were you doing on the stairs at this time of night?"

Gloria was as self-absorbed as a cat. Her painted mouth looked very dark.

"I already told you, *chica,* I heard you arriving and I came to welcome you."

"You're shameless!" shouted Angustias.

My aunt's appearance was pitiful. She had on her immutable hat, the same one she was wearing the day she left, but the feather was twisted and protruded like a fierce horn. She crossed herself and began praying with her hands on her chest.

"Oh, Lord, give me patience! Give me patience, oh, Lord!"

I felt the cold burning the soles of my feet and I shivered violently under my blanket.

What will she say, I was thinking, *when she finds out I used her room?* Granny began to cry.

"Angustias, let the girl go, let the girl go."

She was like a baby.

"I can't believe it's true, Mamá! I can't believe it's true!" Angustias shouted again. "You don't even ask her where she's been. . . . Would you have wanted one of your daughters acting like that? You, Mamá, you didn't even let us to go to parties at our friends' houses when we were young, and you defend this tramp's nighttime gallivanting!"

She raised her hands to her head and took off her hat. She sat on her suitcase and began to moan.

"I'm losing my mind! I'm losing my mind!"

Gloria slipped away like a shadow toward my grandmother's room just as Antonia came snooping and then Juan, squeezed into an old overcoat.

"May I ask what all the shouting's about? Animal!" he said, addressing Angustias. "Don't you realize that tomorrow I have to get up at five and need my sleep?"

"Instead of insulting me you'd be better off asking your wife what she's doing out at this time of night!"

Juan stopped short, his jaw pointing toward my grandmother.

"What does Gloria have to do with this?"

"Gloria's in her room, dear. . . . I mean in my room, with the baby. . . . She went out to the stairs to welcome Angustias, and she thought Gloria was going out. It's a misunderstanding."

Angustias looked at my grandmother in a fury, and Juan, gigantic, was in the middle of all of us. His reaction was unexpected.

"Why are you lying, Mamá? Damn you! . . . And you, you witch, why do you meddle in other people's business? My wife is no concern of yours! Who are you to stop her from going out at night if she wants to? She doesn't have to ask permission from anybody in this house but me, and I'm the only one who can give it . . . so get into your room and stop your howling!"

Angustias, in fact, did go to her room, and Juan stood biting the inside of his cheeks, the way he always did when he was nervous. The maid was so eager she screeched with pleasure from the door of her lair. Juan turned toward her with a raised fist, and then he let it drop, unclenched.

I went into the living room that was my bedroom and I was surprised by the smell of stale air and dust. How cold it was! On the mattress of that divan, as thin as a leaf, all I could do was shiver.

The door opened right after I went in, and once again I saw the figure of Angustias. She stumbled against a piece of furniture in the dark and groaned.

"Andrea!" she shouted. "Andrea!"

"Here I am."

I could hear her breathing heavily.

"I am offering up to the Lord the bitterness that all of you cause me. . . . May I know what your dress is doing in my room?"

I concentrated for a moment. In the silence I could begin to hear an argument in my grandmother's distant bedroom.

"I slept there these past few days," I said at last.

Angustias stretched out her arms as if she were going to fall or feel her way until she found me. I closed my eyes, but she stumbled again and groaned.

"God forgive you for the sorrow you cause me. . . . You're like a crow on my eyes. . . . A crow that would like to be my heir while I'm still alive."

At that moment Gloria's scream crossed the foyer and then the sound of the door to the bedroom she and Juan shared slamming shut. Angustias stood erect, listening. Now there seemed to be stifled sobbing.

"My God! It's enough to drive you mad!" my aunt murmured.

She changed her tone:

"And you, Señorita, I'll settle accounts with you tomorrow. Come to my room as soon as you get up. Do you hear me?"

"Yes."

She closed the door and left. The house, growling like an old animal, was filled with echoes. The dog, behind the maid's door, began to howl, to whimper, and its voice mixed with another of Gloria's screams, and then with her crying, and the more distant crying of the baby. Then the child's weeping became the dominant sound, the one that filled all the corners of the house, which was quiet at last. I heard Juan leave his room again to take his son from my grandmother's room. Then I heard how he walked him monotonously around the foyer, how he talked to him to calm him down and get him to sleep. It wasn't the first time Juan's songs to his son reached me on cold nights. Juan had an unexpected, intimate, almost savage tenderness for the baby. Only once every two weeks would Gloria sleep in my grandmother's room with the boy so that his capricious crying wouldn't wake Juan, who had to leave the house before dawn and spend the day in difficult second jobs from which he would return, exhausted, the next night.

The unfortunate night that Angustias came home was one when my uncle had to get up very early.

Still awake, I heard him leave before the factory sirens pierced the morning fog. The Barcelona sky was still full of sea damp and stars when Juan went out.

I had just fallen asleep, curled up and freezing, when I woke under the impact of Antonia's eyes. That woman exhaled personal amusement.

She screeched:

"Your aunt says you should come. . . ."

And she stood looking at me, her hands on her hips, while I rubbed my eyes and dressed.

When I was completely awake, sitting on the edge of the bed, I found myself in one of my moments of rebellion against Angustias, the strongest I'd had. Suddenly I realized I wouldn't put up with her anymore. That I wouldn't obey her anymore after the days of complete freedom I'd enjoyed in her absence. The disturbances of the night had put my nerves on edge and I felt hysterical, too, weepy and desperate. I realized I could endure everything: the cold that permeated my worn clothes, the sadness of my absolute poverty, the dull horror of the filthy house. Everything except her control over me. That was what had suffocated me when I arrived in Barcelona, what had made me fall into ennui, what had killed off my initiative: that look from Angustias. That hand that quashed my movements, my curiosity about a new life. . . . Yet Angustias, in her way, was an upright, good person among those crazy people. A more complete and vigorous person than the others. . . . I didn't know why that awful indignation with her rose in me, why the mere sight of her long body and especially her innocent delusions of grandeur blocked out the light for me. It's difficult to get along with people of another generation, even when they don't try to impose their way of seeing things on us. And when they do want to make us see with their eyes, for the experiment to be even moderately successful the older people need great tact and sensitivity, and the young need to feel admiration for them.

Rebellious, I didn't respond to her summons for a long time. I washed and dressed to go to the university and arranged the papers in my book bag before deciding to go into her room.

I saw my aunt right away, sitting at her desk. So tall and familiar in her stiff housecoat, as if she had never—not since our first conversation on the morning after my arrival—moved from that chair. As if the light that formed a halo around her graying hair and exaggerated her full lips were the same light. As if she had not yet withdrawn pensive fingers from her forehead.

(The vision of that room in twilight, the chair empty and Román's lively hands, diabolical and attractive, rummaging through the small, prudish desk, was too unreal an image.)

I noticed that Angustias had her languid, helpless air. Her eyes were heavy and sad. For three quarters of an hour she had been sweetening her voice.

"Sit down, child. I need to have a serious talk with you." These were ritual words that I knew all too well. I obeyed, resigned and rigid, ready to jump up, as at other times I'd been prepared to silently swallow all her absurdities. Still, what she said to me was extraordinary:

"You'll be happy, Andrea, because you don't love me; in a few days I'm leaving this house forever. In a few days you'll be able to sleep in my bed, the one you want so much. Look at yourself in the mirror on my armoire. Study at this desk. . . . Last night I became angry with you because what was going on was unbearable. . . . I've committed a sin of pride. Forgive me."

She watched me out of the corner of her eye as she begged my pardon with so little sincerity it made me smile. Then her face became rigid, sown with vertical wrinkles.

"You don't have a heart, Andrea."

I was afraid I'd misunderstood what she said at first. That the fantastic announcement of emancipation wasn't true.

"Where are you going?"

Then she said she was returning to the convent, where she'd spent those days of intense spiritual preparation. It was a cloistered order, and for many years she'd been accumulating the dowry she needed to enter it, and now she was ready. To me, however, the idea of Angustias submerged in a contemplative environment seemed absurd.

"Have you always had a vocation?"

"When you're older you'll understand why a woman shouldn't be alone in the world."

"Do you mean that a woman, if she can't get married, has no choice but to enter a convent?"

"That isn't my idea."

(She moved uneasily.)

"But it's true there are only two paths for a woman. Only two honorable paths.... I've chosen mine, and I'm proud of it. I've acted as a daughter of my family should. As your mother would have done in my position. And God will understand my sacrifice."

She was lost in thought.

(*Where have they gone,* I was thinking, *that family who gathered in the evenings around the piano, protected from the cold by ugly, comfortable green velvet drapes? Where have the modest daughters gone, wearing their enormous hats, who, when they set foot—chaperoned by their father—on the sidewalk of a joyful and swift-paced Calle de Aribau where they lived, lowered their eyes in order to look secretly at the passersby?* I shuddered to think that one of them had died and that her long black braid was kept in an old armoire in a village so far from here. Another, the older one, would soon disappear from her chair, her balcony, taking her hat with her—the last hat in the house.)

Finally Angustias sighed, and I saw her again, just as she was. She brandished a pencil.

"For all this time I've been thinking about you.... There was a moment, when you first arrived, when it seemed to me that my obligation was to be a mother to you. To stay at your side, protect you. You failed me, you disappointed me. I thought I'd find an orphan longing for affection and I've seen a demon of rebellion, a creature who stiffened if I caressed her. You, child, have been my final hope and my final despair. All that's left is for me to pray for you, and oh, how you need it, how you need it!"

Then she said to me:

"If I'd gotten hold of you when you were younger, I'd have beaten you to death!"

And in her voice I could detect a certain bitter gloating that made me feel I'd been saved from certain danger.

I made a move to leave and she stopped me.

"It doesn't matter if you miss your classes today. You have to listen to me. . . . For two weeks I've been asking God for your death . . . or for the miracle of your salvation. I'm going to leave you alone in a house that is no longer what it was . . . because it once was like paradise and now"—Aunt Angustias had a flash of inspiration— "with your uncle Juan's wife, the evil serpent has come in. She has poisoned everything. She, she alone, has driven my mother crazy . . . because your grandmother is crazy, my child, and the worst of it is that I see her throwing herself into the chasms of hell if she doesn't change her ways before she dies. Your grandmother was a saint, Andrea. In my youth, because of her, I lived in the purest of dreams, but now she's gone crazy with age. And the hardships of the war that she apparently tolerated so well have made her crazy. And then that woman, with her flattery, has made her lose her mind completely. I can't understand her attitude any other way."

"My grandmother tries to understand each person."

(I thought of her words *Things are not always what they seem,* when she tried to protect Angustias . . . but did I dare talk to my aunt about Don Jerónimo?)

"Yes, child, yes. . . . And that suits you very well. It's as if you'd lived on your own in a Red zone and not in a convent of nuns during the war. Even Gloria has more excuses than you in her yearning for emancipation and disorder. She's a little street slut, while you've received an education . . . and don't excuse yourself with your curiosity about Barcelona. I've shown you Barcelona."

Instinctively I looked at my watch.

"You listen to me like a person listening to the rain, I can see that ... you wretch! Life will batter you, crush you, flatten you! Then you'll think of me. . . . Oh! I would rather have killed you when you were little than let you grow up like this! And don't look at me so surprised. I know that so far you haven't done anything bad. But you will as soon as I go. . . . You will! You will! You won't control your body and your soul. You won't, you won't. . . . You won't be able to control them."

I saw in the mirror, out of the corner of my eye, the image of my eighteen arid years, enclosed in an elongated body, and I saw the beautiful, shapely hand of Angustias convulsed on the back of a chair. A white hand, with a plump, soft palm. A sensual hand, brazen now, shouting louder with the clenching of its fingers than my aunt was with her impassioned voice.

I began to feel moved and a little frightened, for Angustias's delirium threatened to enclose me and drag me along, too.

She finished, trembling and crying. Angustias rarely wept with sincerity. Weeping always made her ugly, but the hideous sobbing shaking her now didn't cause repugnance in me but a certain pleasure. Something like watching a storm break.

"Andrea," she said at last, gently, "Andrea ... I have to talk to you about other *things.*" She dried her eyes and began to work out the accounts. "From now on you'll receive your allowance directly. You'll give your grandmother whatever you think appropriate to help pay for your food, and you'll take care of budgeting to buy what you need. . . . I don't have to tell you that you should spend as little as possible on yourself. On the day my salary's gone, this house will be a disaster. Your grandmother has always preferred her male children, but those sons"—here it seemed she grew happy—"are going to make her suffer penury. . . . In this house we women have known how to maintain dignity."

She sighed.

"And still do. If only Gloria had never come here!"

———

Gloria, the snake woman, slept curled up in her bed until noon, exhausted and moaning in her sleep. In the afternoon she showed me the marks on her body from the beating Juan had given her the night before; they were beginning to turn black and blue.

IX

Like a flock of crows perching on the branches of the tree where a dead man hangs, Angustias's friends, dressed in black, sat in her room during this time. Angustias was the only person in our house who still grasped desperately at society.

Her friends were the same ones who had waltzed to the rhythms of Granny's piano. The ones whom years and vicissitudes had distanced and who now came back, flapping their wings, when they learned of Angustias's chaste, beautiful death to the life of this world. They'd come from different corners of Barcelona and were of an age as alien to their bodies as adolescence. Few of them had maintained a normal appearance. Swollen or skinny, their features tended to look small or large depending on the circumstances, as if they were fake. I enjoyed looking at them. Some had white hair, which gave them a nobility the others were lacking.

They all remembered the old days in the house.

"Your father, what a fine gentleman, with his full beard . . ."

"Your sisters, how vivacious they were! . . . Lord, Lord, how your house has changed."

"How the times have changed!"

"Yes, the times..."

(And they looked at one another, flustered.)

"Do you remember, Angustias, that green dress you wore the day you turned twenty? The truth is, that evening when we got together, we were a group of good-looking girls.... And that suitor of yours, that Jerónimo Sanz, the one you were so crazy about? Whatever happened to him?"

Somebody steps on the foot of the chattering woman, who falls into surprised silence. A few anguished seconds go by and then all of them start talking at once.

(They truly were like aged, dark birds, their breasts throbbing after flying so much across a very small piece of sky.)

———

"Chica," said Gloria, "I don't know why Angustias hasn't gone away with Don Jerónimo, or why she's becoming a nun when she's no good at praying...."

Gloria was lying on her bed, where the baby was crawling, and she was making an effort to think, perhaps for the first time in her life.

"Why do you think Angustias is no good at praying?" I asked in surprise. "You know how much she likes going to church."

"Because I compare her to your granny, somebody who really knows how to pray, and I see the difference.... Mamá's outside herself, like she was hearing music from heaven; at night she talks to God and the Virgin. She says God can bless all suffering and that's why God blesses me, though I don't pray as much as I should.... And how good she is! She's never left her house and still she understands all kinds of crazy things and forgives them. God hasn't given Angustias any kind of understanding, and when she prays in church she doesn't hear any music from heaven but instead she looks around to see who's come into church in short sleeves and with bare legs.... I think in her heart she doesn't care any more about praying than I do, and I'm no good at praying.... But the truth is," she concluded, "I'm so glad she's leaving! . . . The other night Juan hit me because of her. Just because of her . . ."

"Where were you going, Gloria?"

"Oh, *chica*, it was nothing bad. To see my sister, you know . . . I can tell you don't believe me, but that's where I was going, I swear. It's just that Juan doesn't let me go, and he watches me during the day. But don't look at me like that, don't look at me like that, Andrea, that face you put on really makes me want to laugh."

———

"Bah!" said Román. "I'm glad Angustias is leaving, because right now she's a living piece of the past that interferes with the progress of things. . . . My things. She bothers all of us, she reminds all of us that we aren't mature, rounded, settled people like her, but blindly rushing waters pounding at the earth the best we can in order to erupt where least expected. . . . For all of that I'm glad. When she leaves I'll love her, Andrea, you know? And I'll be touched by the memory of her hideous felt hat with the feather sticking up, to the very end, like a banner . . . indicating that the heart of the home that once was and that the rest of us have lost, is still beating." He turned to me, smiling, as if the two of us shared a secret. "At the same time I'm sorry she's leaving, because I won't be able to read the love letters she receives anymore, or her diary. . . . What sentimental letters and what a masochistic diary! Reading it satisfied all my instincts for cruelty. . . ."

And Román licked his red lips with his tongue.

———

Juan and I seemed to be the only ones with no opinion about how events were developing. I was too astounded, because the only desire in my life had been for people to leave me alone to do what I wanted, and at that moment it seemed the time had come for me to achieve it without any effort on my part. I thought of the muffled battle I'd had for two years with my cousin Isabel until she finally let me leave her and attend the university. When I arrived in Barcelona I was fresh from my first victory, but I immediately found other vigilant eyes watching me and I became accustomed to the game of hiding, resisting.... Now, suddenly, I would find myself without an enemy.

During this time I became humble with Angustias. I'd have kissed her hands if she had wanted that. A terrible joy seemed to hollow out my chest. I didn't think about the others, I didn't think about Angustias: only about me.

I was surprised, however, at the absence of Don Jerónimo in that interminable parade of friends. They were all women except for some big-bellied husband who'd occasionally put in an appearance.

"It's like a wake, don't you think?" shouted Antonia from her kitchen.

At those times macabre thoughts came to all our imaginations.

Gloria told me that Don Jerónimo and Angustias saw each other every morning in church, and she knew it for a fact.... All of Angustias's story was like a novel from the last century.

I remember that on the day Aunt Angustias left, the various members of the family were up almost at dawn. We ran into one another in the house, possessed by nervousness. Juan roared curses at the slightest thing. At the last minute we all decided to go to the station except Román. He was the only one who didn't appear all day. Then, long afterward, he told me he'd been at church very early in the morning, following Angustias and watching how she confessed. I imagined Román with his ears straining toward that long confession, envying the poor priest, old and tired, who dispassionately poured absolution on my aunt's head.

The taxi was full. Three of Angustias's friends came with us, her three closest friends.

The baby was frightened and clutched at Juan's neck. They almost never took him out, and though he was fat, his skin had a sad-looking color in the sun.

On the platform we stood in groups around Angustias, who kissed and embraced us. Granny appeared tearful after the last embrace.

We formed so grotesque a gathering that some people turned around to look at us.

A few minutes before it was time for the train to leave, Angustias climbed into the car and looked at us from the window, hieratic, weeping, sad, almost blessing us, like a saint.

Juan was nervous, making ironic faces in all directions, frightening Angustias's friends—who grouped together as far from him as possible—with his rolling eyes. His legs began to tremble inside his trousers. He couldn't control himself.

"Don't play the martyr, Angustias, you're not fooling anybody! You're feeling more pleasure than a thief with his pockets full. . . . You don't fool me with this farce of sanctity!"

The train began to move and Angustias crossed herself and covered her ears because Juan's voice could be heard all over the platform.

Gloria seized her husband by his jacket, terrified. And he turned with his madman's eyes, in a fury, trembling as if he were about to suffer an epileptic attack. Then he began to run after the train, shouting things that Angustias could no longer hear.

"You're a wretch! Do you hear me? You didn't marry him because your father decided to tell you that a shopkeeper's son wasn't good enough for you. . . . That's whyyyy! And when he came back from America, married and rich, you amused yourself with him, you've been stealing him from his wife for twenty years . . . and now you don't have the courage to go away with him because you think all of Calle de Aribau and all of Barcelona care what you do. . . . And you have contempt for my wife! You evil woman! You and your saint's halo!"

People laughed and followed him to the end of the platform, where he was still shouting after the train had left. Tears ran down his cheeks and he was laughing, satisfied. The trip back to the house was a calamity.

PART TWO

X

I left Ena's house in a daze and had the impression that it must be very late. All the street doors were locked, and the sky was pouring a dense shower of stars over the roofs.

For the first time I felt at large and free in the city, not fearing the phantom of time. I'd had a few drinks that evening. So much heat and excitement rose from my body that I didn't feel the cold or even—at moments—the force of gravity under my feet.

I stopped in the middle of Vía Layetana and looked at the tall building where my friend lived on the top floor. No light could be seen through the closed blinds, though when I had left people were still gathered there, and the comfortable rooms inside must still have been illuminated. Perhaps Ena's mother had sat at the piano again to sing. A chill ran down my spine when I remembered the ardent voice that seemed to burn as it flowed out, enveloping the owner's wasted body in radiance.

That voice had stirred up all the sediment of sentimentality and runaway romanticism of my eighteen years. After she stopped singing I became restless, longing to escape everything else around me. It seemed impossible that the others could keep smoking and eating snacks. Ena herself, though she had listened to her mother with somber, absorbed attention, opened up again, laughing and sparkling among her friends, as if the gathering, spontaneously begun late in the afternoon, would never end. Suddenly I found myself on the street. I'd almost fled, impelled by a restlessness as strong and unspecified as all the others tormenting me at that age.

I didn't know if I needed to walk past silent houses in some sleeping neighborhood, breathing in the black wind from the sea, or feel the lights surging from the signs whose colored bulbs tinted the atmosphere in the center of the city. I still wasn't sure what would do more to calm the almost agonizing thirst for beauty that listening to Ena's mother had left in me. Vía Layetana itself increased my perplexity as it sloped gently down from the Plaza de Urquinaona, where the sky was stained by the red of artificial lights, to the large post office building and the port, bathed in shadows and silvery with starlight above the white flames in the street lamps.

Gravely, in the wintry air, I heard the eleven o'clock bells joining in a concert that came from the towers of old churches.

Vía Layetana, so broad, large, and new, crossed the heart of the old neighborhood. Then I knew what I longed for: I wanted to see the Cathedral enveloped in the charm and mystery of the night. Without thinking anymore, I hurried toward the darkness of the narrow streets that surrounded it. Nothing could calm and astound my imagination like that Gothic city; it sunk among damp houses that were built without style amid those venerable stones, but that the years had also covered with a patina of unique charm, as if they had been infected by beauty.

The cold seemed more intense, channeled in the twisting streets. And the sky turned into glittering strips between roofs that almost touched. The solitude was overwhelming, as if all the residents of the city had died. An occasional lament of air throbbed in the doorways. Nothing else.

When I reached the apse of the Cathedral, I stared at the dance of lights cast by the street lamps against its thousands of nooks and corners, making them romantic and shadowy. I heard a harsh ing, as if someone were attempting to clear his throat in the tal of alleys. A sinister sound that was approaching, accompanied by echoes. I had a few frightened moments. I saw a tall old man with a poverty-stricken appearance emerge from the blackness. I pressed against the wall. He looked at me suspiciously and kept walking. He had a long white beard that the wind divided in two. My heart began to pound with unusual force, and, carried along by the same emotional impulse that had driven me there, I ran after him and touched his arm. Then I began to look nervously through my bag, while the old man watched me. I gave him two pesetas. I saw a spark of irony shine in his eyes. He put the coins in his pocket without saying a word and walked away, dragging behind him the hoarse cough that had terrified me. This human contact in the silent concert of the stones calmed me a little. I thought I was behaving like a fool that night, acting without will, like a sheet of paper in the wind. Still, I hurried until I reached the principal façade of the Cathedral, and when I looked up at it, I found at last the fulfillment of everything I had longed for.

A power greater than the one the wine and music had exerted over me filled me when I looked at the great expanse of shadows of fervent stone. The Cathedral rose in severe harmony, stylized in almost vegetal forms, up to the height of the clean Mediterranean sky. A peace, an imposing clarity, overflowed the marvelous architecture. Around its dark shapes the brilliant night stood out, turning slowly to the rhythm of the hours. I let that profound spell of forms penetrate me for a few minutes. Then I turned to leave.

When I did I realized I wasn't alone. A silhouette that seemed rather satanic to me lengthened in the darkest part of the plaza. I confess in all candor that I felt possessed by all the terrors of my childhood, and I crossed myself. The shape was moving toward me, and I saw it was a man wearing a good overcoat and a hat pulled down over his eyes. He reached me as I was rushing toward the stone steps.

ır name Andrea?"

by something insulting in his way of calling to
n surprise. He stood in front of me and laughed
d large gums.

d of scare girls get when they wander around
it. . . . Don't you remember seeing me at Ena's
house?"

"Ah! . . . Yes, yes," I said sullenly.

(*Damn you!* I thought. *You've robbed me of all the happiness I was going to take away from here.*)

"Well, yes," he continued, satisfied. "I'm Gerardo."

He was motionless, his hands in his pockets, looking at me. I moved toward the stairs to go down, but he held my arm.

"Look!" he commanded.

I saw, at the foot of the stairs, and pressing up against them, a cluster of old houses that the war had turned into rubble, lit by street lamps.

"All this will disappear. A great avenue will go through here, and there'll be enough space and extension to see the Cathedral."

He didn't say anything else and we began to walk down the stone steps together. We'd already gone a fair distance when he said:

"Doesn't it scare you to walk the streets alone? Suppose the wolf comes along and eats you up?"

I didn't answer.

"Are you mute?"

"I prefer to go by myself," I confessed harshly.

"No, absolutely not, my girl. . . . Today I'll walk you home. . . . Seriously, Andrea, if I were your father I wouldn't let you wander around like this."

I gave vent to my feelings by insulting him to myself. I'd seen the boy at Ena's house and had thought he was a fool, and ugly.

We crossed the Ramblas, bustling with animation and lights, and went up Calle de Pelayo to the plaza of the university. There I said good-bye.

"No, no; all the way to your house."

"You're an idiot," I said outright. "Go away right now."

"I'd like to be your friend. You're a very original kid. If you promise that one day you'll phone me to go out with me, I'll leave you here. I like old streets, too, and I know all the picturesque corners in the city. So, is it a promise?"

"Yes," I said, feeling nervous.

He handed me his card and left.

Entering Calle de Aribau was like entering my house. The same watchman as the day I arrived in the city opened the door for me. And Granny, just as she did then, came out to welcome me, freezing with cold. Everyone else had gone to bed.

I went into Angustias's room, which I'd inherited a few days earlier, and when I turned on the light I discovered that a pile of the extra chairs from all over the house had been placed on top of the armoire and were somberly threatening to fall. The piece of furniture that held the baby's clothing had also been installed in the room, as well as a large sewing table with legs that had previously been in the corner of my grandmother's bedroom. The rumpled bed still bore the imprint of Gloria's siesta. I understood immediately that my dreams of independence, isolated from the rest of the house in that inherited refuge, had collapsed. I sighed and began to undress. On the night table was a paper with a note from Juan: *Niece, please don't lock the door. There should always be free access to your room so we can answer the phone.* Obediently I crossed the cold floor again to unlock the door, then I lay down on the bed, wrapping myself voluptuously in the blanket.

On the street I heard someone clapping to call the watchman. A long while after that the whistle of a train as it passed, distant and nostalgic, along Calle de Aragón. The day had brought me the beginning of a new life; I understood that Juan had wanted to spoil things for me as much as he could by letting me know that even though I'd been granted a bed in the house, that was the only thing I'd been given. . . .

On the same night Angustias left, I'd said I didn't want to eat at home and therefore would pay only a monthly rent for my room. I'd seized the opportunity when Juan, still intoxicated and excited by the emotions of that day, had confronted me.

"Well, let's see, niece, with what you contribute to the house . . . because, I'll tell you the truth, I don't feel like supporting anybody. . . ."

"No, what I can pay is so little it's hardly worth it," I said, being diplomatic. "I'll arrange to eat on my own. I'll just pay for my ration of bread and my room."

Juan shrugged.

"Do what you want," he said, in a bad humor.

Granny listened, shaking her head with an air of disapproval, watching Juan's lips. Then she began to cry.

"No, no, she can't pay for her room . . . my granddaughter can't pay for a room in her grandmother's house."

But that's what was decided. I wouldn't have to pay for more than my daily bread.

That day I'd received my allowance for February, and possessed by the charms of being able to spend it, I hurried out and acquired without delay those trifles I'd wanted so much . . . good soap, perfume, and a new blouse to wear to Ena's house: She had invited me to lunch. And some roses for her mother. Buying the roses was particularly gratifying. They were magnificent flowers, expensive in those days. One might say they were beyond my reach. And yet I held them in my arms and gave them as a gift. This pleasure, in which I found the taste for rebellion that was the vice—vulgar, from one point of view—of my youth, subsequently became an obsession.

I thought—lying in my bed—of the warm welcome I'd received from Ena's family at her house and how, since I was accustomed to the dark faces with well-defined features of the people in my house, the number of blond heads around me at the table had begun to make me dizzy.

Ena's parents and her five brothers were blondes. These five brothers, all younger than my friend, had affable, smiling, ordinary faces that became confused in my imagination. Not even the youngest, who was seven and whose missing baby teeth gave him a comical expression when he laughed, and whose name was Ramón Berenguer, as if he were an ancient count of Barcelona, could be distinguished from his brothers except in these two details.

The father seemed to share the same attractive character traits as his offspring and was also a really handsome man, whom Ena resembled. Like her, he had green eyes, though his lacked the strange, magnificent light that animated his daughter's. In him everything seemed simple and open, without malice of any kind. During the meal I remember him laughing as he recounted anecdotes of his travels, because for many years they had lived in different places in Europe. It was as if he'd known me my whole life, and simply because I was at his table he had added me to his patriarchal family.

Ena's mother, on the other hand, gave the impression of being reserved, though she smiled and contributed to the pleasant atmosphere that had been created. Among her husband and children—all of them tall and sturdy—she seemed a strange, rachitic bird. She was very small, and I found it astonishing that her narrow body had supported the weight of a child six times. My first impression of her was of a strange ugliness. Then two or three touches of an almost prodigious beauty in her became evident: silky, very abundant hair that was lighter than Ena's, long golden eyes, and her magnificent voice.

"There, where you see her, Andrea," said the head of the family, "my wife is something of a vagabond. She can't be at peace anywhere and she drags all of us with her."

"Don't exaggerate, Luis," his wife said with a gentle smile.

"Essentially it's true. Of course your father is the one who sends me to the strangest places to represent him and manage his businesses—you see, Andrea, my father-in-law is my employer, too—but you're behind all the moves. You can't deny that if you wanted to, your father would have you living peacefully in Barcelona. The influence you have over him was clear in that London matter.... Of course I'm delighted by your tastes, dear girl; I don't reproach you for them." And he enveloped her in an affectionate smile. "All my life I've liked to travel and see new things.... And I can't control a kind of feverish activity that's almost a pleasure when I enter a new business environment, with people whose psychology is so unfamiliar. It's like beginning the struggle all over again, and one feels rejuvenated...."

"But Mamá likes Barcelona," Ena declared, "more than any other place in the world. I know."

Her mother gave her a special smile that seemed dreamy and amused at the same time.

"I'm always happy anywhere all of you are. And your father's right about my sometimes feeling an urge to travel; of course that's a long way"—her smile grew broader—"from managing my father...."

"And since we're talking about these things, Margarita," her husband continued, "do you know what your father told me yesterday? It's possible that next season we'll be needed in Madrid.... What do you think? The truth is that right now I'd rather be in Barcelona than anywhere else, especially considering that your brother..."

"Yes, Luis, I think we have to talk about it. But now we're boring this child. Andrea, you'll have to forgive us. When all is said and done, we're a family of merchants who end every conversation talking about business...."

Ena had listened to the last part of the conversation with extraordinary interest.

"Bah! My grandfather's a little crazy, I think. So emotional and weepy when he sees Mamá after she's been away and then turning right around and planning to have us leave again. I don't want to leave Barcelona now.... It doesn't make sense! After all, Barcelona's my city and you could say I only got to know it since the war ended."

(She looked at me quickly, and I caught her glance because I knew she'd just fallen in love and this was her supreme and secret argument for not wanting to leave the city.)

In bed on Calle de Aribau, I evoked this conversation in all its detail and was shaken by alarm at the idea of separating from my friend when I'd become so fond of her. I thought the plans of that important old man—Ena's rich grandfather—moved too many people around and wounded too many feelings of affection.

In the agreeable confusion of ideas that precedes sleep my fears were abating, replaced by vague images of empty streets at night. The lofty dream of the Cathedral invaded me again.

I slept, agitated by my final glimpse of the eyes of Ena's mother; as we were saying good-bye, they glanced up at me, fleetingly, with a strange look of anguish and fear.

Those eyes entered my deepest sleep and raised nightmares.

XI

"Niece, don't be stubborn," said Juan. "You'll starve to death."

And he placed his hands on my shoulders in an awkward caress.

"No, thanks; I'm getting on just fine...."

In the meantime I looked at my uncle out of the corner of my eye and saw that things didn't seem to be going too well for him, either. He had caught me drinking the water the vegetables had been cooked in, cold and forgotten in a corner of the kitchen, ready to be thrown out.

Antonia had shouted in disgust:

"What filthy things are you up to?"

I turned red.

"It's just that I like this broth. And since I saw you were going to throw it out..."

Antonia's shouts brought the other people in the house. Juan proposed a reconciliation of our economic interests. I refused.

The truth is I felt happier since I'd disentangled myself from the knot of meals at home. It didn't matter that I spent too much that month and barely had the daily peseta I budgeted for food: Midday is the most beautiful time in winter. A good time to sit in the sun in a park or on the Plaza de Cataluña. At times I thought, with delight, about what was happening at home. My ears filled with the parrot's screeching and Juan's cursing. I preferred my independent wandering.

I learned about delights and flavors I'd never thought of before; for example, dried fruit was a discovery for me. Toasted almonds, or better yet, peanuts, whose pleasures last longer because you have to get them out of their shells, brought me great satisfaction.

The truth is I didn't have the patience to distribute the thirty pesetas I had left on the first day over the thirty days of the month. On Calle de Tallers I found a cheap restaurant and was mad enough to eat there two or three times. I thought the food was better than any I'd ever tasted in my life, infinitely better than anything Antonia prepared on Calle de Aribau. It was a curious restaurant. Dark, with a few sad tables. A self-absorbed waiter served me. People ate quickly, looking at one another and not saying a word. All the restaurants and cafés I'd ever gone into were noisy except that one. It offered a soup I thought was good, made with boiling water and pieces of bread. This soup was always the same, colored yellow by saffron or red by paprika; but on the "menu" its name changed frequently. I left there satisfied and didn't need anything else.

In the morning I took a loaf of bread—as soon as Antonia brought the rations up from the bakery—and ate the whole thing, it was so warm and delicious. At night I didn't eat supper, unless Ena's mother insisted I stay at her house. I'd developed the habit of going to study with Ena on many afternoons, and the family was beginning to consider me as one of their own.

I thought a rebirth was really beginning for me, that this was the happiest time in my life, since I'd never had a friend with whom I'd been so close, or the magnificent independence I enjoyed so much. I spent the last days of the month eating nothing but my ration of bread, the little loaf I devoured in the morning—that was when Antonia caught me drinking the vegetable water—but I was beginning to get used to it, and the proof is that as soon as I received my allowance for March I spent it in exactly the same way. I remember that I felt extraordinarily hungry when I had the new money in my hands, and that it was a sharp, delicious sensation to think I could satisfy that hunger right away. More than any kind of food, what I wanted was candy. I bought a box and went to an expensive movie. I was so impatient that before the lights went out I tore a little piece of the paper to eat some of the cream filling, though I stole sideways glances at the people around me, overwhelmed with embarrassment. As soon as the screen lit up and the theater went dark, I opened the package and swallowed the chocolates one by one. Until then I hadn't suspected that food could be so good, so extraordinary. . . . When the lights went on again there was nothing left in the box. I saw that a woman sitting beside me looked at me out of the corner of her eye and whispered something to her companion. They both laughed.

On Calle de Aribau they were also feeling hunger pangs, but without the compensations I had obtained. I'm not referring to Antonia and Trueno. I suppose the two of them had their sustenance assured, thanks to Román's munificence. The dog was well fed and I often saw it gnawing at juicy bones. The maid also cooked her food separately. But Juan and Gloria were going hungry, and my grandmother, too, and even the baby at times.

For almost two months Román had been traveling again. Before he went away he left some provisions for my grandmother, condensed milk and other treats difficult to find in those days. I never saw the old lady taste them. They would disappear mysteriously and their traces would appear on the baby's mouth.

On the same day Juan invited me to join the family again, he had a terrible argument with Gloria. We all heard them shouting in the studio. I went out to the foyer and saw that the hall was obstructed by the figure of the maid, who was listening at the door.

"I'm sick of all this brazenness," Juan shouted. "Do you hear me? I can't even replace my brushes! Those people still owe us a lot of money. What I can't understand is that you don't want me to go and demand it from them."

"Well, *chico*, you gave me your word you wouldn't get involved, that you'd let me take care of it, and now you can't go back. You know you were very glad when you could sell that trashy painting on credit. . . ."

"I'll strangle you! Bitch!"

The maid sighed with pleasure and I went out to breathe the cold air, heavy with aromas from the stores. The sidewalks, stained with twilight dampness, reflected the lights of the street lamps that had just been turned on.

When I came back, my grandmother and Juan were having supper. Juan was distracted, and my grandmother, holding the baby on her lap, carried on an incoherent conversation as she crumbled bread into the bowl of barley gruel she ate without milk or sugar. Gloria wasn't there. She had gone out a little while after I did.

She still hadn't come back when I got into bed, my stomach aching and empty. I immediately fell into a deep reverie in which the world was moving like a ship on the high seas. . . . Perhaps I was in the dining room of a ship, eating a nice fruit dessert. Somebody screaming for help woke me.

I realized right away that it was Gloria who was screaming and that Juan must be giving her a terrible beating. I sat up in bed, wondering if it was worth going to help her. But the screams continued, followed by the most awful curses and blasphemies in our rich Spanish vocabulary. In his fury, Juan was using both languages, Castilian and Catalan, with stunning facility and abundance.

I stopped to put on my coat and finally went out into the dark house. My grandmother and the maid were knocking at the closed door of Juan's room.

"Juan! Juan! My child, open up!"

"Señorito Juan, open up, open the door!"

Inside we heard curses, insults. Rapid footsteps and stumbling against furniture. The baby, locked in there, too, began to cry, and my grandmother despaired. She raised her hands to bang on the door and I saw her skeletal arms.

"Juan! Juan! The baby!"

Suddenly the door was kicked open by Juan, and Gloria was shoved out, half naked and shrieking. Juan grabbed her and though she tried to scratch and bite him, he caught her under the arm and dragged her to the bathroom. . . .

"My poor boy!" my grandmother shouted as she ran to the baby, who had stood up in the crib, holding on to the railing and whimpering. . . . Then, carrying her grandson, she returned to the brawl.

Juan put Gloria in the bathtub and, without taking off her clothes, ran the icy shower over her. He brutally held her head so that if she opened her mouth she couldn't help swallowing water. Meanwhile, turning to us, he shouted:

"All of you back to bed! Nobody has any business here!"

But we didn't move. My grandmother pleaded:

"For your child's sake, for your baby! Calm down, Juanito!"

Suddenly Juan let go of Gloria—when she had stopped struggling—and came toward us with so much rage that Antonia immediately slipped away, followed by the dog, growling with its tail between its legs.

"And you, Mamá! Take that child away right now where I can't see him or I'll kill him!"

Gloria, on her knees in the bathtub, her head resting on the edge, choking, began to cry with great sobs.

I huddled in a corner of the dark hall. I didn't know what to do. Juan saw me. He was calmer now.

"Let's see if you're good for anything in this life!" he said. "Bring a towel!"

His ribs, protruding beneath his undershirt, were heaving violently.

I had no idea where the linens were kept in that house. I brought my own towel as well as a sheet from my bed, in case it was needed. I was afraid Gloria might catch pneumonia. The cold was awful.

Juan tried to pull Gloria out of the bathtub with a single heave, but she bit his hand. He cursed and began to punch her in the head. Then he grew quiet again, gasping for breath.

"As far as I'm concerned you can go ahead and die, animal!" he finally said to her.

And he walked out, slamming the door, leaving the two of us behind.

I leaned over Gloria.

"Let's go, Gloria! Get out of there now!"

She continued trembling, not moving, and when she heard my voice she began to cry, insulting her husband. She offered no resistance when I began to shake her, trying to get her out of the bathtub. She took off her dripping clothes herself, though her fingers moved with difficulty. Rubbing her body the best I could, I began to feel warm. Then I was overwhelmed by a weariness so awful my knees trembled.

"Come to my room if you like," I said, thinking it was impossible to leave her in Juan's hands again.

She followed me, wrapped in the sheet, her teeth chattering. We lay down together, wrapped in my blankets. Gloria's body was icy and made me cold, but there was no way to avoid it; her wet hair was as dark and viscous as blood on the pillow, and it sometimes brushed against my face. Gloria didn't stop talking. In spite of all this, my need for sleep was so great that my eyes closed.

"The brute . . . The animal . . . After all I've done for him. Because I'm very good, *chica,* very good. . . . Are you listening to me, Andrea? He's crazy. He scares me. One day he's going to kill me. . . . Don't fall asleep, Andreíta . . . What do you think about my running away from this house? You'd do it, wouldn't you, Andrea? Isn't it true that in my shoes you wouldn't let anybody hit you? . . . And I'm so young, *chica.* . . . Román told me one day I was one of the prettiest women he'd ever seen. I'll tell you the truth, Andrea. Román painted me in the Parque del Castillo.... I was amazed to see how good-looking I was when he showed me the picture.... *Ay, chica!* I'm really unlucky, aren't I?"

Sleep weighed on my temples again. From time to time I woke with a start to hear a sob or a louder word from Gloria.

"I'm good, very good.... Even your granny says so. I like to wear a little makeup and have a good time, but *chica,* that's natural at my age.... And what do you think about his not letting me see my own sister? A sister who's been like a mother to me. . . . All because she's a poor woman and doesn't put on airs.... But in her house you eat well. White bread, *chica,* and good sausage.... Oh, Andrea! I'd have been better off marrying a worker. Workers live better than gentlemen, Andrea; they wear espadrilles, but they have good food and good wages. Juan would like to have a factory worker's good wages.... Want me to tell you a secret? Sometimes my sister gives me money when things are very tight. But if Juan found out he'd kill me. I know he'd kill me with Román's pistol.... I heard Román tell him so myself: 'Whenever you want to blow your brains out or the brains of your imbecilic wife, you can use my pistol.' ... Do you know, Andrea, it's not permitted to have weapons. Román's breaking the law...."

Gloria's profile leaned over to observe my sleep. Her profile of a wet rat.

"Oh, Andrea! Sometimes I go to my sister's house just to have a good meal, because she has a good home, *chica,* and she makes money. Whatever you want is there.... Fresh butter, oil, potatoes, ham.... One day I'll take you."

I sighed, completely awake when I heard her talk about food. My stomach began to wait impatiently as I listened to the enumeration treasures that Gloria's sister kept in her pantry. I felt hungrier been before. There, in the bed, I was joined to Gloria ce desire, which had been awakened by her words, the same links that joined me to Román when his music evoked the impotent desires of my soul.

Something like madness took possession of my animal nature when I felt the throbbing of Gloria's neck so close to me as she talked and talked. A desire to bite the palpitating flesh, and to chew. To swallow the good warm blood.... I twisted, shaking with laughter at my own monstrous thoughts, trying to keep Gloria from detecting that shudder in my body.

Outside, the cold began to break into drops that fell against the windows. It seemed that whenever Gloria talked to me for a long time, it rained. That night I thought she was never going to stop. Sleep had fled. Suddenly Gloria whispered, putting her hand on my shoulder.

"Don't you hear that? ... Don't you hear that?"

We could hear Juan's footsteps. He must have been nervous. His footsteps reached our door. They withdrew, receded. Finally they returned and Juan came into the room, turning on the light, which dazed us and made us blink. He had put on his new coat over the cotton undershirt and the trousers he'd been wearing earlier. His hair was uncombed, and dreadful shadows devoured his eyes and cheeks. He looked somewhat comical. He stood in the middle of the room, his hands in his pockets, shaking his head and smiling with a kind of fierce irony.

"Fine. How come you're not still talking? ... What difference does it make if I'm here? ... Don't be afraid, woman, I won't eat you.... Andrea, I know perfectly well what my wife is telling you. I know perfectly well she thinks I'm crazy because I ask a fair price for my paintings.... Do you think the nude I painted of Gloria is worth only ten duros? I spent more than that just on paints and brushes!... This animal thinks my art is the same as a mason's with his fat brush!"

"Go to bed, *chico,* and don't be a pain. This is no time to be bothering anybody with your blessed paintings.... I've seen others who painted better than you and weren't so conceited. You painted me too ugly for anybody to like it. . . ."

"Don't make me lose my patience. Bitch! Either . . ."

Gloria, under the blanket, turned her back and started to cry.

"I can't live like this, I can't . . ."

"Well you'll have to put up with it, you shameless cow! And if you ever touch my paintings again I'll kill you. . . . From now on nobody sells my paintings but me. . . . Understand? Do you understand what I'm telling you? If you ever go into my studio again I'll break your head! I'd rather let everybody die of hunger than . . ."

He paced around the room with so much rage he could only move his lips and make incoherent sounds.

Gloria had a good idea. She got out of bed, bristling with cold, went up to her husband, and nudged him from behind.

"Let's go, *chico*! We've bothered Andrea enough!"

Juan pushed her away roughly.

"Andrea can put up with it! Everybody can put up with it! I have to put up with all of them."

"Come on, let's go to sleep. . . ."

Juan, nervous, began to look all around. As he was leaving, he said:

"Turn out the light so my niece can sleep. . . ."

XII

The early Mediterranean spring began to send its breezes through the still-frozen branches of the trees. There was a free-floating joy in the air, almost as visible as those transparent clouds that sometimes hover in the sky.

"I feel like going to the country and seeing the trees," said Ena, and her nostrils flared a little. "I feel like seeing pines—not these city plane trees that smell sad and decayed from a league away—or maybe what I want even more is to see the ocean. . . . This Sunday I'll go to the country with Jaime and you'll come, too, Andrea. . . . What do you think?"

I knew almost as well as Ena what Jaime was like: his preferences, his laziness, his fits of melancholy—which drove my friend to despair, and charmed her—and his sharp intelligence, though I'd never seen him. On many afternoons, when we were bent over the Greek dictionary, we would interrupt the translation to talk about him. Ena would become prettier, her eyes sweetened by joy. When her mother appeared at the door, we'd instantly stop talking because Jaime was my friend's great secret.

"I think I'd die if they found out at home. You don't know . . . I'm very proud. My mother knows only one side of me: the joking, mischievous person, which is how she likes me. I make everybody in the house laugh at the brash things I say to my suitors. . . . Everybody except my grandfather, naturally; my grandfather almost had an apoplectic fit this summer when I turned down a respectable and very rich gentleman I'd been flirting with. . . . Because I like it when men fall in love, you know? I like to look inside them. To think . . . What kinds of ideas are their thoughts composed of? What do they feel when they fall in love with me? The truth is that thinking it through becomes a pretty boring game, because they play their childish tricks, and they're always the same. Still, for me it's delicious to have them in my hands, to confuse them with their own snares and toy with them like a cat with mice. . . . Well, in fact I often have the chance to amuse myself, because men are idiots and they like me a lot. . . . In my house they're certain I'll never fall in love. I can't turn up now full of illusions, like a fool, and introduce Jaime. . . . Besides, they'd all interfere: uncles, aunts . . . I'd have to show him off to my grandfather like a strange animal . . . then they'd approve because he's rich, but they'd be desperate because he doesn't understand a thing about managing his money. I know what each of them would say. They'd want him to come to the house every day. . . . You understand, don't you, Andrea? I'd end up despising Jaime. If we ever marry, then I'd be obliged to tell them, but not yet. Absolutely not."

"Why do you want me to go to the country with you?" I asked in astonishment.

"I'll tell Mamá that I'm spending the whole day with you . . . and it's always more pleasant to tell the truth. You never interfere with me, and Jaime will love meeting you. You'll see. I've told him so much about you."

I knew that Jaime looked like the Saint George painted on the central panel of Jaime Huguet's altarpiece. The Saint George believed to be a portrait of the prince of Viana. Ena had often told me about it, and together we'd look at a photograph of the painting that she had on her night table. In fact, when I saw Jaime I noticed the resemblance and was struck by the same fine melancholy in his face. When he laughed, the similarity disappeared in a disconcerting way, and he was much more handsome and vigorous than the portrait. He seemed happy with the idea of taking us to the beach at a time of year when nobody went there. He had a very large car. Ena frowned.

"You've ruined the car putting in water and benzene."

"Yes, but thanks to that I can take the two of you wherever you want to go."

We took trips on the four Sundays in March and one more in April. We went to the beach more often than to the mountains. I remember that the sand was dirty with algae from the winter storms. Ena and I ran barefoot along the edge of the water, which was icy, and screamed when it touched us. On the last day it was almost warm and we swam in the ocean. Ena danced a dance of her own invention in response. I was lying on the sand, next to Jaime, and we saw her graceful figure outlined against the Mediterranean, sparkling and blue. Then she came toward us, laughing, and Jaime kissed her. I saw her leaning against him, lowering her golden lashes for a moment.

"How I love you!"

She said it in surprise, as if she'd made a great discovery. Jaime looked at me with a smile, moved and confused at the same time. Ena looked at me, too, and held her hand out to me.

"And you too, darling. . . . You're my sister. Really, Andrea. You see . . . I kissed Jaime in front of you!"

We came back at night on the highway that ran along the ocean. I saw the fantastic lacework formed by the waves in the blackness and the mysterious distant lights of the small boats.

"There's only one person I love as much as I love you two. Maybe more than both of you together . . . or maybe not, Jaime, maybe I don't love her as much as I love you . . . I don't know. Don't look at me like that, you'll have an accident. Sometimes the question torments me: which one do I love more, you or . . ."

I listened carefully.

"You know, darling," said Jaime in a voice that revealed so much enraged irony it approached the peevishness of a child, "it's time you told us the name."

"I can't." And she was silent for a few moments. "I won't tell you for anything in the world. I can have a secret even from the two of you."

What incomparable days! The entire week seemed lightened by them. We'd leave very early and Jaime would wait for us in the car wherever we had arranged. We'd leave the city behind and cross its melancholy suburbs and the somber power of factories, next to which stood tall apartment buildings blackened by smoke. Under the early sun the windows of these dark buildings flashed like diamonds. Flocks of screeching birds, startled by the insistent, hoarse sound of the horn, flew away from the telegraph wires. . . .

Ena sat beside Jaime. In the rear, I'd kneel on the seat and look out the back at the shapeless, portentous mass of Barcelona that rose and spread out as we left it, like a herd of monsters. Sometimes Ena would leave Jaime and climb in the back with me to look out, too, and talk to me about our happiness.

Ena never resembled on weekdays the rash girl, almost childish in her high spirits, that she turned into on Sundays. As for me—and I came from the countryside—she made me see a new meaning in nature I'd never even thought of before. She made me understand the pulsing of damp mud heavy with vital juices, the mysterious emotion of buds that were still closed, the melancholy charm of algae listless on the sand, the potency, the ardor, the splendid appeal of the sea.

"Don't make up history!" she shouted at me in despair when I saw in the Latin Sea a memory of the Phoenicians and the Greeks.

And imagined it (so quiet, resplendent, and blue) furrowed by strange ships.

Ena swam with the delight of someone embracing a beloved. I enjoyed a happiness granted to few human beings: feeling myself carried along in the almost palapable aura radiated by a young couple in love that makes the world more vibrant, throbbing with more odors and resonances, becoming more infinite and profound.

We'd eat at stands along the coast or picnic outdoors in the pines. Sometimes it rained. Then Ena and I would take shelter under Jaime's raincoat, while he calmly got wet. . . . On many afternoons I'd put on a wool jacket or sweater of his. He had a pile of these things in the car as a precaution against the treacheries of spring. That year, however, the weather was marvelous. I remember that in March we came back loaded down with branches of flowering almond and right after that the mimosa began to turn yellow, trembling on garden walls.

These torrents of light pouring into my life because of Ena were embittered by the dismal hues that colored my spirit on the other days of the week. I'm not referring to events on Calle de Aribau, which hardly influenced my life anymore, but to the unfocused vision caused by my nerves, put too much on edge by a hunger I almost didn't feel because it was chronic. Sometimes I'd become angry with Ena over a trifle. I'd leave her house in despair. Then I'd come back without saying a word and begin studying with her again. Ena pretended not to notice and we'd go on as if nothing had happened. Remembering these scenes sometimes made me weep with terror when I thought about them on my walks along the streets in poor districts, or at night when the ache in my head wouldn't let me sleep and I had to remove the pillow for it to go away. I'd think about Juan and how I was like him in many ways. It didn't even occur to me that I was hysterical from lack of food. When I received my monthly stipend, I'd go to Ena's house with flowers and buy candy for my grandmother, and I also acquired the habit of buying cigarettes, which I saved up for the times when food was scarce, since they alleviated the pangs and helped me to dream up incoherent projects. When Román came back from his trips, he'd give me cigarettes as a gift. He watched me with a special smile when I wandered through the house, when I stopped at the kitchen door, sniffing, or when I lay in bed for hours at a time, my eyes open.

On one of the afternoons when I became angry with Ena, my indignation lasted longer than usual. I walked, frowning, carried along by a lengthy, impassioned interior monologue. *I won't go back to her house. I'm sick of her superior smiles. She follows me with her eyes, amused, convinced I'll be back again in two minutes. She thinks I can't do without her friendship. How wrong she is! She plays with me the way she does with everybody else*—I thought unjustly—*her parents, her brothers, the poor boys who fall in love with her, the ones she encourages so she can enjoy watching them suffer.* . . . My friend's Machiavellian character became more and more evident. She seemed almost despicable. . . . I got home earlier than usual. I began to organize my class notes, nervous and almost in tears because I couldn't understand my own writing. At the bottom of my book bag I found the card Gerardo had given me on my first night of freedom, when I met him in the darkness around the Cathedral.

The memory of Gerardo diverted my attention for a moment. I recalled that I had promised to call him so we could go out and visit the picturesque corners of Barcelona. I thought perhaps this could distract me from my thoughts, and without thinking more about it, I dialed his number. He remembered me right away and we made a date to go out the following afternoon. Then, although it was still very early, I went to bed, and I fell asleep watching the dawning of lights in the street through the rectangle of the balcony, a deep sleep, as if I were recuperating from the fatigue of difficult labor.

When I awoke it seemed that something was wrong. It was almost as if someone had told me that Angustias was coming back. It was going to be one of those days that in appearance are like all the rest, inoffensive like the rest, but one on which a very faint stroke suddenly changes the course of our life and moves it into a new period.

I didn't go to the university in the morning, possessed by a stupid insistence on not seeing Ena, though with every hour that passed, it became more painful for me to be angry with my friend, and I thought about her best qualities and her sincere affection for me. The only spontaneous, disinterested affection I'd known until then.

Gerardo came for me in the afternoon. I recognized him because he was waiting at the front door of the building, and he immediately turned toward me, keeping his hands in his pockets, as was his habit. His heavy features had been completely erased from my memory. Now he wasn't wearing a coat or hat. He had on a well-cut gray suit. He was tall and robust and his hair looked like a black man's hair.

"Hello, beautiful!"

That's what he said. And then, with a movement of his head as if I were a dog:

"Let's go."

I felt a little intimidated.

We started walking side by side. Gerardo talked as much as he had on the day I'd met him. I noticed that he spoke like a book, constantly quoting from works he had read. He told me I was intelligent, and that he was, too. Then, that he didn't believe in feminine intelligence. Later, that Schopenhauer had said . . .

He asked if I preferred going to the port or to Montjuich Park. It made no difference to me. I walked beside him in silence. When we crossed streets, he took my arm. We walked along Calle de Cortes to the Exposition gardens. Once there I became more cheerful because the afternoon was blue, gleaming on the domes of the palace and the white cascades of the fountains. Crowds of spring flowers nodded in the wind, invading everything with their flame of colors. We lost our way on the paths of the immense park. On a little square—dark green because of the clipped cypresses—we saw the white statue of Venus reflected in the water. Someone had coarsely painted the lips red. Gerardo and I looked at each other, indignant, and at that moment I liked him. He wet his handkerchief, and with an impulse of his powerful body he climbed the statue and scrubbed the marble lips until they were clean.

From that moment on, we were able to talk more cordially. We took a very long walk. Gerardo spoke to me at length about himself and then he wanted to find out about my situation in Barcelona.

"So you're all alone, eh? You mean you don't have parents?"

He began to annoy me again.

We went to Miramar and sat on the terrace of the restaurant to look at the Mediterranean, which in the twilight had wine-colored reflections. The huge port seemed small, for we had a bird's-eye view of it. At the docks the rusted skeletons of ships sunk during the war broke the surface. To our right I made out the cypresses in the Southwest Cemetery and could almost detect the smell of melancholy facing the open horizon of the sea.

Near us, at little tables on the terrace, people were eating. The walk and the salt air had awakened that cavernous sensation of hunger I always had when I was drowsy. And I was tired. I looked at the tables and the appetizing dishes with avid eyes. Gerardo followed the direction of my glance and said in a contemptuous tone, as if my answering in the affirmative would be barbaric:

"You don't want anything, do you?"

And he took me by the arm, pulling me away from the dangerous place, on the pretext of showing me another splendid view. At that moment he seemed hateful to me.

A short while later, with our backs to the ocean, we were looking at the entire imposing city spread out below us.

Gerardo stood erect as he looked at it.

"Barcelona! So proud and so rich and yet how hard life can be there!" he said pensively.

He was saying this as if it were a confession, and I suddenly felt touched because I thought he was referring to his earlier coarseness. One of the few things I was capable of understanding in those days was indigence, no matter in what guise it appeared: even under Gerardo's good suit and linen shirt. . . . In an impulsive gesture, I placed my hand on his and he pressed it, communicating his warmth to me. At that moment I wanted to cry, not knowing why. He kissed my hair.

Suddenly I stiffened, though we were still close together. In those days I was foolishly innocent—in spite of my pretended cynicism—about those matters. A man had never kissed me and I was certain that the first one who did would be chosen by me over all the rest. Gerardo had barely brushed my hair. I thought it was a consequence of the emotion we had felt together and that I couldn't be ridiculous enough to reject him in indignation. At that moment he kissed me again, gently. I had the absurd feeling that shadows were passing over my face, as if it were dusk, and my heart began to pound furiously, in mindless indecision, as if I were obliged to put up with those caresses. I thought something extraordinary had happened to him, that suddenly he had fallen in love with me. Because at that time I was foolish enough not to realize that he was one of the infinite men born only to be studs, men who with a woman cannot understand any other attitude. Their minds and hearts can go no further. Gerardo suddenly pulled me toward him and kissed me on the mouth. I was startled and shoved him, and felt a rising wave of disgust because of the saliva and heat from his heavy lips. I pushed him with all my strength and began to run. He followed me. He found me trembling slightly, trying to think. It occurred to me that perhaps he had taken the pressure of my hands as a proof of love.

"Forgive me, Gerardo," I said with the greatest innocence, "but, you know? . . . I don't love you. I'm not in love with you."

And I felt relieved at having explained everything to him satisfactorily.

He grasped my arm like a person recovering something that belongs to him, and he looked at me in so vulgar and contemptuous a way that he left me frozen.

Then, in the streetcar we took back, he gave me paternal advice concerning my future conduct and the advisability of not wandering around like a madwoman and going out alone with boys. I almost thought I was listening to Aunt Angustias.

I promised him I wouldn't go out with him again, and he was somewhat taken aback.

"No, *chica*, no, with me it's different. You see, I'm giving you good advice. . . . I'm your best friend."

He was very satisfied with himself.

I was disheartened, as I was on the day a nun at my secondary school, blushing, explained that I was no longer a little girl, that I had become a woman. Out of the blue I remembered the nun's words: "You mustn't be afraid, it isn't a disease, it's something natural sent to us by God." I thought: *So this stupid man is the one who gave me my first kiss. . . . It's very possible that this doesn't matter, either. . . .*

I climbed the stairs of my house, exhausted. Night had fallen. Antonia opened the door with a certain amount of fawning.

"A blond señorita was here asking for you."

Weakened and sad, I almost felt like crying. Ena, who was better than me, had come to see me.

"She's in the living room, with Señorito Román," the maid added. "They've been there all afternoon. . . ."

I stood still for a moment. *Finally she's met Román, just as she wanted to,* I said to myself. *I wonder what she thinks of him?* But not knowing exactly why, a profound irritation replaced my curiosity. At that moment I heard Román beginning to play the piano. I quickly went to the door of the living room, knocked twice, and walked in. Román stopped playing immediately, frowning. Ena was leaning on the arm of one of the damaged armchairs and seemed to wake from a long reverie.

—

On the piano, a candle end—a memory of the nights I'd slept in that room—was burning, and its lengthened, restless flame was the only light in the room.

The three of us looked at one another for a moment. Then Ena ran toward me and embraced me. Román smiled at me affectionately and stood up.

"I'll leave you, little ones."

Ena held her hand out to him and the two of them looked at each other in silence. Ena's eyes were phosphorescent, like a cat's. I began to feel fear. It was something icy on my skin. That was when I had the feeling that a stroke, as fine as a hair, was dividing my life and, as if it were glass, breaking it in two. When I raised my eyes from the floor, Román had left. Ena said:

"I'm leaving, too. It's very late. . . . I wanted to wait for you because sometimes you do crazy things and it's impossible . . . All right, good-bye. . . . Good-bye, Andrea . . ."

She was very nervous.

XIII

The next day it was Ena who avoided me at the university. I had grown so accustomed to being with her between classes that I felt disoriented and didn't know what to do. At the last minute she came over to me.

. "Don't come to the house this afternoon, Andrea. I have to go out. . . . It would be better if you didn't come back until I tell you. I'll let you know. I have something going on right now. . . . You can come and get the dictionaries. . . ." (Because I, who had no text-books, didn't have a Greek dictionary either, and my Latin dictio-nary from secondary school was small and inadequate: I always did translations with Ena.) "I'm sorry," she continued after a moment with an embarrassed smile. "I won't be able to lend you the dictio-naries, either. . . . How annoying! But since exams are coming, I'd better do the translations at night. . . . You'll have to study at the li-brary. . . . Believe me, I'm sorry, Andrea."

"Ena, don't worry about it."

I felt enveloped in the same oppressive feeling as on the previ-ous afternoon. But now it wasn't a presentiment; it was the certainty that something bad had happened. In any case, it was less distressing than that first shudder of nerves I'd felt when I saw Ena looking at Román.

"Well . . . I'm in a rush, Andrea. I can't wait for you because I promised Bonet . . . Ah! There's Bonet, waving to me. Good-bye, darling."

Though it was not her custom, she kissed me on both cheeks, very quickly, and left after warning me again:

"Don't come to the house until I tell you. . . . You just won't find me there, you know? I don't want you to go to the trouble."

"Don't worry."

I watched her leave with one of her least favored suitors, who seemed radiant that day.

From then on I had to get along without Ena. Sunday came, and she, who hadn't said the famous words and merely smiled and greeted me from a distance at the university, also didn't say anything about our excursion with Jaime. Life became solitary for me again. Since it seemed to be something that couldn't be helped, I accepted it with resignation. That was when I began to realize that it is much easier to endure great setbacks than everyday petty annoyances.

At home, Gloria greeted spring—which grew more and more radiant—with an intense nervousness I'd never seen in her. She often cried. My grandmother told me, as if it were a deep secret, that Gloria was afraid she was pregnant again.

"There was a time when I wouldn't have told you . . . because you're a child. But now, since the war . . ."

The poor old woman didn't know in whom she could confide her uneasiness.

Still, nothing like that happened. The air of April and May is an irritant, it stimulates and burns more than the air of the dog days of summer; this was the only thing that happened. The trees on Calle de Aribau—those city trees that, according to Ena, smelled of rot, of a plant cemetery—were covered with delicate, almost transparent little leaves. Gloria, frowning at the window, looked at all this and smiled, then sighed. One day I saw her washing her new dress and trying to change the collar. She threw it to the floor in despair.

"I don't know how to do these things!" she said. "I'm not good for anything!"

No one had told her to do it. She locked herself in her room.

Román seemed to be in excellent humor. Some days he even deigned to talk to Juan. Juan's attitude was pitiful then—he'd laugh at anything and pat his brother's back. Then, as a consequence, he'd have terrible quarrels with his wife.

One day I heard Román playing the piano. He was playing something I recognized. His song of spring, composed in honor of the god Xochipilli. The song that, according to him, brought him bad luck. Gloria was in a dark corner of the foyer making an effort to listen. I went in and watched his hands on the keys. Finally, with a certain irritation, he stopped playing.

"Do you want something, little one?"

Román also seemed to have changed toward me.

"What were you and Ena talking about the other day, Román?"

He looked surprised.

"Nothing in particular, as I remember—what did she tell you?"

"She didn't tell me anything. Since that day we stopped being friends."

"Well, little one . . . I have nothing to do with silly schoolgirl stories. . . . I haven't reached that point yet."

And he left.

The afternoons became particularly long for me. I was used to spending them organizing my notes, then I'd take a long walk and be at Ena's house before seven. She saw Jaime every day after lunch, but then she'd come back at seven to work on a translation with me. Some days she'd spend all afternoon in her house, and that was when the group from the university would get together there.

The boys, infected with literary measles, would read us poems. Finally, Ena's mother would sing something. Those we the days when I'd stay for supper. All of this belonged to the past now (sometimes it terrified me to think about how the elements of my life appeared and dissolved forever as soon as I began to think of them as immutable). Friends stopped gathering at Ena's house because of the menacing shadow of the end of the school year, which was fast approaching. And Ena and I no longer spoke of my returning to her house.

One afternoon I ran into Pons at the university library. He was very happy to see me.

"Do you come here often? I haven't seen you here before."

"Yes, I come to study. . . . I don't have textbooks. . . ."

"Really? I can lend you mine. I'll bring them in tomorrow."

"What about you?"

"I'll ask for them when I need them."

The next day, Pons came to the university with some new, un-opened books.

"You can keep them. . . . This year at home they bought two of each textbook."

I was so embarrassed I felt like crying. But what could I say to Pons? He was enthusiastic.

"Aren't you friends with Ena anymore?" he asked.

"Yes, I just see less of her because of exams. . . ."

Pons was a very childish boy. Small and slim, he had eyes made sweet by very long lashes. One day I saw him at the university in a state of excitement.

"Listen, Andrea, listen to this. . . . I didn't tell you before because we weren't allowed to bring girls. But I talked so much about you, I said you were different . . . well, it's my friend Guíxols and he said yes, understand?"

I'd never heard of Guíxols.

"No, how could I understand?"

their
re

ne. I've never even talked to you about my
:s here, at the university, aren't really my friends.
ırdiaga, mainly . . . well, you'll meet them soon.
writers, painters . . . a completely bohemian
picturesque. No social conventions there . . .
ւսjot, a friend of Guíxols . . . and of mine, naturally . . . wears a scarf
and has long hair. A stupendous guy . . . We meet at Guíxols's studio, he's a painter, very young . . . I mean, young as an artist; after all,
he's already twenty but has enormous talent. So far no girl has gone
there. They're afraid they'll be shocked at the dust and say the kind
of dumb things girls tend to say. But they were interested when I
told them you don't wear any makeup at all and have a very dark
complexion and light eyes. And, I mean, they said to bring you this
afternoon. The studio's in the old district. . . ."

It hadn't even occurred to him that I could turn down his tempting invitation. Naturally, I went with him.

We went on foot, taking a long walk along the old streets. Pons
seemed very happy. He'd always been extraordinarily nice to me.

"Do you know the church of Santa María del Mar?" Pons asked.

"No."

"Let's go in for a moment, if you don't mind. They call it an example of pure Catalan Gothic. I think it's marvelous. It was burned
during the war. . . ."

To my eyes, Santa María del Mar seemed endowed with singular charm, with its peculiar towers and small, ordinary plaza facing
old houses.

Pons lent me his hat, smiling when he saw that I twisted it to
put it on. Then we went in. The nave was large and cool, with a
few pious old women praying there. I looked up and saw broken
stained-glass windows surrounded by stones that the flames had
blackened. This desolation overflowed with poetry and made the
place even more spiritual. We stayed there for a while and then left
by a side door, beside which women were selling carnations and
broom. Pons bought me small bunches of sweet-smelling carna-

tions, red and white. He saw my enthusiasm and his eyes filled with happiness. Then he led me to Calle de Montcada, where Guíxols had his studio.

We went in through a wide entrance guarded by a stone coat of arms. In the courtyard a horse hitched to a cart was eating peacefully and chickens pecked for food, creating an impression of serenity. Rising from the courtyard was a seignorial, dilapidated stone staircase, which we climbed. On the top floor, Pons pulled at a cord hanging on the door. A little bell rang in the distance. Pons barely reached the shoulder of the boy who opened the door. I thought he must be Guíxols. He and Pons embraced effusively. Pons said to me:

"This is Iturdiaga, Andrea. . . . This man just came from the Monastery of Veruela, where he spent a week on the trail of Bécquer. . . ."

From his height, Iturdiaga studied me. He held a pipe between long fingers and I saw that in spite of his imposing appearance, he was as young as we were.

We followed him, crossing a long labyrinth of ramshackle, completely empty rooms, until we reached the one where Guíxols had his studio. A large room, full of light, with several pieces of upholstered furniture—chairs and armchairs, a large settee, and a small table where a handful of brushes had been placed in a glass, like a bouquet of flowers.

Guíxols's work could be seen everywhere: on easels, on the wall, leaning against the furniture, on the floor. . . .

Two or three boys, who stood up when they saw me, were gathered there. Guíxols had the look of an athlete. Strong and very jovial, completely relaxed, almost the antithesis of Pons. Among the others I saw the famous Pujol, who, scarf and all, was terribly shy. Later I saw his paintings, which he made by imitating each detail of Picasso's defects—genius doesn't lend itself to imitation, of course. This wasn't the fault of Pujol or of his seventeen years devoted to slavishly copying the master. The most outstanding of them seemed to be Iturdiaga. He spoke with pompous gestures, almost always shouting. Then I learned he'd written a four-volume novel but couldn't find a publisher for it.

"What beauty, my friends! What beauty!" he said, speaking of the Monastery of Veruela. "I understood religious vocation, mystic exaltation, perpetual enclosure in solitude!... I needed only all of you and love.... I'd be as free as the air if love didn't always hitch me to his wagon, Andrea," he added, addressing me.

Then he became serious.

"The day after tomorrow I fight Martorell—it can't be helped. You, Guíxols, will be my second."

"No, we'll settle it before it gets that far," said Guíxols, offering me a cigarette. "You can be sure I'll settle it.... It's stupid for you to fight because Martorell might have said something obscene to a flower seller on the Rambla."

"A flower seller on the Rambla is a lady like any other woman!"

"I don't doubt it, but you never saw her before, while Martorell is our friend. Maybe a little confused, but an excellent boy. I tell you he's taking the whole thing as a joke. The two of you have to reconcile."

"No, Señor!" shouted Iturdiaga. "Martorell stopped being my friend when ..."

"All right. Now we'll have something to eat if Andrea will be good enough to make us some sandwiches with the bread and ham she'll find hidden behind the door...."

Pons constantly observed the effect his friends had on me and tried to catch my eye to smile at me. I made coffee and we drank it from cups of different sizes and shapes, but all of them fine old porcelain, which Guíxols kept in a glass cabinet. Pons told me Guíxols acquired them at auctions.

I looked at Guíxols's paintings: most of them seascapes. I was interested in a drawing of Pons's head. It seemed Guíxols was lucky and his paintings sold well, though he hadn't yet had a show. Without meaning to, I compared his work to Juan's. Guíxols's was better, no doubt about it. When I heard him talk about thousands of pese-

tas, Juan's voice passed through my ears like a flash of cruelty . . .
"Do you think the nude I painted of Gloria is worth only ten
duros?" I found this "bohemian" atmosphere very comfortable. The
only one who was badly dressed and had dirty ears was Pujol, who
ate with great appetite and in great silence. Despite this, I found
out that he was rich. Guíxols was the son of a very wealthy manu-
facturer, and Iturdiaga and Pons also belonged to families well
known in Catalan industry. In addition, Pons was an only child, and
very pampered, as I learned while he blushed all the way to his ears.

"My father doesn't understand me," shouted Iturdiaga. "How
can he understand me if the only thing he knows is how to pile up
millions? In no way did he want to fund the publication of my novel.
He says it's a lost cause! . . . And the worst thing is that since my last
bit of trouble he keeps me on a short leash and doesn't give me a
cent."

"It was a pretty good one," said Guíxols with a smile.

"No! I didn't lie to him! . . . One day he called me into his room:
'Gaspar, my son . . . have I understood correctly? You said there's
nothing left of the two thousand pesetas I gave you for Christmas'—
this was two weeks after Christmas. I said: 'Yes, Papá, not a cent.' . . .
Then he half closed his eyes like a wild animal and said:

" 'Well, you're going to tell me right now what you spent it on.' I
told him what could be told to a father like mine and he wasn't satisfied. Then it occurred to me to say:

" 'I gave the rest to López Soler, I lent it to the poor man. . . .'
Then you should have seen my father roar like a tiger:

" 'You lent money to a scoundrel like him, who'll never pay you
back! I'm going to give you a beating. . . . If you don't bring me that
money within twenty-four hours, I'll put López Soler in jail and
keep you on bread and water for a month. . . . I'll teach you to squan-
der money . . .'

" 'None of that's possible, my dear father; López Soler's in Bilbao.'

"My father dropped discouraged arms, and then he regained his
strength.

" 'You're going to Bilbao tonight, with your older brother, you imbecile! I'll teach you to waste my money . . .'

"And that night my brother and I were in a sleeping car. All of you know what my brother's like, more serious than most, and with a head like a stone. In Bilbao he visited all my father's relatives and made me go with him. López Soler had gone to Madrid. My brother conferred with Barcelona: 'Go to Madrid,' my father said. 'You know I'm counting on you, Ignacio. . . . I'm determined to educate Gaspar by force.' . . . Once again in the sleeping car to Madrid. There I found López Soler in the Café Castilla and he opened his arms wide, weeping with joy. When he found out why I'd come, he called me a murderer and said he'd kill me before he gave back the money. Then, seeing that my brother Ignacio stood behind me with his boxer's fists, all his friends managed to come up with the money and give it to me. Even Ignacio was satisfied, and he put it in his wallet, while I became López Soler's enemy. . . .

"We returned home. My father made a solemn speech and told me that as a punishment he'd keep the money I recovered, and to recoup the costs of our trip he wouldn't give me money for a week. Then Ignacio, his face serene, took out the twenty-five-peseta bill López Soler had returned to me and handed it to my father. The poor man was like a castle that's collapsing.

" 'What's this?' he shouted.

" 'The money I lent to López Soler, Father,' I replied.

"And that's where the catastrophe of my life begins, dear friends. . . . Now when I was planning to save up to publish the book on my own . . ."

I was very amused, and happy.

"Ah!" said Iturdiaga, looking at a small painting that was turned toward the wall. "Why does the painting of the Truth have its back to us?"

"Romances, the critic, was here earlier, and since he's fifty years old, it didn't seem delicate. . . ."

Pujol stood up quickly and turned the canvas around. On a black background was painted, in large white letters:

LET US GIVE THANKS TO HEAVEN THAT WE ARE WORTH INFINITELY MORE THAN OUR ANCESTORS.—HOMER. The signature was imposing. I had to laugh. I was very comfortable there; the absolute irresponsibility and careless happiness in that atmosphere caressed my spirit.

XIV

The examinations for that year were easy, but I was afraid and studied as much as I could.

"You'll make yourself sick," Pons said. "I'm not worried. Next year will be different, when we have to take the final for the degree."

The truth is I was beginning to lose my memory. I had frequent headaches.

Gloria told me that Ena had come to see Román in his room and Román played his violin compositions for her. About these things, Gloria was always well informed.

"Do you think he'll marry her?" she asked suddenly, with a kind of ardor that spring communicated to her.

"Ena marry Román! What a stupid idea!"

"I'm saying it, *chica*, because she's well dressed, like she comes from a good family.... Maybe Román wants to get married."

"Don't talk foolishness. There's nothing like that between them.... Come on! Don't be ridiculous, Gloria! If Ena came here, you can be sure it was only to hear music."

"And why didn't she come in to say hello to you?"

I was so interested in everything she said that my heart felt as if it would leap out of my chest.

I saw Ena at the university every day. Sometimes we exchanged a few words. But how could we talk about anything intimate? She had distanced me completely from her life. One day I asked politely about Jaime.

"He's fine," she said. "We don't go out on Sundays anymore." (She avoided looking at me, perhaps so I wouldn't see the sadness in her eyes. Who could understand her?)

"Román's traveling," I said abruptly.

"I know," she replied.

We were silent.

"And your family?" I ventured (it was as if we hadn't seen each other in many years).

"Mamá's been sick."

"I'll send her flowers when I can...."

Ena looked at me in a special way.

"You look sick, too, Andrea.... Do you want to go out with me this afternoon? The air will do you good. We can go to Tibidabo. I'd like you to have lunch there with me...."

"Have you finished the important matter that was keeping you so busy?"

"No, not yet; don't be ironic.... But this afternoon I'm going to take a vacation, if you want to spend it with me."

I wasn't happy or sad. It seemed that my friendship with Ena had lost a great deal of its charm after our break. At the same time I sincerely loved my friend.

"Yes, let's go ... if you don't have anything more important to do."

She took my hand and opened my fingers in order to see the confused net of lines on my palm.

"What slender hands!... Andrea, I want you to forgive me if I've behaved badly with you recently. . . . It isn't only with you that I've behaved badly. . . . But this afternoon will be the way it was before. You'll see. We'll run through the pines. We'll have a good time."

In fact, we did have a good time and laughed a lot. With Ena any subject became interesting and animated. I told her stories about Iturdiaga and my new friends. From Tibidabo, behind Barcelona, you could see the ocean. The pines ran in dense, fragrant groves down the mountain, spreading into large forests until they reached the outskirts of the city. Green surrounded and embraced it.

"The other day I went to your house," said Ena. "I wanted to see you. I waited four hours for you."

"Nobody told me."

"I went up to Román's room to pass the time. He was very nice to me. He played music. From time to time he'd call the maid on the phone to see if you'd come back."

I became sad so suddenly that Ena noticed and became sad, too.

"There are things about you I don't like, Andrea. You're ashamed of your family. . . . And yet, Román is a man more original and artistic than most. . . . If I introduced you to my aunts and uncles, you could search with a lantern and not find a spark of spirit. Even my father is an ordinary man, without any sensitivity. . . . Which doesn't mean he isn't good, and besides, he's handsome—you know him—but I would have understood it better if my mother had married Román or someone like him. . . . This is merely an example like any other. . . . Your uncle is a personality. Just with the way he looks at things he knows how to say what he wants. Understand . . . sometimes he seems a little mad. But so do you, Andrea. That's precisely why I wanted to be your friend at the university. You had brilliant eyes and you walked around, so dull, abstracted, not noticing anything. . . . We laughed at you, but secretly I wanted to know you. One morning I saw you leave the university in a torrential rain. . . . It was early in the year—you won't remember this. Most of the kids were huddling in the doorway, and even though I was wearing a raincoat and had an umbrella, I didn't dare go out in that furious downpour. Suddenly I saw you leave, walking the way you always did, without a scarf, your head uncovered. . . . I remember that the wind and rain beat against you and then plastered locks of your hair against your cheeks. I went out after you and the rain was coming down in buckets. You blinked for a moment, as if you were surprised, and then, as if it were a refuge, you leaned against the garden railing. You stood there for at least two minutes until you realized you were still getting wet. It was wonderful. You moved me and made me laugh at the same time. I think that was when I began to be fond of you. . . . Then you got sick . . ."

"Yes, I remember."

"I know it bothers you that I'm Román's friend. I'd already asked you to introduce me to him a long time ago. . . . I understood that if I wanted to be your friend I couldn't even think about anything like that. . . . And the day I went to see you at your house, when you found us together, you couldn't hide your irritation and anger. The next day I saw that you were ready to talk about it. . . . To ask me to explain myself, maybe. I don't know. . . . I didn't want to see you. You have to understand that I can choose my own friends, and I'm very interested in Román, I don't deny it, for reasons of my own and because of his genius and . . ."

"He's a mean-spirited, evil person."

"I'm not looking for goodness or even good manners in people . . . though I think manners are absolutely necessary in order to live with them. I like people who see life with eyes different from everyone else's, who think about things in a way that's different from most people. . . . Maybe it's because I've always lived with people who are too normal and satisfied with themselves. . . . I'm sure my mother and brothers are certain of their indisputable usefulness in this world, and know at every moment what they want, what they think is bad, and what they think is good. . . . And have suffered very little anguish over anything."

"Don't you love your father?"

"Of course I do. This is different. . . . And I'm grateful to Providence that he's so handsome, since I look like him. . . . But I've never understood why he married my mother. My mother was the passion of my entire childhood. I noticed from the time I was very small that she was different from everybody else. . . . I spied on her. I thought she had to be wretched. When I realized she loved my father and was happy I felt a kind of disappointment. . . ."

Ena was serious.

"And I can't help it. All my life I've been running away from my simple, respectable relatives. . . . Simple but intelligent at the same time, in their own way, which is what makes them so unbearable. . . . I like people with that touch of madness that keeps life from being monotonous, even though they're miserable and are always in the clouds, like you. . . . People who, according to my family, are undesirable calamities. . . ."

I looked at her.

"Except for my mother . . . with her, you never know what's going to happen, and this is one of her charms. . . . What do you think my father or grandfather would say about you if they knew what you really were like? If they knew, the way I do, that you go without eating and don't buy the clothes you need so you can have the pleasure of enjoying a millionaire's delicacies with your friends for three days . . . If they knew that you liked wandering around alone at night. That you've never known what you want and that you're always wanting something . . . Bah! Andrea, I think they'd cross themselves when they saw you, as if you were the devil."

She approached and stood in front of me. She placed her hands on my shoulders, looking at me.

"And, darling, this afternoon or whenever your uncle or your house come up, you're just like my relatives. . . . You're horrified at the mere thought of my being there. You think I don't know what that world of yours is like, when in fact it's fascinated me right from the beginning, and I want to find out all about it."

"You're wrong. Román and the rest of them have no merit except being worse than the people you know and living in the midst of ugly, dirty things."

I spoke harshly, knowing I couldn't convince her.

"When I came to your house the other day, what a strange world appeared before my eyes! I was bewitched. I never could have dreamed, in the middle of Calle de Aribau, of a scene like the one Román presented when he played for me, in the candlelight, in that den of antiquities. . . . You don't know how much I thought about you. How interesting I thought you were because you lived in that unbelievable place. I understood you better . . . I loved you. Until you came in . . . Without realizing it, you looked at me in a way that ruined my enthusiasm. So don't be angry with me because I want to go to your house alone and find out about everything. Because there's nothing that doesn't interest me . . . from that witch you have as a maid to Román's parrot. . . . As for Román, don't tell me his only merit is being in that environment. He's an extraordinary person. If you've heard him play his compositions, you have to recognize that."

We rode down to the city in the tram. The mild afternoon air lifted Ena's hair. She was very good-looking. She said:

"Come to the house whenever you want. . . . Forgive me for having told you not to come. That was another matter. You know you're my only friend. My mother asks about you, and she seems alarmed. . . . She was happy I finally found a girl I liked; since I've been old enough to reason I've been surrounded only by boys. . . ."

XV

I came home with a headache and was surprised by the deep silence when it was time for supper. The maid moved around with an unusually light step. In the kitchen I saw her stroking the dog as it rested its large head in her lap. From time to time nervous spasms ran through her like electrical charges and she would laugh, showing her green teeth.

"There's going to be a funeral," she said to me.

"What?"

"The baby's going to die. . . ."

I noticed that the light was on in the married couple's bedroom.

"The doctor's here. I went to the pharmacy for medicines but they didn't want to give me credit because people in the neighborhood know how things are in this house since the poor señor died. . . . Right, Trueno?"

I went into the bedroom. Juan had made a screen for the light so it wouldn't bother the child, who seemed unconscious, flushed with fever. Juan held him in his arms because the boy couldn't lie in the cradle without crying continually. . . . My grandmother seemed stunned. I could see that she was caressing the baby's feet, putting her hands under the blanket wrapped around him. At the same time she said the rosary, and I was surprised she wasn't crying. My grandmother and Juan were sitting on the edge of the big double bed, and in the background, on the bed as well but leaning against the corner of the wall, I saw Gloria, very preoccupied with playing cards. She was sitting Moorish style, disheveled and dirty as usual. I thought she must be playing solitaire. She did that sometimes.

"What's wrong with the baby?" I asked.

"They don't know," my grandmother answered quickly.

Juan looked at her and said:

"The doctor thinks it's the beginning of pneumonia, but I think it's his stomach. It doesn't matter. The boy's strong and he'll tolerate the fever," Juan went on, while he held the baby's head with great delicacy, leaning it against his chest.

"Juan!" Gloria shrieked. "It's time for you to go!"

He looked at the boy with a concern I would have thought strange if I had paid attention to his previous words.

He sweetened his voice a little.

"I don't know if I ought to go, Gloria. . . . What do you think? This baby only wants to be with me."

"I think, *chico,* that we're in no condition to think about it. A chance to quietly earn a few pesetas has fallen from the sky. Mamá and I will be here. And there's a phone in the warehouse, isn't there? We can let you know if he gets worse. . . . And since you're not the only guard there, you could come home. It would just mean you don't get paid the next day. . . ."

Juan stood up. The baby began to moan. Juan hesitated, smiling with a strange expression.

"Go on, *chico,* go on! Give him to Mamá."

Juan put him in my grandmother's arms and the baby began to cry.

"All right! Give him to me."

The baby seemed better in his mother's arms.

"How naughty!" my grandmother said sadly. "When he feels good he only wants me to hold him, and now . . ."

Juan put on his overcoat, pensive, looking at the baby.

"Eat something before you go. There's soup in the kitchen and a loaf in the sideboard."

"Yes, I'll have some hot soup. I'll put it in a cup. . . ."

Before he left he came back to the bedroom.

"I'll leave this coat and wear the old one," he said carefully, taking down a very ragged and stained coat that hung on the rack. "It's not cold now and it can get ruined on a night when you're standing guard. . . ."

You could see he hadn't made up his mind to go. Gloria shouted again:

"It's getting late, *chico*!"

Finally he left.

Gloria cradled the baby impatiently. When she heard the door closing, she sat a while longer, listening, her neck tense. Then she shouted:

"Mamá!"

My grandmother had gone to have her supper, too, and was eating soup and bread, but she left it half eaten and came in right away.

"Let's go, Mamá, let's go! Quick!"

She placed the child in my grandmother's lap, paying no attention to his crying. Then she began to dress in the best clothes she had: a print dress, the unfinished collar still hanging from it, lying wrinkled on the chair, and a necklace of blue beads. To go with the necklace a pair of chunky earrings that were also blue. As usual, she powdered her face heavily to hide her freckles, and she put on lipstick and made up her eyes with trembling hands.

"It was very lucky that Juan had that job tonight, Mamá," she said when she saw my grandmother shaking her head in disapproval as she walked the baby, who had grown very big for her aged arms. "I'm going to my sister's house, Mamá; pray for me. I'm going to see if she'll give me some money for the baby's medicine.... Pray for me, Mamá, poor thing, and don't be angry.... Andrea will stay with you."

"Yes, I'll be here studying."

"Aren't you eating before you leave, child?"

Gloria thought about it for half a minute and then decided to swallow her supper as fast as she could. My grandmother's soup was in the bowl, getting cold and thick. Nobody paid attention to it.

When Gloria left, the maid went to her room with Trueno to sleep. I turned on the light in the dining room—it was the best light in the house—and opened my books. That night I couldn't cope with them—they didn't interest me and I didn't understand them. But two or three hours passed this way. It was the end of May and I had to make an effort in my work. I remember that I became obsessed with the half-empty plate of soup abandoned in front of me. The piece of bitten bread.

I heard something like the buzz of a fly. It was my grandmother walking toward me, crooning to the baby in her arms. Without interrupting the tune, she said to me:

"Andrea, my child . . . Andrea, my child . . . Come say the rosary with me."

It was hard for me to understand her. Then I followed her into the bedroom.

"Do you want me to hold the baby for a little while?"

My grandmother shook her head energetically. She sat down again on the bed. The baby seemed to be sleeping.

"Take the rosary out of my pocket."

"Don't your arms hurt?"

"No . . . no. Go on, go on!"

I began to recite the beautiful words of the Ave Maria. The words of the Ave Maria, which always seemed blue to me. We heard the key in the lock. I thought it was Gloria and turned quickly. It gave me an enormous fright to see Juan. Apparently he couldn't control his uneasiness and had come back before morning. Granny looked so terrified that Juan knew right away. He leaned quickly over the baby, who was sleeping, flushed, his mouth half open. But then he straightened up.

"What's Gloria done? Where is she?"

"Gloria's resting a little . . . or maybe not . . . No! Isn't that right, Andrea? She went out to get something at the pharmacy. . . . I don't remember. You tell him, Andrea my child . . ."

"Don't lie to me, Mamá. Don't make me curse!"

Once again he was exasperated. The boy awoke and began to whimper. He picked him up for a moment, crooning without taking off his coat, still wet from the street. From time to time he muttered a curse. Growing more and more agitated. Finally he left the baby in my grandmother's lap.

"Juan! Where are you going, child? The baby's going to cry. . . ."

"I'm going to bring Gloria back, Mamá, drag her back by her hair if I have to, back to her son. . . ."

His entire body trembled. He slammed the door. My grandmother began to cry, at last.

"Go with him, Andrea! Go with him, child, he'll kill her! Go!"

Without thinking about it, I put on my coat and ran down the stairs after Juan.

I ran in pursuit as if my life depended on it. Terrified. Seeing street lamps and people coming toward my eyes like blurred images. The night was warm but heavy with dampness. A white light magically illuminated the tender green branches of the last tree on Calle de Aribau.

Juan walked quickly, almost running. At first I didn't so much see him as guess at him in the distance. I thought in despair that if he decided to take a streetcar, I wouldn't have money to follow him.

We reached the plaza of the university when the clock on the building struck twelve-thirty. Juan crossed the plaza and stopped at the corner where the Ronda de San Antonio ends and a dark Calle de Tallers begins. A river of lights ran down Calle de Pelayo. The signs winked their eyes in a tiresome game. Streetcars passed in front of Juan. He looked all around as if orienting himself. He was too thin and his coat hung on him, it swelled in the wind and played around his legs. I was there, almost beside him, not daring to call to him. What good would it have done if I had called to him?

My heart pounded with the exertion of running. I saw him take a few steps toward the Ronda de San Antonio and followed him. Suddenly he turned around so quickly that we were face-to-face. Still, he seemed not to notice but passed me, going in the opposite direction, not seeing me. Again he reached the plaza of the university, and now he went down Calle de Tallers. We didn't run into anyone there. The street lamps seemed dimmer and the pavement was broken. Juan stopped again where the street forks. I remember a public fountain there, its spigot not closed all the way, and puddles forming on the stone pavement. Juan looked for a moment toward the sound of the frame of light that marked where the street ended in the Ramblas. Then he turned his back and moved down Calle de Ramalleras, which was just as narrow and twisting. I ran to follow him. From a closed warehouse came the smell of straw and fruit. The moon rose over an adobe wall. My blood ran with me, pounding through my body.

Each time we saw the Ramblas at an intersection, Juan gave a start. He moved his deep-set eyes in all directions. He bit the inside of his cheeks. On the corner of Calle de Carmen—better lit than the others—I saw him stop, his right elbow resting in the palm of his left hand, pensively stroking his cheekbones, as if caught up in a huge mental effort.

Our journey seemed to have no end. I had no idea where he wanted to go and almost didn't care. An obsession with following him had taken root in my mind, an idea that so captivated me I no longer even knew why I was doing it. Then I realized we could have taken a route that was half as long. We crossed and went through part of the San José market. Our steps echoed under the high roof.

In this enormous place, a multitude of closed stalls presented a dead appearance, and there was great sorrow in the occasional dim, yellowish lights. Large rats, their eyes gleaming as if they were cats, fled noisily at our approach. Some stopped in their tracks, very fat and thinking perhaps of confronting us. There was an indefinable smell of rotting fruit, scraps of meat and fish. . . . A watchman eyed us suspiciously as we passed, heading for the alleys in the back, running one behind the other.

When we reached Calle del Hospital, Juan hurried toward the lights of the Ramblas, which he'd seemed to be avoiding until then. We found ourselves on the Rambla del Centro. I was almost beside Juan. He seemed to pick up my scent unconsciously because he was constantly looking behind him. But though his eyes often passed over me, he didn't see me. He looked suspicious, like a thief avoiding people. I think a man said something obscene to me. I'm not even certain, though it's likely people tried to interfere with me and laughed at me a good number of times. I didn't think for a moment about where this adventure might lead me, or what I would do to calm someone whose fits of rage I knew so well. I know it reassured me to think he wasn't carrying a weapon. Otherwise my thoughts trembled with the same excitation that squeezed my throat until I almost felt pain. Juan went onto Calle del Conde del Asalto, swarming with people and lights at that hour. I realized this was the beginning of the Barrio Chino. "The devil's glitter" that Angustias had told me about looked impoverished and gaudy and had a great abundance of posters with portraits of male and female dancers. The doors of the cabarets with featured attractions seemed like shacks at a fair. The music was bewildering as it came from every side in discordant waves that combined in disharmony. Passing quickly through a human wave that made me desperate at times because it kept me from seeing Juan, I had a vivid memory of a carnival I'd seen when I was little. The people were truly grotesque: a man passed by, his eyes heavy with makeup under a broad-brimmed hat. His cheeks were rouged. Everyone seemed disguised with bad taste, and the noise and the smell of wine brushed past me. I wasn't even frightened, just like that day when I shrank against my mother's skirt and listened to the laughter and ridiculous contortions of the people in masks. All of that was merely the frame to a nightmare, unreal like everything external to my pursuit.

I lost sight of Juan and was terrified. Someone pushed me. I looked up and saw at the end of the street the mountain of Montjuich enveloped, with its gardens, in the purity of the night. . . .

At last I found Juan. Poor man, he was standing still. Looking into the lit show window of a dairy store, where there was a row of delicious flans. He was moving his lips and with his hand he pensively held his chin. *This is the moment,* I thought, *to put my hand on his arm. To make him see reason. To tell him that Gloria surely is home.* . . . I didn't do anything.

Juan resumed walking, going—after looking around to orient himself—down one of those dark fetid alleys that open their mouths there. Again the pilgrimage turned into a hunt in shadows that grew darker and darker. I lost track of the streets we went down. The houses were close together, tall, oozing dampness. Behind some doors you could hear music. We passed a couple in a coarse embrace, and I stepped into a mud-filled puddle. It seemed that some streets had a reddish breath, diluted in the darkness. Others, a bluish light . . . Some men passed and their voices sounded gruff in the silence. My head cleared for a few moments and I approached Juan so he could see I was with him. When Juan and I were alone again I relaxed, paying attention only to the sound of his footsteps.

I remember we were going down a black, utterly silent alley, when a door opened and a drunk was thrown out with such bad luck that he fell against Juan, making him stumble. An electrical charge seemed to run down Juan's back. In the blink of an eye he punched the man in the jaw and then stood and waited for him to come to. After a few minutes they were entangled in a savage fight. I could barely see them. I heard their panting and their curses. From an invisible window, a rasping voice broke through the air above us: "What's going on here?"

Then I was surprised by the animation that suddenly filled the street. Two or three men and a few boys, who seemed to spring from the earth, surrounded the men who were fighting. A half-opened door threw a stream of light onto the street, and it blinded me.

Terrified, I tried to remain invisible. I had no idea what might happen in the next few minutes. Above that inferno—as if witches were riding through the sky over the street—we heard hard, piercing voices. Women's voices egging on the fighters with their quips and laughter. In a kind of delusion it seemed to me that fat faces floated in the air, like the balloons children let go of sometimes.

I heard a roar and saw that Juan and his opponent had fallen and were rolling in the mud on the street. No one intended to separate them. A man shone a flashlight on them and then I saw that Juan was pulling on the other man's neck to bite him. One of the onlookers threw a bottle at Juan, making him spin around and fall in the mud. A few seconds later he sat up.

At that moment somebody shrieked an alarm similar to the firemen's bell or the special horn on a police car that has so much impact in the movies. In an instant Juan and I were alone. Even his drunken opponent had disappeared. Juan staggered to his feet. We heard stifled giggles above us. I, who had been frozen in a strange inaction, reacted suddenly, leaping with feverish speed, a kind of madness, toward Juan. I helped him to stand upright, and I straightened his clothes, wet with blood and wine. He was gasping.

In my head I heard the reverberation of my heartbeats. The noise deafened me.

"Let's go!" I tried to say. "Let's go!"

My voice didn't come out and I began to shove Juan. I would have liked to fly. I knew or believed that police would be arriving soon, and I got Juan onto another street. Before we turned the second corner, we heard footsteps. Juan had a strong reaction but let himself be led by me. I leaned against his shoulder and he put his arms around me. A group passed by. They were individuals who stamped their feet when they walked and made jokes. They didn't say anything to us. A little while later we had separated. My uncle leaned against a wall, his hands in his pockets, and a street lamp shone its light on the two of us.

He looked at me, realizing who I was. But he didn't say anything because he no doubt found it natural for me to be in the heart of the Barrio Chino that night. I pulled a handkerchief out of his pocket so he could wipe away the blood dripping down over one eye. I tied it around his head and then he leaned on my shoulder, turning his head and trying to orient himself. I began to feel very tired, which happened to me frequently in those days. My knees were trembling so much that it became difficult for me to walk. My eyes were full of tears.

"Let's go home, Juan! . . . Let's go!"

"Do you think the punches have made me crazy, Andrea? I know very well why I've come here. . . ."

He became enraged again, and his jaw trembled.

"Gloria must be home by now. She only went to see her sister to ask her to lend her money for medicine."

"Lies! She's shameless! Who told you to get mixed up in what doesn't concern you?" He calmed down a little. "Gloria doesn't have to ask that witch for money. Today they promised her on the phone that tomorrow at eight we'd have a hundred pesetas that they still owe me for a painting. . . . So why is she asking for money? As if I didn't know that her dear sister doesn't even give her the time of day! . . . But she doesn't know that today I'll break her head! She can behave badly with me, but for her to be worse than animals are with their pups, I won't have that. I'd rather see the bitch die once and for all! . . . What she likes is to drink and carry on in her sister's house. I know her. But if she has the brains of a rabbit . . . like you! Like all women! . . . But at least let her be a mother, the miserable . . . !"

All of this was peppered with curses that I remember very well, but why should I repeat them?

He was talking as we walked. Leaning on my shoulder and pushing me at the same time. In those fingers that clutched at me I felt pierced by all the energy of his nerves. And at each step, each word, his strength grew sharper.

I know we walked again along the same street where the fight had taken place, enveloped now in silence. Juan sniffed like a dog looking for a trail. Like one of the mangy dogs we sometimes saw rooting around in filth. . . . The light of the moon rose above that weariness and decay. You only had to look up at the sky to see it. Down below, in the alleys, you forgot about it.

Juan began banging at a door. The echoes of his blows answered him. Juan kept kicking and banging for a long time, until the door opened. Then he pushed me to one side and went in, leaving me in the street. I heard something like a muffled scream inside. Then nothing. The door slammed in my face.

Suddenly I was so tired that I sat in the doorway, my head in my hands, not thinking of anything. Then I began to laugh. I covered my mouth with my hands, which were trembling because my laughter was stronger than I was. The running, the exhausting pursuit was all for this! . . . What would happen if they didn't come out all night? How would I find the way back home by myself? I think I began to cry then. A long time passed, perhaps an hour. Dampness rose from the softened ground. The moon illuminated the top of a house in a bath of silver. The rest was in darkness. I began to feel cold in spite of the spring night. Cold and vague fear. I began to tremble. The door opened behind me and a woman's head looked out, cautiously, calling to me:

"*Pobreta! . . . Entra, entra.*"

I found myself in a closed store that sold food and drinks and was lit solely by a low-watt bulb. Juan was next to the counter, turning a filled glass around and around in his fingers. From another room came an animated sound, and a stream of light filtered beneath a curtain. Undoubtedly they were playing cards. *Where's Gloria?* I thought. The woman who opened the door for me was very fat and had dyed hair. She wet the tip of a pencil on her tongue and wrote something down in a book.

"So it's time now for you to find out about your affairs, Juan. It's time you know that Gloria's supporting you.... Coming here ready to commit murder is all very nice ... and my idiot sister puts up with everything instead of telling you that the only people who want your pictures are ragpickers.... And you with all your gentle-man's airs on Calle de Aribau ..."

She turned to me:

"*Vols una mica d'aiguardent, nena?*"

"No, thank you."

"*Que delicadeta ets, noia!*"

And she began to laugh.

Juan listened somberly to her tongue-lashing. I couldn't even imagine what had happened while I was on the street. Juan no longer had the handkerchief around his head. I noticed that his shirt was ripped. The woman continued:

"And you can thank God, Joanet, that your wife loves you. With the body she has she could put some good horns on you without all the scares the *pobreta* goes through just to come here and play cards. So the great gentleman can think he's a famous painter ..."

She began to laugh, shaking her head. Juan said:

"If you don't shut up, I'll strangle you! Pig!"

She stood erect, threatening.... But then her expression changed and she smiled at Gloria, who was coming through a side door. Juan heard her come in, too, but appeared not to see her as he looked at his glass. Gloria seemed tired. She said:

"Let's go, *chico!*"

And she took Juan's arm. No doubt he'd seen her earlier. God only knows what had happened between them.

We went out to the street. When the door closed behind us, Juan put an arm across Gloria's back, leaning on her shoulders. We walked for a while in silence.

"Did the boy die?" asked Gloria.

Juan shook his head and began to cry. Gloria was frightened. He embraced her, pressed her to his chest, and went on crying, shaken by spasms, until he made her cry, too.

XVI

Román came in the house impetuously, as if he'd been rejuvenated.
"Have they brought my new suit?" he asked the maid.
"Yes, Señorito Román. I took it upstairs...."
Trueno, lazy and fat, began to get up to greet Román.
"This Trueno," said my uncle, frowning, "is becoming too deca-
dent.... My friend, if you keep on this way, I'll slit your throat as if
you were a pig...."
The smile froze on the maid's face. Her eyes began to shine.
"Don't make jokes, Señorito Román! Poor Trueno. He gets better-
looking every day!... Isn't that right, Trueno? Isn't that right, my
darling?"
The woman sat on her heels and the dog put its paws on her
shoulders and licked her dark face. Román watched the scene with
curiosity, his lips curved into an undefinable expression.
"In any event, if the dog keeps on this way I'll kill him.... I don't
like so much happiness and so much swelling up."
Román turned and went out. As he passed he caressed my
cheeks. His black eyes were shining. The skin on his face was dark
and hard, with a multitude of wrinkles, small and deep as if made

with a penknife. In his brilliant, curly black hair, a few white strands. For the first time I thought about Román's age. I thought about it precisely on that day, when he seemed younger.

"Do you need money, little one? I want to give you a present. I made a good business deal."

I don't know what impelled me to respond:

"I don't need anything. Thanks, Román. . . ."

He wore a half-smile, confused.

"All right. I'll give you cigarettes. I have some terrific ones . . ."

He seemed to want to say something else. He stopped as he was leaving.

"I know *those two* are going through a good period now," and he pointed ironically at Juan's room. "I can't be away from home for so long. . . ."

I didn't say anything. Finally he left.

"Did you hear?" Gloria said. "Román bought himself a new suit . . . and some silk shirts, *chica*. . . . What do you think of that?"

"I think it's fine." I shrugged.

"Román's never thought about his clothes. Tell me the truth, Andrea. Do you think he's in love? Román falls in love very easily, *chica!*"

Gloria was getting uglier. During the month of May her face had become very thin and her narrow eyes looked sunken.

"Román liked you, too, in the beginning, didn't he? Now he doesn't like you. Now he likes your friend Ena."

The idea that my uncle could have been interested in me as a woman was so idiotic I was stunned. *How are our actions and words interpreted by minds like hers?* I thought in astonishment, looking at Gloria's white forehead.

I went outside, still thinking about these things. I walked quickly, distracted, but I realized that an old man with a red nose was crossing the street and coming toward me. And possessed by my usual discomfort, I crossed to the other side but couldn't avoid our meeting in the middle. He was out of breath as he passed close to me, lifted his old cap, and greeted me.

"Good morning, Señorita!"

The rogue's eyes were shining with anxiety. I greeted him with a nod of my head and fled.

I knew him very well. He was the "poor" old man who never asked for anything. Leaning against the wall at a corner of Calle de Aribau, dressed with a certain decency, he stood for hours, leaning on his cane and watching. It didn't matter if it was cold or hot: He was there, not whining or shouting like the other beggars, always liable to be picked up and taken to the poorhouse. He only greeted passersby with respectful courtesy, and they sometimes took pity on him and placed some money in his hand. He couldn't be reproached for anything. I felt a special antipathy toward him that grew over time and became more intense. He was my unavoidable charge, which is why I think I hated him so much. It didn't occur to me at the time, but I felt obliged to give him alms and was ashamed when I didn't have any money to give him. I had inherited the old man from Aunt Angustias. I remember that whenever she and I went out, my aunt would deposit five céntimos in that reddened hand raised in polite greeting. And she would stop to talk to him in an authoritarian voice, obliging him to tell her lies or truths about his life. He answered all her questions with the meekness Angustias desired. . . . At times his eyes slipped away in the direction of some "client" he was longing to greet and whose view my aunt and I were blocking as we stood there on the sidewalk. But Angustias went on with her interrogation:

"Answer me! Don't get distracted! . . . Is it true that your little grandson can't go into the orphanage? And that your daughter finally died? And . . . ?"

At last she concluded:

"You can be sure I'll find out the truth in all this. It can cost you dearly if you're deceiving me."

Since that time he and I had been connected by an inevitable bond, because I'm sure he guessed at my dislike for Angustias. A gentle smile would pass over his lips between his decent silver beard and mustache, while his eyes, dancing with intelligence, fired at me occasionally. I'd look at him in despair.

Why don't you send her packing? I'd ask without speaking.

His eyes continued to flash.

"Yes, Señorita. God bless you, Señorita! Ay, Señorita, what the poor go through! May God go with you, Señorita, and the Virgin of Montserrat, and the Virgin of the Pillar!"

At last, humble and fawning, he received his payment of five céntimos.

"One must be charitable, my child. . . ."

From then on I felt antipathy for the old man. On the first day I had money I gave him five pesetas so that he too would feel free of Aunt Angustias's miserliness and as happy as I was; on that day I'd wanted to share myself, merge with all the creatures in the world. When he began his string of praises, he irritated me so much that before I ran away in order not to hear him, I said:

"Oh, please, be quiet!"

The next day, and the day after that, I didn't have any money to give him. But his greeting and his dancing eyes pursued me, obsessed me, on that little piece of Calle de Aribau. I devised a thousand tricks to escape him, to deceive him. Sometimes I took the long way around, going up toward Calle Muntaner. This was when I acquired the habit of eating dried fruit on the street. Some nights, when I was hungry, I'd buy a paper cone of almonds at the stand on the corner. It was impossible for me to wait until I got home to eat them. . . . Then two or three barefoot boys would always follow me.

"Just one almond! We're hungry!"

"Don't be mean!"

Ah! Damn you! I'd think. *You've had something hot in some Social Services dining hall. Your stomachs aren't empty.* I'd look at them in a rage.

I elbowed them out of the way. One day, one spit at me. . . . But if I walked past the old man, if I was unlucky enough to meet his eyes, I'd give him the entire cone that I was carrying, and sometimes it was almost full. I don't know why I did that. He didn't inspire the slightest compassion in me, but his mild eyes put my nerves on edge. I'd put the almonds in his hand as if I were throwing them in his face, and then I'd almost tremble with fury and unsatisfied hunger. I couldn't bear him. As soon as I collected my stipend, I'd think about him, and the old man would have his salary of five pesetas a month, which represented one day less of food for me. He was so good a psychologist, and so sly, that he no longer thanked me. But what he couldn't dispense with was his greeting. Without his greeting I'd have forgotten about him. It was his weapon.

That day was the beginning of my vacation. Exams were over and I found myself at the end of a school year. Pons had asked me:

"What do you plan to do this summer?"

"Nothing, I don't know . . ."

"And when you finish school?"

"I don't know that either. I'll teach, I suppose."

(Pons had the ability to ask me unnerving questions. As I was saying I'd teach, I understood clearly that I could never be a good teacher.)

"Wouldn't you rather get married?"

I didn't answer.

I'd gone out that afternoon attracted by the warm day, and I wandered without a fixed destination. At the last minute I decided to go to Guíxols's studio.

Right after I crossed paths with the old beggar, I saw Jaime, as distracted as I was. He was sitting in his car, which he had parked at the sidewalk on Calle de Aribau. The sight of Jaime brought back many memories, among them my desire to see Ena again. He was smoking, leaning on the steering wheel. I realized I'd never seen him smoke before. He happened to look up and see me. His movements were very agile; he jumped from the car and seized my hands.

"You've come at just the right time. I really wanted to see you. . . . Is Ena in your house?"

"No."

"But will she come?"

"I don't know, Jaime."

He seemed befuddled.

"Do you want to take a ride with me?"

"Yes, I'd love to."

I sat beside him in the car, I looked at his face, and it seemed bathed in thoughts that had nothing to do with me. We left Barcelona along the Vallvidrera highway. We were soon enveloped in pines and their warm scent.

"You know that Ena and I aren't seeing each other anymore?" Jaime asked me.

"No. I haven't seen her very much lately, either."

"Still, she goes to your house."

I flushed slightly.

"It isn't to see me."

"Yes, I know; I guessed as much . . . but I thought you saw her, that you talked to her."

"No."

"I wanted you to tell her something for me, if you see her."

"Yes?"

"I want her to know that I have confidence in her."

"All right, I'll tell her."

Jaime stopped the car and we walked along the highway among the reddish and golden tree trunks. That day I was in a special frame of mind for observing people. I asked myself, as I had done earlier with Román, how old Jaime could be. He was standing beside me, very slim, looking at the splendid view. Vertical lines were forming on his forehead. He turned toward me and said:

"I turned twenty-nine today . . . What's wrong?"

I was astounded because he had answered my silent question. He looked at me and laughed, not knowing how to account for my expression. I told him.

We stayed there for a while, almost without speaking, in perfect harmony, and then, by mutual consent, we went back to the car. When he started the engine, he asked me:

"Are you very fond of Ena?"

"Very. There's no one I love more."

He looked at me quickly.

"All right . . . I should say what the poor say . . . God bless you! . . . But that isn't what I'm going to say; instead I'll tell you that you shouldn't leave her alone now, you should be with her. . . . Something strange is happening to her. I'm certain of that. I think she's very unhappy."

"But why?"

"If I knew, Andrea, we wouldn't have quarreled and I wouldn't have to ask you to be with her; I'd do it myself. I think I behaved badly with Ena, I refused to understand her. . . . Now that I've thought it over, I follow her in the street, I do the stupidest things to see her, and she won't even listen to me. She runs away as soon as she catches sight of me. Just last night I wrote her a letter. She hasn't read it because I knew she'd tear it up and I didn't mail it; I think I'm getting too old to write twelve-page love letters. Still, I'd have sent it to her house eventually if you hadn't shown up. I'd rather you tell her. Will you? Tell her I have confidence in her and I'll never ask her about anything. But I need to see her."

"Yes, I'll tell her."

We didn't speak anymore after this. Jaime's words seemed confused to me, and at the same time I was moved by their vagueness.

"Where shall I drop you off?" he asked as we entered Barcelona.

"Calle de Montcada, if you don't mind."

He drove me there in silence. At the door of the old palace

where Guíxols had his studio, we said good-bye. At that moment Iturdiaga showed up. I noticed that Jaime and he greeted each other coldly.

"Do you all know that this señorita arrived by car?" said Iturdiaga when we were in the studio.

"We have to warn her about Jaime," he added.

"Oh, yes? Why?"

Pons looked at me sorrowfully.

It was Iturdiaga's opinion that Jaime was a disaster. His father had been a famous architect and he belonged to a wealthy family.

"In short, a spoiled rich kid," said Iturdiaga. "Somebody without initiative who never in his life thought about doing anything."

Jaime was an only child and had planned to pursue the same profession as his father. The war had interrupted his studies, and when it was over, Jaime found himself an orphan with a fairly large fortune. He needed two more years to become an architect, but he hadn't worried about finishing. He devoted himself to having a good time and not doing anything all day. In Iturdiaga's opinion, he was a contemptible being. I remember Iturdiaga as he said these things: He sat with crossed legs and his face of an avenging angel, almost on fire with indignation.

"And when are you going to begin studying for the state exam, Iturdiaga?" I said with a smile when he stopped.

Iturdiaga gave me an arrogant look. He spread his arms.... Then he continued his diatribe against Jaime.

Pons hadn't stopped watching me and this began to annoy me.

"Last night, for example, I saw this Jaime in a club on the Paralelo," said Iturdiaga, "and he was alone in his corner and more bored than an old maid."

"And you, what were you doing?"

"Being inspired. Finding characters for my novels ... Besides, I have a waiter who gives me real absinthe ..."

"Bah! Bah! ... It's probably green-colored water," said Guíxols.

"No, Señor! ... But, all of you, listen to me. I've wanted to tell you my new adventure since I got here, and I've been distracted. Just last night I met my soulmate, the ideal woman. We fell in love without saying a word. She's a foreigner. Probably Russian or Norwegian. She has Slavic cheekbones and the dreamiest, most mysterious eyes I've ever seen. She was in the same club where I saw Jaime, but she seemed out of place there. Her clothes were very elegant and she was with a peculiar guy who devoured her with his eyes. She didn't pay much attention to him. She was bored and seemed nervous. . . . Then she looked at me. . . . It was only for a second, friends, but what a look! She told me everything with that look: her dreams, her hopes . . . Because I must tell you that she isn't mercenary, this is a girl as young as Andrea, delicate, very pure . . ."

"I know you, Iturdiaga. She's probably forty years old, and dyes her hair, and was born in Barcelona. . . ."

"Guíxols!" shouted Iturdiaga.

"Forgive me, *noi*, but I know how you are. . . ."

"All right, but that's not the end of the adventure. At that moment the guy who was with her came back because he had gone to pay the bill, and they both stood up. I didn't know what to do. When they reached the door, the girl turned and looked back into the club, as if she were looking for me. . . . Friends! I jumped out of my seat, I left my coffee without paying . . ."

"So it was coffee and not absinthe."

"I left the coffee without paying for it and ran after them. That was when my unknown blonde and her escort got into a cab. . . . I don't know what I felt. There are no words to express the heartbreak I felt. . . . Because when she looked at me for the last time, she did it with real sadness. It was almost a call for help. I spent all day today half crazy, looking for her. I have to find her, my friends. A thing like this, so powerful, happens only once in your life."

"But you, because you're a privileged being, it happens to you every week, Iturdiaga. . . ."

Iturdiaga got up and began to walk around the studio, puffing on his pipe. A little while later, Pujol came in with a very dirty Gypsy girl, whom he wanted to propose as a model for Guíxols. She was young and had an enormous mouth full of white teeth. Pujol strutted around with her and held her arm. He wanted us to know he was her lover. I knew my presence hindered his conversation and for that reason he was angry with me that day, when he had wanted to show off to his friends. Pons had brought wine and pastries, and by contrast seemed delighted. He wanted to celebrate the successful end of the year. We had a good time. They had the Gypsy girl dance, and she turned out to be very graceful.

We left the studio fairly late. I wanted to walk home and Iturdiaga and Pons accompanied me. The night seemed splendid, with its breath as warm and pink as blood in a vein opened gently over the street.

As we walked up Vía Layetana, I couldn't help looking toward Ena's house, remembering my friend and the strange message Jaime had given me for her. I was thinking about this when I saw her actually appear before my eyes. She was holding her father's arm. They were a magnificent couple, so good-looking and elegant. She saw me, too, and smiled. No doubt they were returning home.

"Wait a minute," I said to the boys, interrupting Iturdiaga in the middle of a sentence. I crossed the street and went toward my friend. I reached her just as she and her father were walking into the building.

"Can I speak to you for a moment?"

"Of course. You don't know how happy I am to see you. Do you want to come up?"

This was the equivalent of an invitation to supper.

"I can't, my friends are waiting for me. . . ."

Ena's father smiled.

"I'm going up, girls. Come up soon, Ena."

He waved to us. Ena's father was Canarian, and though he'd spent most of his life away from the islands, he retained the habit of speaking in the special, affectionate manner of his homeland.

"I saw Jaime," I said quickly, as soon as he was gone. "I was out with him today and he gave me a message for you."

Ena looked at me with a closed expression.

"He said he has confidence in you, that he won't ask you anything and needs to see you."

"Ah! All right, fine, Andrea. Thanks, darling."

She pressed my hand and went into the building, leaving me with a certain disappointment. She hadn't even let me see her eyes.

When I turned I saw Iturdiaga, who had leaped across the street with his long legs through a surging wave of cars. . . .

He looked in a daze toward the entrance, where the elevator was going up with Ena inside.

"It's her! The Slavic princess! . . . I'm an imbecile! I realized it just as she was saying good-bye to you! For God's sake! How is it possible that you know her! Talk to me, please! Where was she born? Is she Russian, Swedish, maybe Polish?"

"She's Catalan."

Iturdiaga was stunned.

"Then, how is it possible she was in a club last night? How do you know her?"

"She's at school with me," I said vaguely, as Iturdiaga took my arm to cross the street.

"And all these men who are with her?"

"The one today was her father. The one yesterday, you understand, I don't know. . . ."

(And as I was saying this to Iturdiaga, I could see a clear image of Román. . . .)

I was distracted all the way home, thinking that you always move in the same circle of people no matter how many turns you seem to make.

XVII

The month of June was passing and the heat increased. From the corners full of dust, from the grimy wallpaper in the rooms, a flock of hungry bedbugs started to emerge. I engaged in a fierce struggle against them that sapped my strength every morning. I saw in horror that the other people in the house didn't seem to notice anything wrong. The first day I began a thorough cleaning of my room, with disinfectant and hot water, Granny looked in and shook her head in disapproval.

"Girl! Girl! Let the maid do that!"

"Leave her alone, Mamá. This is happening to my niece because she's dirtier than the rest of us," said Juan.

I wore my bathing suit to do this repugnant chore. It was the same blue bathing suit I'd worn in the village the previous summer to swim in the river. The river ran deep as it passed my cousin's garden, bending in delicious curves, its banks full of bulrushes and mud. . . . In spring it was turbid, heavy with the seeds of trees and images of flowering orchards. In summer it filled with green shadows that trembled between my arms when I swam. . . . If I let myself be carried along by the current, those shadows carried reflections that shone in my open eyes. At twilight the water took on a re. ocher color.

In that same faded bathing suit that now was becoming stained with soap, I'd stretched out on the beach next to Ena and Jaime during the spring and had gone into the cold blue sea under the raw light of April.

As I washed down my bed with boiling water and skinned my fingers when I touched the esparto brush, the thought of Ena came to me enveloped in so much darkness and sadness that it eventually depressed me more than everything in my surroundings. Sometimes I felt like crying as if it were me, not Jaime, whom she had betrayed and deceived. It was impossible for me to believe in the beauty and truth of human feelings—as my eighteen years conceived of them at the time—when I thought that everything reflected in Ena's eyes—until they became radiant and at the same time filled with sweetness, in a look she had only when she was with Jaime—had vanished in a moment, leaving no trace.

That spring she and Jaime had seemed different from all other human beings, as if they'd been made divine by a secret I imagined as high and marvelous. For me their love had illuminated the meaning of existence, simply because it existed. Now I considered myself bitterly cheated. Ena constantly avoided me, she was never home if I called, and I didn't have the courage to visit her.

Since the day I gave her Jaime's message, I hadn't heard anything else about my friend. One afternoon, depressed by the silence that surrounded me, it occurred to me to call Jaime, and I was told he'd left Barcelona. This made me realize that his attempt to approach her had been a failure.

I would have liked to enter Ena's thoughts, open her soul wide, and finally understand her strange mode of being, the reason for her obstinacy. As I despaired, I convinced myself that I loved her dearly, since I couldn't think of any other attitude to have toward her except to make the effort to understand her even when that seemed impossible.

nán in the house, my heart beat wildly with the
n questions. I'd have liked to follow him, spy on
unters with Ena. Sometimes, carried away by this
onging, I'd climb a few sections of the stairs that
om his room when I suspected Ena was there. The
image ía caught in a beam of light on that same staircase
embarrassed me and made me call a halt to my intentions.

Román was affectionate and ironic with me. He kept giving me
small gifts and tapping me lightly on my cheeks, as was his custom,
but he never invited me now to come up to his room.

On one occasion he saw me in the middle of my scrubbing
and it seemed to make him very happy. I looked at him in a criti-
cal, somewhat strained way, as I usually did at that time and—as
always—he seemed not to notice. His white teeth gleamed.

"Good, Andrea! I see you've become a real little wife. . . . I like to
think I have a niece who'll know how to make a man happy when
she marries. Your husband won't have to darn his socks himself, or
feed the children, isn't that right?"

What's this about? I thought. I shrugged.

The door of the dining room was open behind Román. At that
moment I saw him turning in that direction.

"Hey! What do you say to that, Juan? Wouldn't you like to have
a hardworking little wife like our niece?"

Then I realized that Juan was in the dining room, feeding the
baby—who after his illness had become very fussy—his bowl of
milk. He hit the table with his fist and made the bowl jump. He
stood up.

"I have enough with my wife, you hear? And our niece isn't good
enough to lick the ground she walks on. Do you hear me? I don't
know if you intentionally ignore all the shameless things your niece
does so you can worship her; but nobody's as sly as she is. . . . She's
only good for playacting and trying to humiliate other people—
that's what she's good for, that and getting together with you!"

Terrified, I understood the reason for Juan's recent hostility toward me. He was always giving orders for his room to be cleaned, in vain, and when he saw me on the first day holding the kitchen soap, he snatched it from me almost brutally, saying he "needed it," and took it to the studio, where he no longer painted but spent hours holding his head and staring at the floor with wide-open eyes. That's how I saw him a short while later, when I discovered the maid spying on him through the crack in the half-closed door. When she heard me, Antonia quickly straightened up, then raised her finger to her lips, smiling at me, and obliged me—with the threat of touching me with her dirty hands—to look as well. On her face Antonia had the moronic joy of a child throwing stones at an imbecile. My heart contracted at the sight of that man, so tall in his chair, surrounded by the desolation of useless household junk, crushed by the weight of absurdity.

Which was why, during that time when the heat seemed to spur him and incite him to a frenzy, I never answered his insults. He jumped up in exasperation at Román's provocation, responding to the blow. Román laughed. Juan continued shouting.

"Our niece! A terrific example! . . . Loaded down with lovers, running around Barcelona like a dog . . . I know her. Yes, I know you, you hypocrite!" He came to the door to screech at me as Román was leaving.

I mopped up the water spilled on the floor, and against my will my hands began to tremble. . . . I made an effort to see the humorous side of the matter, even if I only imagined my hypothetical lovers, and I couldn't. I picked up the bucket of dirty water and left the room to spill it out.

"Don't you see how quiet that wicked girl is?" Juan shouted. "Don't you see how she can't answer?"

Nobody paid attention to him. Antonia sang in the kitchen, crushing something in the mortar. Then, in one of his typical rages, he crossed the foyer and went to pound on the door of his own room. Gloria—who no longer tried to hide it when she went to play cards—was sleeping, tired because she had gone to bed late.

The door gave way to his shoving and I heard Gloria's frightened screams when Juan attacked and started beating her. The baby, who had been quiet in the dining room, began to cry, too, with huge tears.

Selfishly I went into the bathroom. The water that streamed over my body felt lukewarm, incapable of refreshing or cleaning my flesh.

———

The city, when it begins to be enveloped in the heat of summer, has a beauty that's oppressive and a little sad. Barcelona seemed sad to me as I looked at it from the window in my friends' studio at dusk. From there you could see a panorama of flat roofs and tiled roofs enveloped in reddish vapors, and the steeples of ancient churches seemed to sail through waves. Overhead, the cloudless sky changed its simple colors. From dusty blue it moved to bloodred, gold, amethyst. Then night fell.

Pons was with me in the window alcove.

"My mother wants to meet you. I'm always talking about you. She wants to invite you to spend the summer with us on the Costa Brava."

Behind us we could hear the voices of our friends. Everyone was there. Iturdiaga's voice dominated.

Pons stood beside me, biting his nails. He was so nervous and childish he tired me a little, and at the same time I was very fond of him.

That afternoon we were celebrating the last of our gatherings for a while because Guíxols was going away for the summer. Iturdiaga's father had wanted to send him to Sitges with the rest of the family, but he'd categorically refused to go. Since Iturdiaga's father took only a few days of vacation at the end of the summer, he was, at heart, pleased that Gaspar would be with him for meals.

"I'm convincing him! I'm convincing him!" Iturdiaga shouted. "Away from the pernicious influence of my mother and sisters, my father becomes more reasonable. . . . He's calculating how much it would cost him to publish my book. . . . And he's proud I've become an art critic. . . ."

I turned around.

"You've become an art critic?"

"At a well-known paper."

I thought it was a little astonishing.

"What kind of art have you studied?"

"None. All you need to be a critic is sensitivity, and I have that. And friends . . . I have them, too. At Guíxols's first show I plan to say that he's reached the culmination of his style. On the other hand, I'll go after the famous ones, the ones nobody dares to challenge. . . . My success is guaranteed."

"Don't you think it's a little premature to say I've reached the culmination of my art? After a statement like that I'd only have to look after my brushes and rest on my laurels," said Guíxols.

But Iturdiaga was too enthusiastic to listen to reason.

"Look! They're beginning to light the bonfires!" shouted Pujol, his voice filled with false notes. . . .

It was Saint John's Eve. Pons said to me:

"Think about it for five days, Andrea. Think about it until Saint Peter's Day. That's my saint's day and my father's. We'll have a party at home and you'll come. You'll dance with me. I'll introduce you to my mother and she'll be able to persuade you better than I can. Remember, if you don't come, the day won't have any meaning for me. . . . Then we'll go on vacation. Will you come to the house, Andrea, on Saint Peter's Day? Will you let my mother persuade you to come to the beach?"

"You just said I have five days to answer."

At the same time I was saying this to Pons I felt a longing, a vehement desire to be nonchalant. To free myself. To accept his invitation and lie on the beaches he was offering me, feeling the hours pass as they did in a children's story, and escape the crushing world around me. But I was stopped by the uncomfortable feeling Pons's infatuation produced in me. I believed that accepting his offer bound me to him with other ties that made me uneasy because they seemed false.

In any case, the idea of attending a dance, even one in the afternoon—for me the word *dance* evoked an exciting dream of evening clothes and gleaming floors, the effect of my first reading of the story of Cinderella—touched me, because I, who knew how to let myself be surrounded by the music and slide along to its rhythms and in fact had done that often by myself, had not "really" danced with a man, not ever.

Pons squeezed my hand nervously when we said good-bye. Behind us Iturdiaga exclaimed:

"Saint John's Eve is the night for witchcraft and miracles!"

Pons leaned toward me.

"I have a miracle to ask for tonight."

At that moment I ingenuously wanted the miracle to happen. With all my strength I wanted to be able to fall in love with him. Pons immediately noticed my new tenderness. He only knew how to squeeze my hand to express everything.

When I reached the house, the air was already crackling, hot with the enchantment of that unique night of the year. On this Saint John's Eve it was impossible for me to sleep. The sky was completely clear and still I felt electricity in my hair and fingertips, as if there were a storm. My chest was heavy with a thousand daydreams and memories.

I looked out Angustias's window, in my nightgown. I saw the sky reddened in places by the brilliance of the flames. Even Calle de Aribau burned with excited shouting for a long time, since two or three bonfires had been lit at various intersections with other streets. A short while later boys jumped over the embers, their eyes red with the heat, the sparks, and the bright magic of the fire, to hear the name of their beloved called out by the ashes. Then the shouting began to die down. People dispersed for the open-air celebrations. Calle de Aribau was resonant, still in flames, silent. You could hear fireworks in the distance and the sky over the houses was lit up by brilliant streaks. I thought of the country songs on Saint John's Eve, the night for falling in love if you picked the magic clover in the overheated fields. I leaned on my elbows in the darkness of the balcony, aroused by passionate desires and images. It seemed impossible to withdraw from the spot.

More than once I heard the footsteps of the watchman responding to distant hand claps. Later I was distracted by the noise of our building door closing and I looked down at the sidewalk and saw that it was Román leaving the house. I watched him walk and then stop under the street lamp to light a cigarette. Even if he hadn't stopped in the light, I would have recognized him. The night was very clear. The sky looked sown with golden light. . . . I spent time watching his movements, his body outlined in black, astonishingly proportioned.

At the sound of footsteps, he raised his head, as intense and nervous as a small animal, and I looked up, too. Gloria was crossing the street, coming toward us. (Toward him, down there on the sidewalk, toward my eyes in the darkness of my elevated position.) No doubt she was coming back from her sister's house.

As she walked past Román, Gloria looked at him as she usually did, and the light set her hair ablaze and illuminated her face. Román did something that I thought was extraordinary. He tossed away his cigarette and went toward her with his hand outstretched in greeting. Gloria stepped back in astonishment. He grasped her arm and she shoved him ferociously. Then they stood facing each other, talking for a few seconds in a confused murmur. I was so interested and surprised that I didn't dare to move. From where I watched, the couple's movements seemed like the steps in an Apache dance. Finally, Gloria slipped away and went into the house. I saw Román light another cigarette, toss it away, too, take a few steps, walk away, then finally turn around, determined to follow her.

In the meantime, I heard the apartment door open and Gloria come in. I heard her tiptoe across the dining room toward the balcony. Probably she wanted to see if Román was still in the same spot. All of this began to move me deeply, as if I were directly involved. I couldn't believe what I had seen with my own eyes. When I heard Román's key scraping at the apartment door, the excitement made me tremble. He and Gloria met in the dining room. I heard Román say in a very clear whisper:

"I told you I have to talk to you. Come with me!"

"I don't have time for you."

"Don't talk like a fool. Come with me!"

I heard them walk to the balcony and close the glass behind them. What was happening was as incomprehensible to me as if I were dreaming it. What if it were true that the witches of Saint John really did exist? What if they had made me see visions? I didn't even think I was committing an ugly act of spying when I returned to Angustias's window. The balcony was very close. I could almost hear their breathing. Their voices were clear in my ears against the great background of silence that muffled the distant explosion of fireworks and the music at the celebrations.

I heard Román's voice:

"You only think about these petty things.... Have you forgotten our trip to Barcelona in the middle of the war, Gloria? You don't even remember the purple lilies that grew in the castle park.... Your body was so white and your hair as red as fire in the middle of those purple lilies. I've often thought about you just as you were then, though apparently I've mistreated you. If you come up to my room you can see the canvas I painted of you. I still have it...."

"I remember everything, *chico*. All I've done is think about it. I was hoping you'd remind me one day so I could spit in your face...."

"You're jealous. Do you think I don't know you love me? Do you think I don't know that on so many nights, when everything was quiet, you came with a ghost's footsteps to my door? On many nights this winter I've heard you crying on the stairs...."

"If I was crying, it wasn't for you. I love you as much as I love the

hog they take to the slaughterhouse. That's h[c]
you think I won't tell Juan about this? I wa[s]
wanting you to talk to me so your brother
suaded who you are. . . ."

"Don't raise your voice! You have a lot t[c]
quietly. . . . You know I can present your husband with w[ith]
saw how you came one night to offer yourself to me in my room
and how I kicked you out. . . . I could have done it already if I'd
wanted to take the trouble. Don't forget that there were a lot of soldiers in the castle, Gloria, and some of them live in Barcelona. . . ."

"That day you got me drunk and you were kissing me. . . . When
I went to your room I loved you. You humiliated me in the worst
way. You hid your friends up there, and they died laughing, and you
insulted me. You told me you weren't prepared to steal what belonged to your brother. I was very young, *chico.* When I went to you
that night I thought of myself as separated from Juan, I planned to
leave him. The priest hadn't blessed us yet, don't forget that."

"But you were carrying his child, don't forget that either. . . .
Don't play the puritan tonight, it won't work with me. . . . Maybe I
was blind then, but I want you now. Come up to my room. Let's finish it once and for all."

"I don't know what your intentions are, *chico,* because you're a
traitor like Judas. . . . I don't know what happened with that Ena,
with that blond girl you bewitched, that you talk to me like this."

"Leave her alone! . . . She isn't the one who can satisfy me, it's
you; be happy with that, Gloria."

"You made me cry a lot, but I've been waiting for this moment. . . . If you think I'm still interested in you, you're wrong. If you
think I'm desperate because you take that girl up to your room,
then you're even dumber than Juan. I hate you, *chico.* I've hated you
since the night you humiliated me, when I forgot about everything
because of you. . . . And do you want to know who denounced you
so they'd shoot you? Well it was me! Me! Me! . . . Do you want to

hose fault it was that you were in jail? It was mine. And do
want to know who would denounce you again if she could? Me!
ow I'm the one who can spit in your face, and I do."

"Why do you say so many stupid things? You're boring me. Don't
expect me to beg you. . . . You love me, woman! Look, let's finish dis-
cussing this in my room. Come on! Let's go!"

"Be very careful about touching me, you pig, or I'll call Juan. I'll
scratch out your eyes if you come any closer!"

During the last part of the conversation, Gloria raised her voice
so much that it broke into a hysterical screech.

I heard my grandmother's footsteps in the dining room. Since
they were standing on the balcony, my grandmother could see their
silhouettes outlined against the light of the stars.

Román hadn't become agitated; only his voice had a nervous
ring that I'd noticed since the first words he said:

"Be quiet, idiot! . . . I don't intend to raise a finger to force you.
You can come on your own, if you want to . . . but if you don't come
tonight, don't bother to look in my face ever again. I'm giving you
your last chance. . . ."

He left the balcony. He bumped into my grandmother.

"Who is it? Who is it?" said the old woman. "God save me,
Román, you must be crazy, child!"

He didn't stop. I heard a door slam. My grandmother, shuffling
her feet, approached the balcony. Her voice sounded frightened
and helpless:

"Girl! . . . Girl! Is that you, Gloria, my child? Yes? Is that you? . . ."

Then I realized that Gloria was crying. She shouted:

"Go to bed, Mamá, and leave me in peace!"

After a while she ran to her room, sobbing:

"Juan! Juan! . . ."

My grandmother came over to her.

"Be still, girl, be still. . . . Juan's gone out. He told me he couldn't
sleep. . . ."

There was a silence. I heard footsteps on the stairs. Juan came in.

"Both of you are still up? What's going on?"

A long pause.

"Nothing," Gloria said finally. "Let's go to sleep."

Saint John's Eve had become too strange for me. Standing in the middle of my room, my ears alert to the murmurs in the house, I felt the taut muscles in my neck begin to hurt. My hands were cold. Who can understand the thousand threads that join people's souls and the significance of their words? Not the girl I was then. I lay down on the bed, almost sick. I remembered the words in the Bible, in a completely profane way: "They have eyes and see not, ears and hear not." . . . My eyes, round with so much opening wide, my ears, wounded with listening, had failed to capture a vibration, a profound note in all of that. . . . It seemed impossible that Román had pleaded with Gloria like a lover. Román, who charmed Ena with his music . . . It was impossible that he had pleaded with Gloria, suddenly, with no motive, when I had seen him mistreat and mock her in public. My ears didn't detect this motive in the nervous tremor of his voice, and my eyes couldn't see it in the dense, brilliant mass of blue night that came in through my balcony. . . . I covered my face so I couldn't see the excessive, incomprehensible beauty of the night. At last I fell asleep.

I was dreaming about Ena when I awoke. Imperceptibly my fantasy had linked her to the words, the pettiness, the betrayals, of Román. The bitterness I always felt in those days when I thought about her filled me completely. Impulsively I hurried to her house, not knowing what I would say to her, wanting only to protect her from my uncle.

My friend wasn't there. They told me it was her grandfather's saint's day and that she'd spend the whole day in the great "tower" the old gentleman had in Bonanova. When I heard this, I was filled with a strange exaltation; I thought it was necessary to find Ena at any cost. To talk to her right away.

I crossed Barcelona in a streetcar. I remember that it was a wonderful morning. All the gardens in Bonanova were filled with flowers and their beauty gripped my spirit, which was already too full. I also seemed to be overflowing—as the lilacs, the bougainvillea, the honeysuckle, overflowed the garden walls—so great was the affection, the anguished fear I felt for the life and dreams of my friend. . . . Perhaps in the entire story of our friendship I had not experienced moments as beautiful and as childish as the ones I felt during that useless excursion past gardens on a radiant Saint John's morning. . . .

At last I reached the door of the house I was looking for. A wrought-iron entrance through whose grillwork I could see a lawn, a fountain, and two dogs. . . . I didn't know what I was going to say to Ena. I didn't know how I would tell her again that Román would never be good enough to join his life to hers, so luminous, so well loved by a good and noble creature like Jaime. . . . I was certain that as soon as I began to speak, Ena would laugh at me.

A few long minutes went by, filled with sun. I was leaning against the metal of the high garden fence. There was an intense aroma of roses, and a bumblebee flew over my head, creating a deep peaceful echo. I didn't have the courage to ring the bell.

I heard the door to the house—a glass door that opened onto a white terrace—opening noisily and I saw little Ramón Berenguer appear, accompanied by a cousin with black hair. The two boys ran down the stairs to the garden. I suddenly felt terrified, as if my hand had been seized at the moment of cutting a stolen flower. I began to run, too. I couldn't help it; I was escaping. . . . I laughed at myself when I caught my breath, but I didn't go back to that fence. As impulsively as the exaltation and affection I'd felt that morning for Ena, I began to be overcome by a deep depression. As the day ended, I no longer intended to leap across the distance that she herself had opened between us. I thought it better to let matters take their course.

———

I heard the dog howl on the stairs as it came down, terrified, from Román's room. Its ear bore the red mark of a bite. I shuddered.

Román had been locked in his room for three days. According to Antonia, he was composing music and smoking constantly, so that he was enclosed in an excruciating atmosphere. Trueno must have known something about the mood this atmosphere produced in its owner. The maid, when she saw the dog wounded by Román's teeth, began to shake like a leaf, and tended to the animal, almost howling herself.

I looked at the calendar. Three days had passed since Saint John's Eve. Three more days until Pons's party. My soul pounded with impatience to escape. It almost seemed as if I loved my friend Pons when I thought he would help me to realize this desperate longing.

XVIII

The memory of nights on Calle de Aribau comes to me now. Those nights that ran like a black river beneath the bridges of the days, nights when stagnant odors gave off the breath of ghosts.

I remember the first autumn nights and how they intensified my first moments of disquiet in the house. And the winter nights, with their damp melancholy: the creak of a chair interrupting my sleep and the shudder of my nerves when I discovered two small shining eyes—the cat's eyes—fixed on mine. In those icy hours there were certain moments when life broke with all sense of modesty before my eyes and appeared naked, shouting sad intimacies, which for me were only horrifying. Intimacies that the morning took care to erase, as if they'd never existed. . . . Later came the summer nights. Sweet, dense Mediterranean nights over Barcelona, with golden juice flowing from the moon, with the damp odor of sea nymphs combing their watery hair over white shoulders, over the scales of golden tails. . . . On one of those hot nights, hunger, sadness, and the power of my youth brought me to a swoon of feeling, a physical need for tenderness as avid and dusty as scorched earth with a presentiment of the storm.

First thing, when I lay wearily on the mattress, came the headache, empty and throbbing, tormenting my skull. I had to lie with my head low, without a pillow, to feel the pain slowly fade, crossed by a thousand familiar sounds from the street and the house.

This was how sleep came, in increasingly indolent waves, until the deep, complete oblivion of body and soul. The heat flung its breath at me, as irritating as the juice of nettles, until, oppressed as in a nightmare, I'd wake again.

Absolute silence. On the street, from time to time, the watchman's footsteps. Far above the balconies, the tiled roofs, the flat roofs, the brilliance of the stars.

Uneasiness made me jump out of bed, for these luminous, impalpable threads that come from the world of stars affected me with forces impossible to define, but real.

I remember one night when there was a moon. My nerves were on edge after a day that had been too turbulent. When I got out of bed I saw in Angustias's mirror my entire room filled with the color of gray silk, and in the middle of it, a long white shadow. I approached and the phantom approached with me. At last I saw my own face in a blur above my linen nightgown. An old linen nightgown—made soft by the touch of time—weighed down with heavy lace, which my mother had worn many years before. It was unusual for me to stand looking at myself this way, almost without seeing myself, my eyes open. I raised my hand to touch my features, which seemed to run away from me, and what appeared were long fingers, paler than my face, tracing the line of eyebrows, nose, cheeks, conforming to my bone structure. In any case there I was, Andrea, living among the shadows and passions that surrounded me. Sometimes I doubted it.

Pons's party had taken place that afternoon.

For five days I'd tried to store up expectations for that flight from my ordinary life. Until then it had been easy for me to turn my back on what lay behind me, to think about starting a new life at any moment. And on that day I'd had a kind of presentiment of other horizons. Something like the awful tension that seizes me at times in the railroad station when I hear the whistle of the train pulling out or when I walk along the port and in a mouthful of air the smell of ships comes to me.

My friend had telephoned in the morning and his voice filled me with tenderness for him. The feeling of being expected, of being loved, awoke a thousand woman's instincts in me; an emotion like triumph, a desire to be praised, admired, to feel like Cinderella in the fairy tale, a princess for a few hours after a long period of concealment.

I recalled a dream I'd often had in my childhood, when I was a sallow, skinny girl, one of those whom visitors never call pretty and whose parents receive vague consolations. . . . Those words that children, pretending to be absorbed and removed from the conversation, eagerly pick up: "When she grows up she'll certainly be a pretty girl," "Children can surprise us as they grow up." . . .

Half asleep, I saw myself running, stumbling, and at the impact I'd feel something detach from me, like a dress or a chrysalis that breaks and falls, wrinkled, at one's feet. I saw people's astonished eyes. When I ran to the mirror, I contemplated, trembling with emotion, my astonishing transformation into a blond princess—blond, just as the stories describe—immediately endowed, through the grace of my beauty, with the attributes of sweetness, charm, and goodness, and the marvelous trait of generously scattering my smiles. . . .

This fairy tale, repeated so often during the nights of my childhood, made me smile, as with lightly trembling hands I tried to arrange my hair elegantly and make my least old dress, carefully ironed for the party, look pretty.

Perhaps, I thought, blushing a little, *that day is today.* If Pons's eyes found me pretty and attractive (and my friend had said as much with awkward words, or more eloquently without them, very often), it was as if the disguise had already fallen.

Perhaps the meaning of life for a woman consists sole,
ered like this, looked at so that she herself feels radiant w.
looking at, not in listening to the poisons and stupidi
but in experiencing fully the joy of her own feelings an
her own despair and happiness. Her own wickedness or g

And so I escaped from the house on Calle de Aribau ai almost
had to cover my ears in order not to hear the piano that Román was
tormenting.

My uncle had spent five days locked in his room. (According to
what Gloria told me, he hadn't gone out even once.) And that
morning he had appeared in the house, scrutinizing the changes
with his penetrating eyes. In some corners he noticed the missing
furniture, which Gloria had sold to the rag dealer. Cockroaches
scurried around those clear spaces.

"You're stealing from my mother!" he shouted.

My grandmother came to the rescue immediately.

"No, child, no. I sold them, they're mine; I sold them because I
needed to, because it's my right. . . ."

It was so incongruous to hear that unfortunate old woman talk of
rights when she was capable of dying of hunger so there'd be more
for others, or of cold so the baby would have another blanket in his
cradle, that Román smiled.

In the afternoon, my uncle began to play the piano. From the
door to the gallery I saw him in the living room. Sunbeams branched
out behind his head. He turned toward me and saw me, too, and
also gave me a lively smile that covered over all his thoughts.

"You've become too good-looking to want to listen to my music,
hmm? You run away, like all the women in this house. . . ."

He pressed the keys with passion, forcing them to give the sense
of a splendid spring. His eyes were red, like those of a man who's
had a good deal of alcohol or hasn't slept for several days. When he
played, his face filled with wrinkles.

And so I ran away from him, as I had done on other occasions.
On the street I remembered only his gallantry. *In spite of everything,*

...ought, *Román makes the people around him come to life. He really knows what's going on. He knows I'm full of hope this afternoon.*

Linked to the idea of Román, the thought of Ena came to mind involuntarily. Because I, who had so wanted to prevent those two from ever meeting, could no longer separate them in my imagination.

"Do you know that Ena came to see Román on the afternoon of Saint John's Eve?"

Gloria had told me this, looking at me out of the corner of her eye:

"I saw her myself when she ran out, down the stairs, like Trueno was running the other day. . . . The same way, *chica*, like she was crazy. . . . What do you think of that? . . . She hasn't come back since then."

I covered my ears, there on the street on my way to Pons's house, and looked up at the treetops. The leaves already had a hard green consistency. The fiery sky shattered against them.

Back in the dazzling street, I again became an eighteen-year-old girl going to dance with her first suitor. An agreeable, lighthearted expectation completely silenced those echoes of other people.

Pons lived in a splendid house at the end of Calle Muntaner. In front of the fence around the garden—so citified the flowers smelled of wax and cement—I saw a long line of cars. My heart began to pound in a way that was almost painful. I knew that in a few minutes I'd have to enter a happy, unthinking world. A world that revolved around the solid pedestal of money, with an optimistic view I knew something about from listening to the conversations of my friends. It was the first time I was going to a society party, since the gatherings at Ena's house, which I had attended, had an intimate character imbued with a literary and artistic purpose.

I remember the marble entrance and its pleasant coolness. My confusion before the servant at the door, the shadowy foyer decorated with plants and vases. The scent of a woman wearing too many jewels who came to shake the hand of Pons's mother, whose indefinable glance at my old shoes crossed the yearning look of Pons, who was watching her.

She was tall, imposing. She smiled as she spoke to me, as if the smile had come to rest—forever—on her lips. It was too easy then to hurt me. In a moment I felt anguish because of my shabby clothes. I placed a not-very-certain hand on Pons's arm and went into the living room with him.

There were a good number of people there. In a small adjacent room the "adults" devoted themselves principally to eating and laughing. A fat woman is set in my memory, her face congested with laughter at the moment she puts an almond pastry in her mouth. I don't know why I have this image eternally fixed in the midst of all the confusion and movement. The young people were eating and drinking, too, and talking as they constantly moved around. There was a preponderance of pretty girls. Pons introduced me to a group of four or five, saying they were his cousins. I felt very shy with them. I almost felt like crying, for in no way did this emotion resemble the radiant sensation I had anticipated. Felt like crying with impatience and rage . . .

I didn't dare to move away from Pons, and in terror I began to sense that he was becoming a little nervous as he faced those pretty, malicious eyes observing us. Finally someone called my friend over for a moment and he left me—with an apologetic smile—alone with the girls and two young boys I didn't know. For all that time I didn't know what to say. I wasn't having a good time at all. I saw myself in a mirror, white and gray, dowdy among the bright summer dresses all around me. Absolutely serious in the midst of everyone's animation, and I felt ridiculous.

Pons had disappeared from my visual horizon. At last, when the music filled the room with a slow fox-trot, I found myself completely alone by a window, watching the others dance.

The dance ended with the sound of conversation, and nobody came over to me. I heard Iturdiaga's voice and quickly turned around. Gaspar was sitting with two or three girls to whom he was showing I don't know what plans and explaining his future projects. He was saying:

"Today this rock is inaccessible, but to reach it I'll construct a cable car and my castle-house will have its foundations on the same peak. I'll marry and spend twelve months a year in this fortress, with no other company but that of my beloved wife, listening to the hum of the wind, the scream of the eagles, the roar of the thunder. . . ."

A very pretty young girl, who was listening to him open-mouthed, interrupted:

"But that can't be, Gaspar . . ."

"What do you mean, Señorita? I have the plans! I've spoken to the architects and engineers! Are you going to tell me it's impossible?"

"What's impossible is your finding a woman who wants to live with you there! . . . Really, Gaspar . . ."

Iturdiaga raised his eyebrows and smiled with haughty melancholy. His long blue trousers ended at shoes that shone like mirrors. I didn't know if I should go over to him, for I felt humble and desperate for company, like a dog. . . . At that moment I was distracted by hearing his name, Iturdiaga, spoken with absolute clarity behind me, and I turned my head. I was leaning against a low window, open to the garden. There, on one of the narrow paved paths, I saw two men walking and undoubtedly talking about business. One of them, enormous and stout, bore a certain resemblance to Gaspar. Their discussion was so animated that they had stopped a few steps from the window.

"But in that case, do you realize how much we can make in the war? Millions, man, millions! . . . This isn't child's play, Iturdiaga . . . !"

They continued on their way.

A smile came to my lips, as if in fact I'd seen them riding across the reddened sky of evening (a magician's hood covering the worthy heads of important men) astride the black specter of war fly over the fields of Europe. . . .

Time passed too slowly for me. For an hour, for two, perhaps, I was alone. I observed the maneuvers of those people who, when I caught sight of them, began to obsess me. I think I was distracted when I saw Pons again. He was red-faced and happy, drinking a toast with two girls, separated from me by the entire width of the room. I also held my solitary glass in my hand and looked at it with a stupid smile. I felt a wretched, useless sadness there by myself. The truth is I didn't know anyone and felt out of touch. It seemed as if a pile of illustrations that I'd arranged in the shape of a castle to pass the time had fallen at a single gust, as if it were a children's game. Illustrations of Pons buying carnations for me, Pons promising me ideal summer vacations, Pons leading me by the hand, out of my house and toward happiness. My friend—who had pleaded so much that he'd succeeded in moving me with his affection—no doubt felt embarrassed by me that afternoon. . . . Perhaps it had all been ruined by his mother's first glance at my shoes. . . . Or perhaps it was my fault. How would I ever understand how these things worked?

"Poor thing, you're very bored. . . . This son of mine is a boor! I'll get him right away!"

Pons's mother had surely been watching me for some time. I looked at her with a certain rancor because she was so different from how I had imagined her. I saw her approach my friend, and after a few moments he was at my side.

"Forgive me, Andrea, please. . . . Would you like to dance?"

The music was playing again.

"No, thanks. I'm not comfortable here and I'd like to leave."

"But why, Andrea? . . . You can't be angry with me? . . . I tried so often to come over to you. . . . I was always stopped on the way. . . . Still, I was happy you didn't dance with anybody else; I looked at you sometimes. . . ."

it. He was bewildered. He seemed about to cry.

cousins walked by and asked an absurd question:

rel?"

forced smile of a movie star. A smile so amused

when I remember it. Then I saw Pons turn red, and it rose up in me like a demon from my heart, making me suffer.

"I can't find the slightest pleasure in being with people *like that*," I said, "like that girl, for example."

Pons looked hurt and aggressive.

"What do you have to say about that girl? I've known her my whole life, she's intelligent and good.... Maybe you think she's too good-looking. You women are all alike."

Then I turned red, and he, immediately repentant, tried to grasp one of my hands.

Is it possible, I thought, *that I'm the protagonist in a ridiculous scene like this?*

"I don't know what's wrong with you today, Andrea. I don't know why you're not the way you always are...."

"It's true. I'm not feeling well.... Look, the fact is I didn't want to come to your party. I only wanted to congratulate you and leave, you know? ... But when your mother greeted me, I was so confused.... You can tell I'm not even properly dressed. Didn't you see that I wore old sports shoes? Didn't you notice?"

Oh! something inside me thought, making a disgusted face. *Why am I saying so many idiotic things?* Pons didn't know what to do. He looked at me in astonishment. His ears were red and he looked very small in his elegant dark suit. He shot an instinctive, anguished glance toward his mother's distant silhouette.

"I didn't notice anything, Andrea," he stammered, "but if you want to leave ... I ... don't know what I can do to stop you."

After the long pause that followed, I began to feel a certain discomfort because of my words.

"I'm sorry for what I said about your guests, Pons."

We walked in silence to the foyer. The ugliness of the large,

ostentatious vases made me feel more confident and certain and relieved some of my tension. Pons, suddenly shaken, kissed my hand
when we said good-bye.

"I don't know what happened, Andrea; first the marquise
arrived—you know, Mamá is a little old-fashioned about that; she's
very respectful of titles. Then my cousin Nuria took me out to the
garden. . . . Well, she told me she loved me . . . no . . ."

He stopped and swallowed.

It made me laugh. Now it all seemed comical to me.

"Is she that very pretty girl who talked to us a moment ago?"

"Yes. I didn't want to tell you. Naturally, I wouldn't want to tell
anybody. . . . Later . . . You see, Andrea, I couldn't be with you. After
all, it was very courageous of her to do what she did. She's a fascinating girl. She has thousands of suitors. She uses a perfume . . ."

"Yes, of course."

"Good-bye . . . So . . . when will we see each other again?"

And he turned red once more, because he still was really very
young. He knew perfectly well, just as I did, that from now on we'd
run into each other only by accident, at the university, perhaps,
after vacation.

The air outside was burning hot. I stood there, not knowing what
to do with a long Calle Muntaner sloping down in front of me.
Overhead the sky, almost blue-black, was becoming heavy, even
threatening, without a single cloud. There was something terrifying in the classical magnificence of that sky flattened over the silent
street. Something that made me feel small and crushed by cosmic
forces like the hero in a Greek tragedy.

So much light, so much burning thirst of asphalt and stone,
seemed to choke me. I walked as if I were traveling over the deserted road of my own life. Looking at the shadows of people who
fled my side, unable to grasp them. Constantly, irremediably chew-
ing on solitude.

Cars began to drive by. A streetcar crowded with passengers
climbed the hill. The broad avenue of the Diagonal passed in front

of my eyes with its walks, its palm trees, its benches. Finally I found myself sitting on one of these benches in a stupid posture. Exhausted and sore, as if I'd made a great effort.

I thought, *It's useless to race if we always have to travel the same incomprehensible road of our personality.* Some creatures were born to live, others to work, others to watch life. I had a small, miserable role as spectator. Impossible to get out of it. Impossible to free myself. A dreadful grief was the only reality for me then.

The world began to tremble behind a pretty gray mist that the sun made iridescent in seconds. My parched face absorbed those tears with pleasure. My fingers wiped them away with rage. I was there for a long time, crying, in the intimacy afforded me by the indifference of the street, and so it seemed to me that slowly my soul was being washed.

In reality, my disillusioned little girl's sorrow didn't merit all the bother. I had quickly read a page of my life that wasn't worth thinking about anymore. As far as I was concerned, greater sorrows had left me indifferent even to ridicule . . .

I ran back along Calle de Aribau, almost from one end to the other. I'd spent so much time sitting in the midst of my thoughts that the sky was growing pale. The street displayed its soul at dusk, its shop windows lit like a string of yellow or white eyes looking out from dark sockets. . . . A thousand odors, sorrows, stories, rose from the paving stones, climbed to the balconies or entrances along Calle de Aribau. An animated wave of people coming down from the elegant solidity of the Diagonal encountered the one coming up from the restless world of the university plaza. A mix of lives, qualities, tastes—that's what Calle de Aribau was. And I: one more element on it, small and lost.

I reached my house, from which no invitation to a marvelous summer vacation would save me, back from my first dance, where I hadn't danced. I walked listlessly, wanting to lie down. Before my eyes, which hurt a little, the street lamp was turned on, as familiar now as the features of a loved one, rising on its black arm in front of the entrance.

At that moment I saw with astonishment Ena's mother coming out of my house. She saw me, too, and came toward me. As always, the charm of her sweetness and simple elegance touched me deeply. Her voice brought to my ears a world of memories.

"What luck running into you, Andrea!" she said. "I've been waiting for you quite a while in your house. . . . Do you have a moment? May I invite you to have an ice cream somewhere?"

PART THREE

XIX

When we were first facing each other in the café, just as we sat down, I was still the introverted, embittered child whose dream had been shattered. Then I became filled with the desire to hear what Ena's mother was about to tell me. I forgot about myself and finally found peace.

"What's wrong, Andrea?"

The formal address—*usted*—on her lips became tender and familiar. It made me want to cry, and I bit my lip. She had looked away. When I could see her eyes, shadowed by the brim of her hat, they had a feverish glaze.... By now I was calm and she was the one who smiled at me a little fearfully.

"Nothing's wrong."

"It's possible, Andrea . . . for days I've been discovering strange shadows in everyone's eyes. Hasn't it ever happened to you? You attribute your state of mind to everyone around you?"

It seemed that by smiling she was trying to make me smile, too. She said everything in a lighthearted tone.

"And why haven't you come to the house recently? Are you angry with Ena?"

"No"—I lowered my eyes—"but I think she's bored with me. It's natural...."

"Why? Ena is very fond of you.... Yes, yes, don't put on that distracted expression. You're the only female friend my daughter has. That's why I came to talk to you...."

I saw that she was toying with her gloves, smoothing them. She had extremely delicate hands. The tips of her fingers withdrew gently at the slightest contact. She swallowed.

"It's very difficult for me to talk about Ena. I never have with anyone; I love her too much for that.... You might say I adore Ena, Andrea."

"I'm very fond of her, too."

"Yes, I know ... but, how could you understand this? Ena, for me, is different from my other children; she's above everyone else in my life. The affection I feel for her is something extraordinary."

I understood. More because of her tone than her words. More because of the ardor in her voice than what she said. She frightened me a little.... I'd always thought the woman was on fire. Always. When I heard her sing on the first day I saw her in her house, and then when she looked at me in such a way that I picked up only a shudder of anguish.

"I know Ena is suffering now. Do you understand what that means for me? Until now her life had been perfect. It seemed that any step she took was a success. Her laughter gave me the sensation of life itself.... She's always been so healthy, so uncomplicated, so happy. When she fell in love with that boy, Jaime ..."

(To my surprise, her smile was sad and mischievous at the same time.)

"When she fell in love with Jaime, it was all like a good dream. Her finding a man who could understand her just as she was leaving adolescence and needed him, was to my eyes like the fulfillment of a marvelous natural law...."

I didn't want to look at her. I was nervous. I thought: *What does this woman want to learn from me?* In any event, I was determined not to betray any of Ena's secrets, regardless of how much her mother seemed to know. I decided to let her speak and not say a word.

"You see, Andrea, I'm not asking you to tell me anything my daughter wanted to keep to herself. You don't need to. Besides, I beg you never to tell Ena everything I know about her. I know her very well and I know how hard she can become sometimes. She'd never forgive me. On the other hand, someday she'll tell me these stories herself. Whenever something happens to Ena, I live for the day when she'll tell me about it. . . . She never disappoints me. The day always comes. So I'm asking for your discretion and also for you to listen to me. . . . I know that Ena often goes to your house and not precisely to visit you. . . . I know she's been going out with a relative of yours named Román. I know that since she has, her relationship with Jaime has cooled or ended altogether. Ena herself seems to have changed completely. . . . Tell me, what's your opinion of your uncle?"

I shrugged. "This has made me think, too. . . . I believe the worst thing is that Román is attractive in his way, though he isn't an admirable person. If you don't know him it's impossible to explain."

"Román?" Her smile made her almost beautiful, it was so profound. "Yes, I know Román. I've known Román for many years. You see, we were at the Conservatory together. He was only seventeen when I met him and he strutted like a peacock in those days, thinking the world would be his. . . . He seemed to have extraordinary talent, though it was limited by his laziness. The professors had great hopes for him. But then he went down. In the end, the worst in him prevailed. . . . When I saw him again a few days ago I had the impression of a man who's finished. But he still has his theatricality, his look of an Eastern wizard about to discover some mystery. He still has his snares and the art of his music. . . . I don't want my daughter to let herself be caught by a man like that. . . . I don't want Ena to cry over or be ruined by . . ."

Her lips were trembling. She realized she was talking to me and the color of her eyes changed with the effort to control herself.

Then she closed them and let her tumultuous words overflow like water that breaks through the dikes and carries away everything.

"My God! Of course I know Román. I've loved him too long, my child, not to know him. His magnetism and attractiveness, what can you tell me about them that I don't already know, that I haven't suffered deep inside, with the intensity of first love that seems impossible to soften and calm? I know his defects so well that even now, pressed and embittered by his life, if it's anything like what I suppose, the mere idea that my daughter can be attracted by them, just as I was, is an unimaginable horror for me. After all these years I didn't expect this trick of fate—it's so cruel. . . . Do you know what it means to be sixteen, seventeen, eighteen years old and obsessed only with a succession of expressions, states of mind, movements, that taken together form the something that at times seems unreal and is a person? . . . No, what anguish! What can you know with those serene eyes of yours? And you don't know anything about wanting to contain what overflows, about an impossible modesty concerning one's feelings. Crying alone was the only thing I was permitted during my adolescence. I did and felt everything else surrounded by watchful eyes. . . . To see a man alone, even from a distance, the way I spied on Román then, even from a corner on Calle de Aribau, in the rain, in the morning, my eyes fixed on the entrance where he would appear with his student's portfolio under his arm, almost always hitting his brother's back in a game of puppies who've just awakened? No, I could never wait there alone. I had to bribe the maid, who chaperoned me, who was curious and irritated by those empty periods of waiting that destroyed all her notions about what love is. . . . I respect to an extraordinary degree Ena's independence when I think of that woman's black mustache and bulging eyes. Her yawns beneath the umbrella on winter mornings. . . . One day I managed to obtain my father's consent for Román and me to give a piano and violin recital of Román's compositions at home. It was an amazing success. The people who came were electrified. . . . No, no, Andrea, no matter how long I live I'll never feel again an emotion like the one I felt for those few minutes. Like the one that destroyed me when Román smiled at me with eyes that were almost wet. A little while later, in the garden, Román became aware of the ecstatic adoration I felt for him and he played with me with the cynical curiosity of a cat playing with the mouse it's just caught. That was when he asked for my braid.

" 'You're not capable of cutting it off for me,' he said, his eyes flashing.

"I'd never even dreamed of a happiness greater than his asking me for something. The magnitude of the sacrifice was so great, however, that I trembled. My hair, when I was sixteen, was my one beauty. I still wore a braid, a single thick braid that fell over my chest down to my waist. It was my pride. Román looked at it day after day with his immutable smile. At times his look made me cry. Finally I couldn't bear any more and after a sleepless night, almost with my eyes closed, I cut it off. The mass of hair was so thick and my hands shook so much that it took me a long time. Instinctively I tightened my neck as if an incompetent executioner were trying clumsily to cut it. The next day, when I looked in the mirror, I burst into tears. Ah, how stupid youth is! . . . At the same time a humble pride consumed me entirely. I knew that no one else could have done the same thing. Nobody loved Román the way I did. I sent him my braid with the somewhat feverish solicitude, which to the cold-hearted seems so vulgar, of a heroine in a romantic novel. I didn't receive even a line from him in response. In my house it was as if a true misfortune had befallen the family. As punishment I was kept indoors for a month. . . . Still, it was all easy to endure. I'd close my eyes and see in Román's hands the golden rope that was a piece of myself. In this way I felt repaid in the best coin. . . . Finally I saw Román again. He looked at me with curiosity. He said:

" 'I have the best of you at home. I've stolen your beauty.' And then he concluded impatiently: 'Woman, why did you do something so stupid? Why do you act like my dog?'

"Now, seeing things from a distance, I ask myself how we can reach that capacity for humiliation, how we can become so sick, as if there is room in our human faculties for a great deal of pleasure in pain.... Because I was sick. I had a fever. I couldn't get out of bed for some time; that was the poison, the obsession that filled me.... And you ask if I know Román? I studied all his corners, all his folds for infinite, solitary days.... My father became alarmed. He made inquiries, the maid spoke of my 'manias.'... And this pain of being discovered, being exposed down to the most intimate corners? A pain as if our skin were being stripped away to observe the network of veins throbbing between our muscles.... They kept me in the country for a year. My father gave Román money so he'd leave Barcelona for a while and not be there when I returned, and he was brazen enough to take it and sign a receipt that recorded the fact.

"I remember my return to Barcelona very well. The languid fatigue of the train—you can't imagine the quantity of shawls, hats, gloves, and veils we needed in those days for a four-hour trip. I remember my father's large automobile waiting for us at the station; we bounced on its seats in our fur coats and the noise of its motor deafened us. I'd spent an entire year without hearing Román's name and then each tree, each drop of light—that baroque, unmistakable light of Barcelona—carried his scent to me until my nostrils dilated in anticipation....

"My father embraced me, very moved—because, like Ena, I'm the only daughter among several sons. As soon as I had the chance, I told him I wanted to continue my piano and voice lessons. I believe it was the first thing I said to him.

" 'Fine. Aren't you ashamed, even a little, to run after that boy this way?'

"My father's eyes blazed with anger. Don't you know my father? He has the most sullen and also the sweetest eyes I've ever seen.

" 'So there's no other man for you? So it has to be you, my daughter, who pursues a fortune hunter?'

"My father's words wounded all my lover's pride in the object of

my affections. I defended Román. I spoke of hi[s]
splendid generosity. My father listened to me cal[m,]
put that receipt in my hands.

" 'You can look at it when you're alone. I don'[t]
when you do.'

"We never spoke of Román again. Our soul's reactions are curious. I'm sure that, secretly, I could have gotten past that new insult.
With the eyes of my family watching me, it seemed impossible to
continue showing my love for that man. It was like a moral shrug of
my shoulders. I married the first suitor my father liked, I married
Luis. . . .

"Today, as you know, Andrea, I've forgotten the whole story, and
I'm content."

It embarrassed me to listen to her. I, who heard every day the
most vulgar words in our language, and listened unperturbed to
Gloria's conversations filled with the most barbaric materialism—I
blushed at that confession of Ena's mother and began to feel uncomfortable. In those days I was bitter and intransigent, like youth
itself. Everything in the story that spoke of failure and repression
repelled me. The fact that she would recount her miseries to another person almost made me feel ill.

When I looked at her, I saw that her eyes were filled with tears.

"But how am I going to explain these things to Ena, Andrea?
How am I going to tell someone I love so much what I might have
said in a confessional, devoured by anguish, what I've told you? . . .
Ena knows me only as a symbol of serenity, of clarity. . . . I know she
couldn't bear for this image that she's deified to have its feet made
of the clay of passions and madness. She would love me less. . . . And
every atom of her love is vital to me. She's the one who has made
me the person I am now. Do you think she could destroy her own
creation? . . . The work between us has been so delicate, so silent
and profound!"

Her eyes darkened, her long cat's pupils contracted. Her fa[ce] a vegetal, extremely delicate quality: In an instant it would age, becoming covered with subtle wrinkles, or it would open like a flower. . . . I didn't understand how I could have thought she was ugly.

"Look, Andrea. When Ena was born, I didn't love her. She was my first child but I hadn't wanted her. The early days of my marriage were difficult. It's curious the extent to which two people who live together and don't understand each other can be strangers. Fortunately for him, Luis was so busy all day he didn't have much time to think about our discordant intimacy. In spite of everything, he was thrown off-balance by a wife who barely spoke. I remember him glancing at his watch, at my shoes, at the rug, on those interminable evenings we spent together, when he smoked and I tried to read. Between us there was an almost infinite distance and I was convinced that as the years passed the separation would become deeper and deeper. Sometimes I'd see him get up nervously and go to the window. Finally he stopped suggesting any form of diversion to me. . . . He liked me to be perfectly dressed and our house to be comfortable and luxurious. . . . Once I had achieved all that, the poor man didn't know what it was that was missing from our life.

"If he sometimes took my hand, with an awkward smile, he seemed astonished at the passivity of my fingers, which were too small in his. He'd look up, and his entire face seemed possessed by a childish distress when he glanced at me. At those times I felt like laughing. It was like revenge for all the failure in my earlier life. For once I felt strong and powerful. For once I understood the pleasure that made Román's soul vibrate when he mortified me. Luis would ask:

" 'Do you feel nostalgic for Spain?'

ould shrug and say no. The hours slipped past, quickly cut-
h of a life that was completely gray. . . . No, Andrea, I
child of my husband's then. And yet it came. Each
elt seemed like another of life's brutalities
any others I'd had to endure. When they told

me it was a girl, a strange grief combined with my unwillingness. I didn't want to see her. I lay in the bed and looked away.... I remember it was autumn, and through the window I could see a sad, gray morning. Branches of a large tree, the color of dry gold, were pushing, almost creaking, against the glass. The infant, next to my ear, began to cry. I felt remorse for having let her be born to me, for having condemned her to carrying my inheritance. I began to weep with a faint sorrow that because of me, this wailing thing could become a woman someday. And moved by a compassionate impulse— almost as embarrassing as the one we feel when we put a coin in the hand of some unfortunate creature we see on the street—I held that piece of my flesh against my body and let it nurse, sucking and devouring and conquering me, for the first time, physically ...

"From that moment Ena was more powerful than me; she enslaved me, she subjugated me. She made me marvel at her vitality, her strength, her beauty. As she grew, I looked at her with the same astonishment I'd feel if I saw all my unfulfilled longings growing in one body. I had dreamed of health, of energy, of the personal success that had been denied me, and I watched them develop in Ena from the time she was very little. You know, Andrea, that my daughter is like a radiant light of strength and life.... I understood, humbly, the meaning of my existence when I saw all my pride, my strength, my best desires for perfection, being realized so magically in her. I could look at Luis with new eyes and appreciate all his qualities because I'd first seen them reflected in my daughter. It was she, the little girl, who revealed to me the fine warp of life, the thousand sweetnesses of renunciation and love, which is not only passion and blind egoism between the body and soul of a man and the body and soul of a woman, but is invested with what we call understanding, friendship, tenderness. It was Ena who made me love her father, who made me want more children, and—since she required a mother adequate to her perfect, healthy human qualities—who made me consciously shed my sickly complaints, my narrow egotism. . . . Open myself to others and discover unimagined horizons. Because before I created her, almost by force, with my own blood and bones, my own bitter substance, I was an unbalanced, mean-spirited woman. Dissatisfied and egotistical ... A woman who'd rather die than have Ena suspect that in me. ...."

We were silent.

There was nothing more to say at this point, since it was easy to understand this language of blood, pain, and creation that begins with physical substance itself when one is a woman. It was easy to understand this, knowing that my own body was prepared— carrying the seeds—for this labor of life's continuation. Though everything in me then was acid, and incomplete, like hope, I understood it.

When Ena's mother finished speaking, my thoughts harmonized entirely with hers.

I became frightened and found that people had started to shout again around me (like the wave that, immobile and black for a moment, crashes against the cliff and explodes into clamor and foam). My eyes saw all the lights in the café and on the street at the same time when she spoke again.

"That's why I want you to help me. ... Only you or Román could help me, and he refused. I'd like Ena to be embarrassed about Román without knowing the wretched part of my past that you know now. My daughter is not the sickly creature I was. She'd never let herself be carried away by the same fevers that consumed me. ... I don't even know how to ask you to do something concrete. When they're upstairs, in Román's room, making music, I'd like somebody to dissipate the shadows, the false charm, simply by turning on the light. I'd like someone who isn't me to talk to Ena about Román, and lie, if necessary. ... Tell her that he's hit you, emphasize his sadism, his cruelty, his turbulence. ... I know that what I'm requesting is too much. ... Now I'm the one asking you: Do you know this side of your uncle?"

"Yes."

"Well, then, will you try to help me? Above all, don't leave Ena, as you have until now. . . . If she believes anyone, it'll be you. She values you more than she's let you know. I'm sure about that."

"As far as I'm concerned, you can be sure I'll try to help you. But I don't believe these things do any good."

(My soul rustled inside like crumpled paper. The way it had rustled when Ena pressed Román's hand one day in front of me.)

Her head hurt. I could almost touch the pain.

"If only I could take her away from Barcelona! . . . You must think it's ridiculous that I can't impose my authority in a matter like summer vacation. But my husband can't possibly leave his business now and Ena defends herself, shields herself behind her desire not to leave him alone. . . . What she accomplishes is that Luis gets angry at my insistence and half joking and half in earnest accuses me of monopolizing the daughter we both prefer. He tells me to go away with the boys and leave Ena with him. He's enthusiastic because usually she's not very generous with demonstrations of affection, but recently she's been showing him extraordinary tenderness. I spend entire nights not sleeping. . . ."

(And I imagined her open-eyed next to her husband's tranquil sleep. Bones aching because of stiff postures so as not to wake him . . . Alert to the creaking of the bed, the ache of sleepless eyelids, her own internal anguish.)

"On the other hand, Andrea, I've tried telling ridiculous or offensive anecdotes about Román. My memory is full of those anecdotes. . . . But I don't venture down that path very often. If Ena looks at me, I feel that I'll blush as if I were guilty. As if my daughter's eyes were going to transfix me. . . . My father has promised me that starting in September Luis will take charge of the Madrid office. . . . But so many things can happen between now and then. . . ."

She stood up to leave. She had not found relief in speaking to me. Before she put on her gloves, she passed her hand over her forehead in a mechanical gesture. A hand so fine I wanted to turn her palm toward my eyes and marvel at its tenderness, as I sometimes like to do with the underside of leaves.

In a moment I saw that she was moving away, that as I sank into the heavy stupor our talk had produced in me, the small, slim figure was disappearing into the crowd.

Later, in my room, the night filled with disquiet. I thought about the words of Ena's mother:

"I've asked for Román's help and he refused to give it to me." At last, the señora had seen that man alone—and I don't know why Román made me feel sad; he seemed to me like an unfortunate man—the one she'd pursued with her thoughts years ago. She'd seen the small room, the small theater in which, over time, Román had finally enclosed himself. And her bitter eyes had guessed what could bewitch her daughter there.

When it was almost dawn, a cortege of dark clouds, like extremely long fingers, began to float across the sky. At last, they put out the moon.

XX

Morning came and it seemed as if I could hear it arrive—my eyes still closed—like Aurora in a large chariot whose wheels were crushing my skull. The noise deafened me—the crack of bones, the shudder of wood and metal on the pavement. The clang of the streetcar. A confused murmur of leaves on the trees merged with lights. A distant shout:

"*Drapaireee...!*"

The doors of a balcony opened and closed nearby. The door of my room opened wide, pushed by a current of air, and I had to open my eyes. I found the room filled with a soft light. It was very late. Gloria was going to the balcony of the dining room to call to the ragman shouting in the street and Juan stopped her, grabbing her arm and slamming the glass door with a tremendous bang.

"Leave me alone, *chico!*"

"I told you not to sell anything else. Do you hear me? What's in this house doesn't belong only to me."

"And I'm telling you we have to eat...."

"I earn enough for that!"

n't. You know very well why we aren't starv-

me, you bitch!"

ico!"

the shoulders, exasperated.

I saw Gloria fall and hit her head against the balcony door. The glass rattled and cracked. I heard her screaming on the floor.

"I'll kill you, damn you!"

"I'm not scared of you, you coward!" Gloria's piercing voice trembled.

Juan picked up a pitcher of water and threw it at her when she tried to stand. This time there was broken glass, though he had poor aim. The pitcher shattered against the wall. One of the pieces ricocheted and cut the hand of the baby; he was sitting in his high chair and watching everything with round, serious eyes.

"The baby! Imbecile! What a rotten mother—look what you've done to your son!"

"Me?"

Juan rushed at the child, who was terrified and at last began to cry. And he tried to quiet him with loving words, picking him up. Then he carried him away to treat the cut.

Gloria was crying. She came into my room.

"Did you see what an animal he is, Andrea? An animal!"

I was sitting on the bed. She sat down, too, rubbing the back of her neck, painful because of her fall.

"You realize I can't live here? I can't. . . . He'll kill me, and I don't want to die. Life's very sweet, *chica*. You're a witness. . . . Weren't you a witness, Andrea, when even he realized I was the only one doing anything to keep us from starving to death that night he found me playing cards? . . . Didn't he say so in front of you, didn't he cry and kiss me? Tell me, didn't he kiss me?"

She wiped her eyes and her small nose shortened in a smile.

"In spite of everything, there was something comical in all of

that, *chica*.... A little comical. You know ... I told Juan I was selling
his paintings to houses that handled art objects. Actually I was selling them to ragmen, and with the five or six duros they gave me, I
could play cards at night in my sister's house.... Friends of hers,
men and women, get together there at night. My sister likes that
very much because they spend on liquor and she makes money on
that. Sometimes they stay till dawn. They're good players and they
like to make bets. I almost always win.... Almost always, *chica*.... If
I lose, my sister lends me money when I'm short and then I return
it with a little interest when I win again.... It's the only honorable
way to have a little money. I tell you that sometimes I've brought
home forty or fifty duros at a time. It's very exciting to gamble,
chica.... That night I'd won, I had thirty duros in front of me.... And
what a coincidence, imagine, it was just as well that Juan showed up,
because I was playing against a very ignorant man and I cheated a
little.... Sometimes you have to do that. Well, anyway, he has a
crossed eye. A strange man, you'd enjoy meeting him, Andrea. The
worst thing is that you never know where he's looking and what he's
seen or hasn't seen.... He's a smuggler and had something to do
with Román. You know Román does crooked business?"

"And Juan?"

"Ah, yes, yes! It was an exciting moment, *chica*—we were all quiet
and Tonet said:

" 'Well, I don't think anybody's going to fool me....'

"I was just a little scared inside.... And that was when we begin
to hear a banging at the street door. A friend of my sister's,
Carmeta—a very good-looking girl, you can take my word ... she
said:

" 'Tonet, I think it's for you.'

"And Tonet, who was already listening, very suspicious, got up
like a shot because he was on the run at the time. My sister's husband said ... well, my sister's husband isn't her husband, you know,
but he's just like one; well, he said:

" 'Get to the roof and then go to Martillet's house. I'll count to twenty before I open up. I think there's only one or two people down there....'

"Tonet started running up the stairs. It sounded like they were going to knock the door down. My sister, who's more diplomatic, went to open the door. Then we heard Juan ranting and my brother-in-law frowned because he doesn't like sentimental stories. He ran to see what was going on. Juan argued with him. Even though my brother-in-law's a fat man, and two meters tall, you know that crazy people are very strong, *chica,* and Juan was like a crazy man. He couldn't hold Juan back; but when he pushed past him and was pulling back the curtain, my brother-in-law punched him in the back and knocked him down, headfirst, into our room. It made me sad, poor thing. (Because I love Juan, Andrea. I was head over heels when I married him, you know?) I lifted his head, kneeling beside him, and began to tell him I was there to earn money for the baby. He shoved me away and got up, not very steady on his feet. Then my sister put her hands on her hips and delivered a speech. She told him that she herself had made propositions to me about men who would have paid a lot and that I refused because I loved him, though I was always going through hell because of him. Always silent, and suffering because of him. Juan, poor thing, was quiet, his arms hanging, looking at everything. He saw that the bets were on the table, that Carmeta and Teresa were there with two nice guys who are their boyfriends. He saw that things were serious there, it wasn't a party.... My sister told him I'd won thirty duros while he was planning to kill me. Then my brother-in-law began to belch in the corner, where he was standing with his hands on his waist, and it looked like Juan would go over to him and start fighting again in a frenzy ... but my sister is a wonderful woman, *chica.* You've met her, and she said:

"'Now, Joanet, have a little drink with me and in no time your wife will settle up her winnings with these friends and go home to take care of your *nen.'*

"Then my head began working overtime. Then, when my sister

took Juan into the shop, I began to think that if Juan came it was because you or your grandmother had phoned him, and at that time of night the most likely thing was that the baby was dead. . . . Because I think a lot, *chica*. You wouldn't think so, would you? Well, I think a lot.

"I felt so sad and sorry I couldn't count my money that was on the table where we were playing. . . . Because I love the *nen* a lot; he's really cute, isn't he? Poor thing!

"Carmeta's so good, she settled up for me. And there was no more talk about my having cheated. . . . Then I saw you with Juan and my sister. Imagine the daze I was in, I almost wasn't surprised. I could think only one thing: *The* nen's *dead, the* nen's *dead.* . . . And then you could see that Juan really loved me when I said that to him. . . . Because men really fall in love with me, *chica*. They can't forget me so easily—don't kid yourself. . . . Juan and I had loved each other so much. . . ."

We were silent. I began to dress. Gloria was calming down, and she stretched her arms lazily. Suddenly she stared at me.

"What strange feet you have! So skinny! They look like Christ's feet!"

"Yes, that's true"—in the end, Gloria always made me smile—"while yours are like the feet of the muses. . . ."

"Very pretty, aren't they?"

"Yes."

(They were small, white feet, shapely and childlike.)

We heard the street door. Juan was going out. My grandmother appeared, wearing a smile.

"He took the baby out for a walk. . . . This son of mine is so good! . . . Naughty girl"—she was talking to Gloria— "why do you answer back and get him involved in arguments? A know that with men you always have to give in?"

Gloria smiled and caressed my grandmother. Sh mascara. Another ragman went by and she called window. My grandmother shook her head in agit

"Quick, quick, girl, before Juan or Román comes back.... Imagine if Román comes back! I don't want to think about it!"

"These things are yours, Mamá, not your son's. Isn't that right, Andrea? Am I going to let the baby go hungry just to save this junk? Besides, Román owes Juan money. I know ..."

My grandmother left, avoiding—as she said—complications. She looked very thin. Beneath the tangle of white hair her transparent ears protruded.

While I showered and then, in the kitchen, while I ironed my dress—under the bitter eyes of Antonia, who never tolerated intrusions into her kingdom very well—I heard Gloria's shrill voice and the hoarse one of the *drapaire* arguing in Catalan. I thought of something that Gloria had told me a long time ago, referring to the story of her and Juan: "It was like the end of a movie. It was like the end of all sadness. We were going to be happy...." That happened a very long time ago, when, overcoming all the madness of the war, Juan came back to the woman who'd given him a child, to make her his wife. They hardly remembered that.... But not long ago, on that desperate night, which Gloria's talk had recalled for me, I'd seen them again fused into one until they could feel the pounding of each other's blood, loving each other, leaning on each other in the same sorrow. And it was like the end of all hatred, all incomprehension.

If on that night—I thought—*the world had ended or one of them had died, their story would have been completely closed and beautiful, like a circle.* That's how it happens in novels, in movies, but not in life.... I was realizing, for the first time, that everything goes on, turns gray, is ruined in the living. That there is no end to our story until death comes and the body decays. ...

"What are you looking at, Andrea? ... What are you looking at in the mirror with those wide-open eyes?"

Gloria, in a good mood now, appeared at my back as I finished dressing. Behind her I saw my grandmother, her face radiant. The old lady feared those sales that Gloria made. She firmly believed that the ragmen were doing us a huge favor by accepting old furniture, and her heart pounded in alarm as Gloria argued with the buyer. Trembling, she would pray before her dusty altar that the Mother of God would soon free her daughter-in-law of this humiliation. When the terrible man left, she breathed more easily, like a child leaving the doctor's office.

I looked at her with affection. Where she was concerned, I always felt a vague remorse. Some nights, when I came back to the house during times of great penury, when I couldn't afford to eat lunch or supper, I'd find on my night table a plate with some unappetizing vegetables, boiled for many hours, or a crust of bread left there by "accident." Driven by a need stronger than I was, I'd eat those mouthfuls that the poor creature had deprived herself of, and I'd be disgusted with myself when I did. The next day I'd hover clumsily near my grandmother. I detected so sweet a smile in her light eyes when she looked at me that I was moved as if the roots of my spirit were clutching at me, and I wanted to cry. If, impelled by my feelings, I'd put my arms around her, I'd encounter a little body, hard and cold as if made of wire, inside of which beat a surprisingly strong heart.

Gloria leaned toward me, touching my back through my blouse with a certain satisfaction.

"You're thin, too, Andrea. . . ."

Then quickly, so that my grandmother wouldn't hear her:

"Your friend Ena is coming to Román's room this afternoon."

(A turbulence rose inside me.)

"How do you know?"

"Because he just asked the maid to go up and clean it and buy liquor. . . . I'm not a fool, *chica*"—and then, narrowing her eyes—"your friend is Román's mistress."

I turned so red that she became frightened and moved away from me. My grandmother observed us with uneasy eyes.

"You're like an animal," I said, furious. "You and Juan are like beasts. Can't there be anything else between a man and a woman? Can't you conceive of anything else in love? Oh! You're filthy!"

The violence of my feelings pressed inside my head, making me shed tears. At that moment I was terrified for Ena. I loved her and couldn't bear those corrosive words about her life.

Gloria twisted her mouth into a rictus that was an ironic smile, but it calmed me because I realized that she was about to cry, too. My grandmother, frightened and aggrieved, said:

"Andrea! My grandchild talking like that!"

I said to Gloria:

"Why do you think something so vile about a girl who's my friend?"

"Because I know Román very well.... Want me to tell you something? Román tried to be my lover after I married Juan.... You see, what can you expect from a man like that?"

"All right. But I know Ena.... She belongs to a class of human beings that you can't imagine, Gloria.... She might be interested in Román as a friend, but ..."

(I found relief in saying these things aloud and at the same time began to find the conversation with Gloria about my friend repugnant. I stopped speaking.)

I turned to leave the apartment. My grandmother touched my dress as I passed her.

"Child! Child! So this is my little granddaughter who never gets angry! Jesus, Jesus!"

I don't know what bitter, salty taste I had in my mouth. I slammed the door as if I were just like them. Just like all of them ...

I was so nervous I kept feeling tears in my eyes, even on the street. The sky looked heavy with hot, oppressive clouds. Other people's words, old words, began to pursue me and dance in my ears. Ena's voice: "You eat too little, Andrea, and you're a hysteric...." "You're a hysteric, you're a hysteric...." "Why are you crying if you're not a hysteric? ..." "What reasons do you have to cry? ..." I saw that people were looking at me with a certain surprise and I bit my lips with rage when I realized it.... *I'm making nervous faces like Juan.... Now I'm going crazy, too.... People have been driven crazy by hunger....*

I went down the Ramblas to the port. The thought of Ena had a softening effect, she inspired so much affection in me. Her own mother had assured me of her esteem. She, so loved, so radiant, admired and valued me. I felt exalted at the thought that a providential mission had been asked of me. But I didn't know if my intervention in her life would really do any good. Gloria's telling me of her visit this afternoon filled me with uneasiness.

I was at the port. The enclosed ocean presented its brilliant oil stains to my eyes; the smell of pitch, of ropes, penetrated me deeply. The ships were enormous, their sides extremely high. At times the water seemed to tremble as if struck by a fish's tail, a small boat, an oar. I was there on that summer afternoon. From some deck, perhaps, Nordic blue eyes would see me as a tiny brushstroke on a foreign print.... I, a Spanish girl with dark hair, standing for a moment on a dock in the port of Barcelona. In a few seconds, life would move on, displacing me to some other point. I'd find myself with my body framed by another print.... *Perhaps,* I thought at last, overcome as always by my martyrized instincts, *eating somewhere.* I had very little money, but I did have some. Slowly, I went toward the carefree bars and restaurants of Barceloneta. On sunny days, blue or white, they sound their joyful marine note. Some have terraces where people with good appetites eat rice and shellfish, stimulated by the warm, red odors of summer rising from the beaches or the inner harbors of the port.

That day a gray, burning wind blew from the sea. I heard someone say it was storm weather. I ordered beer and some cheese and almonds. ... The bar where I was sitting was in a two-story house, stained indigo and adorned with nautical implements. I was at one of the little tables on the street and it almost seemed that the ground beneath me would begin to vibrate, driven by some hidden motor, and take me far away ... and open horizons for me once again. This longing, always repeated in my life, that would blossom under any pretext.

I sat there for a long time. . . . My head hurt. At last, very slowly, the sacks of wool of the clouds weighing on my shoulders, I returned to my house. I made some detours. I stopped. . . . But, as the hours unwound, it seemed that an invisible thread was pulling at me from Calle de Aribau, from the front door, from Román's room at the top of the house. . . . Half the afternoon had gone by when that force became irresistible and I walked through our building door.

As I climbed the stairs, the familiar, anodyne silence with which it was impregnated seized me in its claws. Through a broken window I could hear—on one of the landings—a maid singing in the courtyard.

Román and Ena were up there and I had to go there, too. I didn't understand why I was so sure about my friend's presence. Gloria's suppositions were not enough to make me so certain. Like a dog searching for someone, I sensed her presence in my nostrils. I, who was used to allowing the course of events pull me along, was moved by this behavior that apparently was going to force matters.

As I climbed each step I had the impression that my shoes were growing heavier. All the blood in my body went down to my legs, and my face paled. When I reached Román's door, my hands were icy and perspiring at the same time. I stopped there. To my right, the open door to the roof gave me the idea of walking through it. I couldn't stand indefinitely in front of Román's room and I couldn't decide to knock, either, though I heard something like a murmur of conversation. I needed a small interlude to calm down. I went out to the flat roof. Beneath an increasingly menacing sky there appeared—like a flock of enormous white birds—the panorama of roofs almost falling down on me. I heard Ena's laugh. A laugh in which the forced notes made me shiver. The little window of Román's room was open. On an impulse, I got down on all fours, like a cat, and crawled, in order not to be seen, to the opening and sat down under it. Ena's voice was loud and clear:

"For you, Román, it all turned out to be too simple a deal. What did you think? That I'd marry you? That I'd go around in a panic my whole life, like my mother, fearing your demands for money?"

"Now you'll listen to me . . ." Román spoke in a tone I'd never heard him use before.

"No. There's nothing else to say. I have all the proofs. You know you're in my hands. Finally this nightmare will end. . . ."

"But you're going to listen to me, aren't you? Even if you don't want to. . . . I've never asked your mother for money. I don't believe you have any proof of blackmail. . . ."

Román's voice slithered like a serpent as it reached me.

Rapidly, without thinking about it, I slid along the wall, left the roof, and hurled myself at my uncle's door, banging on it. They didn't answer and I knocked again. Then Román opened the door.

At first I didn't realize he was so pale. My eyes drank in the image of Ena, who seemed very much at ease, sitting and smoking. She gave me a sullen look. The fingers holding the cigarette trembled a little.

"Opportunity's your name, Andrea," she said coldly.

"Ena, darling . . . I thought you were here. I came up to say hello. . . ."

(That's what I wanted to say, or something like that. Still, I don't know if I managed to finish the sentence.)

Román seemed to react. His intense eyes took in Ena and me.

"Go on, little one, be a good girl . . . go away."

He was very agitated.

Unexpectedly, Ena got to her feet with her elastic and very rapid movements, and I found that she was beside me, grabbing my arm before Román and I had time to think about it. In confusion, I felt her heart pounding as she came close to my body. I couldn't say if it was her heart or mine that was frightened.

Román began to smile, with the beautiful, strained smile I knew so well.

"Do what you like, little ones." He was looking at Ena, not at me, only at Ena. "But I'm surprised by this sudden departure when we were in the middle of our conversation, Ena. You know it can't end this way. . . . You know that."

I don't know why Román's amiable, tense tone frightened me so much. His eyes glittered as he looked at my friend, just as Juan's eyes glittered when his brain was about to explode.

Ena pushed me toward the door. She made a slight, mocking bow.

"We'll talk another day, Román. Until then don't forget what I've told you. Good-bye!"

She was smiling, too. Her eyes were brilliant as well, and she was extremely pale.

It was at that moment I realized that Román had kept his right hand in his pocket the whole time. That he was holding something. I don't know what swerve of my imagination made me think about his black pistol when my uncle intensified his smile. It was a matter of seconds. I threw my arms around him like a madwoman and yelled at Ena to run.

I felt Román's shove and saw his face, finally free of that anguished tension. Swept clean by a tremendous anger.

"Idiot! Did you really think I was going to shoot you both?"

He looked at me, his serenity recovered. I'd been hit in the back when I collided with the staircase railing. Román passed his hand across his forehead to push away his curly hair. To my eyes, in rapid descent—it had happened on other occasions—his features aged prematurely. Then he turned his back on us and went back into his room.

My body hurt. A gust of dusty air banged the door to the roof. In the distance I heard the hoarse warning of thunder.

I found Ena waiting for me on a landing. Hers was the mocking glance of her worst moments.

"Andrea, why are you so tragic, darling?"

Her eyes wounded me. She raised her head and her lips curved in unbearable scorn.

I felt like hitting her. Then my fury struck me as a despair that made me turn my head and race down the stairs, almost killing myself, blinded by tears. . . . The familiar physiognomies of the doors, their mats, their shining or opaque knockers, the nameplates announcing the occupation of each tenant . . . PRACTITIONER, TAILOR . . . danced, threw themselves at me, disappeared, devoured by my tears.

And so I reached the street, scourged by the uncontainable explosion of suffering that made me run, removing myself from everything. And so, bumping into passersby, I raced down Calle de Aribau toward the plaza of the university.

XXI

That stormy sky entered my lungs and blinded me with sorrow. The odors of Calle de Aribau filed quickly through the grief-stricken mist that enveloped me. Odor of perfume shop, pharmacy, food store. Odor of street that a dust cloud bears down on, in the belly of a suffocatingly dark sky.

The plaza of the university appeared as still and enormous as in a nightmare. As if the few pedestrians crossing it, and the automobiles and streetcars, had been attacked by paralysis. Someone remains in my memory with one foot raised: That's how strange my vision of everything was and how quickly I forgot what I'd seen.

I found I was no longer crying, but my throat ached and my temples were throbbing. I leaned against the university garden railing, as I had on that day Ena remembered. A day on which, apparently, I didn't realize that rain was pouring down on me. . . .

An old sheet of paper blew against my knees. I looked at the thick air, crushed against the earth, which was beginning to make the dust and leaves fly around in a macabre dance of dead things. I felt the pain of solitude, more unbearable, because repeated, than the one that had assailed me when I left Pons's house the other day.

Now it was like a punishment that my weeping had ended. It scraped inside me, wounding my eyelids and my throat.

I didn't think or expect anything when I sensed a human presence next to me. It was Ena, agitated, as if she had been running. I turned slowly—it seemed as if the springs in my body weren't working, as if I were sick and any movement was difficult for me. I saw that her eyes were filled with tears. It was the first time I'd seen her cry.

"Andrea!... Oh! Andrea, what an idiot...!"

She made a face as if she were going to laugh and began to cry even harder; it was as if she were doing my crying for me, her tears eased my anguish so much. Incapable of saying anything, she held out her arms, and we embraced there, on the street. Her heart— hers, not mine—was racing, pounding next to me. We stood there for a second. Then I abruptly pulled away from her tenderness. I saw that her eyes were drying rapidly and now her smile blossomed easily, as if she had never cried.

"You know I love you very much, Andrea?" she said. "I didn't know I loved you so much.... I didn't want to see you again or anything else that could remind me of that damn house on Calle de Aribau.... But, when you looked at me like that, when you left..."

"I looked at you 'like that'? Like how?"

What we said didn't matter to me. What mattered was the comforting feeling of companionship, of consolation, like an oil bath on my soul.

"Well... I don't know how to explain it. You looked at me with desperation. And besides, since I know you love me so much, and so faithfully. Just like I love you, don't think..."

She made incoherent statements that seemed full of sense to me. Up from the asphalt came an odor of wet dust. Large, hot drops were falling, and we didn't move. Ena put her arm around my shoulder and pressed her soft cheek against mine. All our reticence seemed to erupt. Our bad moments were stilled.

"Ena, forgive me for this afternoon. I know you can't stand people spying on you. I never did it before today, I swear. . . . If I interrupted your conversation with Román it was because I thought he was threatening you. . . . I know it may be ridiculous. But that's what I thought."

Ena moved away to look at me. Laughter floated on her lips.

"But that's what I needed, Andrea! You came from heaven! You really didn't know you were saving me? . . . If I've been mean to you it was because of too much strain on my nerves. I was afraid to cry. And now you see, now I have. . . ."

Ena took a deep breath, as if this had relieved her of a thousand fiery emotions. She crossed her hands behind her, almost stretching, ridding herself of all her tension. She didn't look at me. It seemed as if she weren't actually speaking to me.

"The truth is, Andrea, that deep down I've always valued your fondness for me as something extraordinary, but I never wanted to admit it. True friendship seemed like a myth until I met you, just as love seemed like a myth until I met Jaime. . . . Sometimes"—Ena smiled with a certain timidity—"I think about what I've done to deserve these two gifts from fate. . . . I assure you I was a terrible, cynical girl. I never believed in any golden dream, and in contrast to what happens to other people, I've been showered with the most beautiful realities. I've always been so happy. . . ."

"Ena, didn't you fall in love with Román?"

I asked the question in so faint a murmur that the rain, falling steadily now, drowned out my voice. I repeated the question:

"Tell me, didn't you fall in love?"

Ena brushed me quickly with an indefinable glance from eyes that were too brilliant. Then she looked up at the clouds.

"We're getting wet, Andrea!" she shouted.

She pulled me toward the doorway of the university, where we took shelter. Her face looked fresh under the drops of rain, and a little pale, as if she had suffered fevers. The storm unleashed cataracts of rain; it came down in sheets, accompanied by violent

claps of thunder. We didn't speak for a while, li:
that calmed me and made me green again, like th

"How beautiful!" said Ena, and her nostrils fla
know if I fell in love with Román . . ." she continu
dreamy expression. "I was very interested in him!

She laughed quietly.

"I've never made anyone so desperate, so humiliated. . . ." I
looked at her in some surprise. She saw only the curtain of rain that
fell before her eyes, illuminated by flashes of lightning. The earth
seemed to boil, heave, rid itself of all its poisons.

"Ah! What a pleasure! To know that someone is pursuing you,
that he thinks he's caught you, and then you escape, and he's out-
witted. . . . What a strange game! . . . Román has a swinish spirit, Andrea. He's attractive, and a great artist, but deep down he's so
mean-spirited and coarse! . . . What kind of woman has he been
used to? I suppose creatures like the two shadows I saw haunting
the stairs when I went up to see him. . . . That horrible maid your
family has, and the other woman who's so peculiar, the one with red
hair—I know now her name is Gloria. . . . And maybe someone very
sweet and timid, like my mother. . . ."

She looked at me out of the corner of her eye.

"You know my mother was in love with him when she was
young? . . . That was the reason I wanted to meet Román. Then,
what a disappointment! I began to hate him. . . . Doesn't that happen
to you, when you make up a legend about a specific person, and you
see what lies under your fantasies and that he's really worth even
less than you, and you begin to hate him? Sometimes my hatred for
Román grew so enormous he noticed it and turned his head, as if it
were charged with electricity. . . . What strange days when we were
first getting to know each other! I don't know if I was unhappy or
not. I was obsessed with Román. I avoided you. I quarreled with
Jaime over some stupid thing and then I couldn't bear to be with
him. I think I felt that if I saw Jaime again I'd have to abandon the

.ure. And then I felt too involved, almost intoxicated by all of
... If I'm with Jaime I become good again, Andrea, I'm a different woman. . . . If you could only see, sometimes I'm afraid to feel
the dualism of the forces that drive me. When I've been too sublime
for a while, I feel like scratching somebody. . . . Like doing a little
harm."

She seized my hand, and at my instinctive attempt to withdraw
it, she smiled with indulgent tenderness.

"Do I frighten you? Then why do you want to be my friend? I'm
not an angel, Andrea, though I love you so much. . . . There are people who fill my heart, like Jaime, my mother, and you, each in a different way. . . . But a part of me needs to expand and give free rein
to its poisons. Do you think I don't love Jaime? I love him very
much. I couldn't bear it if my life were separate from his. I desire
his presence, his entire personality. I admire him passionately. . . .
But there's something else: curiosity, a malignant disquiet in my
heart, that can never rest. . . ."

"Did Román make love to you? Tell me."

"Make love to me? I don't know. He was desperate with me, so
angry he could have strangled me at times. . . . But he holds himself
in check very well. I wanted to make him lose control of his nerves.
I succeeded only once. . . . It was more than a week ago, Andrea, the
last time I came to see him before today. I came five times to see
Román and I always tried to let somebody know. Because deep
down, Román has always inspired a little fear in me. I knocked at
the door of your house, when I knew you wouldn't be there, and I
asked for you. Those two peculiar women, who felt a special antipathy toward me as soon as they saw me, suited me very well. I
knew they'd be like two bodyguards. But you have no idea how
much that charged atmosphere began to amuse me. At times I even
forgot the feeling of being continually on my guard. I laughed
there, openly, I was excited and enthusiastic. I'd never had a field
of experimentation like that. . . . Those were the moments when

Román would come over slowly to sit beside me. But when I noticed the heat of his body, an inexplicable rage rose up in me; it was hard to make the effort to hide it. Then, still laughing, I'd move to the other side of the room.

"I was driving him crazy. When he thought I was languid, half overcome by his music, by the almost perverse confidential tone he gave to our conversation, I'd suddenly stand up on the divan.

" 'I feel like jumping!' I'd say to him.

"And I'd begin to do it, almost touching the ceiling with my leaps, the way I do when I play with my brothers. When he heard me giggling, he didn't know if I was crazy or stupid. . . . Not for a moment did I stop watching him out of the corner of my eye. After its first movement of involuntary surprise, his face remained impenetrable, as always. . . . That wasn't what I wanted, Andrea. If you knew how Román made my mother suffer when she was young . . ."

"Who told you the story?"

"Who? . . . Ah! Yes! . . . Papá did. Papá did once when Mamá was sick and talked about Román when she was feverish. . . . The poor man was very moved that night, he thought she was going to die."

(I had to smile to myself. In only a day or two, life seemed different from the way I'd always conceived of it. Complicated and very simple at the same time. I thought that the most painful and jealously guarded secrets are perhaps the ones that everyone around us knows. Stupid tragedies. Useless tears. That's how life began to seem then.)

Ena turned toward me, and I don't know what ideas she saw in my eyes. Suddenly she said:

"But don't think I'm better than I am, Andrea. . . . Don't try to find excuses for me. . . . That wasn't the only reason I wanted to humiliate Román . . . how can I explain what a thrilling game it became for me? . . . It was an increasingly fierce battle. A battle to the death. . . ."

Ena was surely looking at me as she spoke. I thought I could feel her eyes on me the whole time. I could only listen while I stared at the rain, whose fury ebbed and flowed, increasing at certain moments and then almost stopping.

"Listen, Andrea, I couldn't think about Jaime or you or anybody then; I was completely absorbed in this duel between Román's coldness and control of his nerves and my own malice and safety. . . . Andrea, the day I could finally laugh at him, the day I escaped from between his hands when he thought he had firm hold of me, was something splendid. . . ."

Ena was laughing. I turned toward her, a little frightened, and she looked very beautiful, her eyes shining.

"You can't even imagine a scene like the one that ended my relationship with Román last week, Saint John's Eve, to be precise. I remember it very well . . . I escaped . . . just like that, running down the stairs, almost killing myself. . . . I left my bag and gloves in his room, even my hair clips. But Román stayed there, too. . . . I've never seen anything more abject than his face. . . . You want to know if I fell in love with him? . . . With that man?"

I began to look at my friend, seeing her for the first time as she really was. Her eyes were shadowed under the discordant, changeable lights coming from the sky. I felt I could never judge her. I ran my hand along her arm and leaned my head on her shoulder. I was very tired. A multitude of thoughts were becoming clear in my mind.

"This happened on Saint John's Eve?"

"Yes. . . ."

We didn't speak for a while. In that silence, without being able to avoid it, the image of Jaime came to me. It was a case of thought transmission.

"The person I've treated the worst in all of this is Jaime, I know that," said Ena.

Her face was childish again, a little peevish. She looked at me and there was no more defiance or cynicism in her glance.

"Each time I thought about Jaime it was such torment, if you only knew! But I couldn't control the demons that had taken hold of me.... One night I went out with Román and he took me to the Paralelo. I was very tired and bored when we went into a café filled with people and smoke. I thought it was a trick of my imagination when I saw Jaime's eyes looking into mine; he was behind the smoke, behind the heat, and he didn't say hello to me. All he did was look at me.... That night I cried a long time. The next day you brought me a message from him, do you remember?"

"Yes."

"I didn't want anything else but to see Jaime and reconcile with him. I was so moved when we met! Then everything went wrong, I don't know if it was my fault or his. Jaime had promised to be understanding, but in the course of our conversation he became agitated.... Apparently he'd followed me and found out about the life and miracles of Román. He said your uncle was an undesirable involved in the dirtiest kind of smuggling. He explained that business to me.... Finally, he began to make accusations, desperate because I was 'at the mercy of a bandit like him.' . . . It was more than I could stand and the only thing I could think of to do was to begin an impassioned defense of Román. Hasn't that awful thing ever happened to you? You become enmeshed in your own words and then you find you can't get out? . . . Jaime and I were in despair when we separated that day. . . . He left Barcelona, did you know?"

"Yes."

"Maybe he thinks I'll write to him . . . do you think so?"

"Of course."

Ena smiled at me and leaned her head against the stone of the wall. She was tired. . . .

"I've talked so much, haven't I, Andrea? So much . . . aren't you sick of me?"

"You still haven't told me the most important thing. . . . You still haven't told me why, if you broke off with him on Saint John's Eve, you were in my uncle's room today. . . ."

Ena gazed out at the street before she answered. The storm had eased and the sky looked stained and turbulent, its colors yellow and gray. The sewers swallowed up the water that ran along the curbs.

"All right if we leave, Andrea?"

We began to walk aimlessly. Our arms were entwined.

"Today," Ena said, "I risked everything when I went back to Román's room. He wrote me a few lines saying he had some things of mine in his room and wanted to return them to me. . . . I understood he wasn't going to leave me alone so easily. I thought of my mother and had the notion that, like her, I'd spend the rest of my life running away if I didn't make a stand. . . . That was when I had the idea of using what Jaime had learned as a safeguard against Román. With that as my only security, I went there. I was prepared to see him for the last time. . . . Don't think I wasn't afraid. I was terrified when you arrived. Terrified, Andrea, and even regretting my impulse . . . because Román is crazy, I believe he's crazy. . . . When you knocked at the door, I was about to collapse, my nervous tension was so high. . . ."

Ena stopped in the middle of the street to look at me. The street lamps had just gone on and were glistening on the black ground. The washed trees gave off their green fragrance.

"Do you understand, Andrea, do you understand, darling, that I couldn't say anything to you, except to insult you on the stairs? Those moments seemed erased from my existence. When I realized that it was I, Ena, who was alive, I found myself running down Calle de Aribau, looking for you. Finally, when I turned the corner, I found you. You were leaning against the university garden wall, very small and lost under a stormy sky. . . . That's how I saw you."

XXII

Before Ena finally left to spend her vacation at a beach in the north, the three of us, Ena, Jaime, and I, went out again as we had in the better days of spring. I felt changed, however. Each day my head grew weaker and I felt softened, with tears in my eyes over anything. The simple joy of lying under a cloudless sky next to my friends, which seemed perfect to me, escaped at times into a vagueness of imagination similar to dreaming. Blue distances buzzed in my brain with the sound of a blowfly, making me close my eyes. When I opened them, I could see the hot sky through the branches of the carob trees, heavy with the chirping of birds. It was as if I had died centuries before and my entire body, turned to fine dust, was dispersed over oceans and broad mountains, so scattered, light, and vague was the sense I had of my flesh and bones. . . . Sometimes I found Ena's troubled eyes on my face.

"Why are you sleeping so much? I'm afraid you're very weak."

This affectionate concern regarding my life was going to end as well. Ena was supposed to leave in a few days and wouldn't come back to Barcelona after the summer. Her family planned to move directly from San Sebastián to Madrid. I thought that when I began the new term I'd be in the same spiritual solitude as the year before. But now I carried a larger burden of memory on my shoulders. A burden I found somewhat wearing.

On the day I went to say good-bye to Ena, I felt terribly depressed. In the din of the station, Ena appeared surrounded by blond brothers and hurried along by her mother, who seemed possessed by a feverish haste to leave. Ena threw her arms around my neck and kissed me over and over again. I felt my eyes filling with tears. It was cruel. She spoke into my ear:

"We'll see each other very soon, Andrea. Trust me." I thought she meant that she'd return shortly to Barcelona, married to Jaime, perhaps.

When the train pulled out, Ena's father and I were left in the large railroad station. Ena's father, suddenly alone in the city, seemed a little overwhelmed. He invited me to take a cab with him and seemed disconcerted when I said no. He kept looking at me with his kind smile. I thought he was one of those people who didn't know how to be alone with their own thoughts even for a moment. Who might not have any thoughts. Still, I found him extraordinarily likable.

I intended to go back to the house from the station, taking the long way in spite of the humid, oppressive heat that gripped everything. I began walking, walking ... Barcelona had been left infinitely empty. The July heat was awful. I passed the closed, desolate Borne market. The streets were dirty with ripe fruit and straw. Some horses, hitched to their wagons, were kicking. I suddenly thought of Guíxols's studio and went down Calle de Montcada. The majestic courtyard, with its dilapidated carved stone staircase, was the same as always. An overturned wagon held traces of its load of alfalfa.

"Nobody's there, Señorita," the concierge told me. "Señor Guíxols is away. Nobody comes anymore, not even Señor Iturdiaga— he went to Sitges last week. Señor Pons isn't in Barcelona, either. ... But I can give you the key, if you want to go up; Señor Guíxols gave me permission to give it to any of you. ..."

It hadn't been my intention when I went there, following the thread of my memories, to go into the studio, which I already knew was closed. And yet I accepted her offer. It suddenly seemed like an attractive prospect, being protected for a while by the empty peace of the house, the coolness of its ancient walls. The enclosed air still had a faint smell of varnish. Behind the door where Guíxols usually kept his provisions I found a forgotten bar of chocolate. The paintings were carefully covered with white cloths and seemed like specters wrapped in shrouds. Souls of the memory of a thousand happy conversations.

I reached Calle de Aribau when it was already growing dark. When I left the studio I had resumed my long, discouraging trek through the city.

When I went into my room, I found the hot smell of closed windows and tears. I made out the shape of Gloria, lying on my bed and crying. When she realized that someone was coming in, she turned over in a fury. Then she became calmer when she saw who it was.

"I was sleeping a little, Andrea," she said.

I saw that the light could not be turned on because someone had taken the lightbulb. I don't know what moved me to sit on the edge of the bed and take Gloria's hand, wet with perspiration or with tears, between mine.

"Why are you crying, Gloria? Do you think I don't know you're crying?"

Since I was sad that day, the sadness of other people didn't seem offensive to me.

At first she didn't answer. After a while she murmured:

"I'm scared, Andrea!"

"But why, Gloria?"

"Before you never asked anybody anything, Andrea. . . . You're nicer now. I'd really like to tell you what I'm scared of, but I can't."

There was a pause.

"I wouldn't want Juan to know I've been crying. I'll say I fell asleep if he notices that my eyes are puffy."

———

That night, I don't know what bitter throbbing was in things, like evil omens. I couldn't sleep, which happened to me frequently during that time, when weariness tormented me. Before I decided to close my eyes, I groped clumsily around the marble top of the night table and found a piece of bread from the day before. I ate it eagerly. My poor grandmother rarely forgot to leave her little gifts. At last, when sleep finally took possession of me, it was like a coma, almost like an antechamber to final death. My exhaustion was terrible. I think someone had been screaming for a long time before the awful screams managed to penetrate my ears. Perhaps it was only a matter of a few seconds. But I remember that they had formed part of my dreams before they forced me to return to reality. I'd never heard that kind of screaming in the house on Calle de Aribau. It was the lugubrious shriek of a maddened animal, and it made me sit up in the bed and then jump out of it, trembling.

I found the maid, Antonia, on the floor of the foyer, her legs spread in a tragic kick, revealing her dark inner places, and her hands clutching at the tiles. The street door was wide open and the curious faces of neighbors were beginning to look in. At first I had only a comic vision of the scene, I was so bewildered.

Juan, who had come in half dressed, kicked the street door so it would slam in their faces. Then he began to slap the woman's distorted face and asked Gloria for a pitcher of cold water to throw on her. At last the maid began to pant and gulp more freely, like a defeated animal. But immediately, as if this had been only a truce, she returned to dreadful screams.

"He's dead! He's dead! He's dead!"

And she pointed upward.

I saw Juan's face turn gray.

"Who? Who's dead, you stupid woman . . . ?"

Then, without waiting for her to answer, he ran to the door, racing like a madman up the stairs.

"He slit his throat with his razor," Antonia concluded.

And finally she started to cry in despair. It was rare to see tears on her face. She looked like a figure in a nightmare.

"He told me to bring him up coffee early, he was leaving on a trip.... He told me early this morning!... And now he's lying on the floor, bleeding like an animal. Ah! Oh! Trueno, my dear child, you've lost your father...."

All over the house you could hear something like the sound of rain getting heavier. Then shouts, warnings. We were paralyzed, but through the open door we could see people from the other apartments going up to Román's room.

"You have to tell the police," shouted the stout medical practitioner on the third floor, coming down the stairs in a state of great excitement.

The women in our house huddled together stupidly, trembling; we heard him but didn't dare react to these incredible events. Antonia was still screaming, and hers was the only voice heard from the strange, compact group formed by her, Gloria, my grandmother, and me.

At a certain moment I felt my blood begin to flow again, and I went to close the door. When I returned I saw my grandmother making her presence real to me for the first time. She seemed shrunken, weighed down by the black veil that she undoubtedly had put on to go to her daily Mass. She was shaking.

"He didn't commit suicide, Andrea . . . he repented before he died," she said childishly.

"Yes, darling, yes . . ."

My affirmation didn't console her. Her lips were blue. She stammered when she spoke. Her wet eyes wouldn't let her tears flow openly.

"I want to go upstairs . . . I want to be with my Román."

I thought the best thing was to humor her. I opened the door and helped her, step by step, up the staircase I knew so well. I didn't even realize I wasn't dressed and that only a robe covered my nightgown. I don't know where the people came from who crowded the stairs. At the entrance you could hear the voices of police officers trying to contain that avalanche. They let us pass, staring at us. I felt my head clear for moments at a time. At each step I felt a new wave of anguished fear and repugnance. My knees began their nervous dance, making it difficult for me to walk. Juan was coming down, desolate, yellow. Suddenly he saw us and stopped in front of us.

"Mamá! Damn it!"—I don't know why the image of my grandmother unleashed his rage. He shouted at her in a fury: "Back home this instant!"

He raised his fist as if he were going to hit her and the people began muttering. My grandmother wasn't crying, but her chin trembled in a childish pout.

"He's my son! He's my boy! . . . I have the right to go up! I have to see him. . . ."

Juan became quiet. His eyes looked around, scrutinizing the faces watching him eagerly. He seemed indecisive for a moment. At last, brusquely, he gave in.

"You, niece, downstairs! You haven't lost anything!" he said.

Then he put his arm around his mother's waist and, almost dragging her, helped her go up. I heard my grandmother begin to cry, leaning on her son's shoulder.

When I went into our apartment I found that a crowd of people had come in, too, and spread out, invading every corner and prying into everything with sympathetic murmurs.

Making my way through those people, pushing past some of them, I managed to reach the isolated corner of the bathroom. I took refuge there, and locked the door.

Mechanically, not knowing how, I found myself in the dirty tub, naked as I was every day, ready to receive the water from the shower. I saw myself reflected in the mirror, miserably skinny, my teeth chattering as if I were dying of the cold. The truth is it was all so horrible that it surpassed my capacity for tragedy. I turned on the shower and I think I began to laugh nervously when I found myself like that, as if it were a day like any other. A day when nothing had happened. *I believe I'm hysterical,* I thought, as the water fell, pounding me and refreshing me. The drops slid along my shoulders and chest, formed canals on my belly, ran down my legs. Román was lying upstairs, bloody, his face broken in two by the grimace of those who are damned when they die. The shower continued to fall on me in cool, inexhaustible cataracts. I heard the human noise growing louder on the other side of the door; I felt as if I would never move from there. I seemed imbecilic.

Then they began to bang on the bathroom door.

XXIII

The days that followed were submerged in the most intense darkness because someone immediately closed all the balconies, almost nailing them shut. Almost preventing even a breath of outside air from coming in. A heavy, ill-smelling heat enveloped everything, and I lost my sense of time. Hours or days were all the same. Days or nights seemed identical. Gloria got sick and nobody paid attention to her. I sat beside her and saw that her fever was very high.

"Have they taken that man away yet?" she asked constantly.

I brought her water. It seemed she'd never grow tired of drinking. Sometimes Antonia came in and looked at her with an expression so full of hate that I preferred to spend all the time I could with Gloria.

"She won't die, the witch! She won't die, the murderer!" Antonia would say.

From the maid I also learned the details of the end of Román's life. Details I heard as if through a mist. (It seemed to me that I was losing my ability to see clearly. That the outlines of things were disappearing.)

Apparently, on the night before his death, Román had called Antonia on the phone, saying he'd just come back from his trip—Román had been away—and that he needed to leave again first thing in the morning. "Come up and help me pack and bring me all the clean clothes I have; I'll be away for a long time...." These, according to Antonia, had been Román's last words. The idea of cutting his throat must have been a sudden impulse, a rapid fit of madness that attacked him while he was shaving. His cheeks were covered with lather when Antonia found him.

Gloria montonously asked for details about Román.

"And the paintings? Didn't they find the paintings?"

"What paintings, Gloria?" I bent over her with a gesture that my weariness made languid.

"The picture of me that Román painted. My picture with the purple lilies..."

"I don't know. I don't know anything. I can't find out anything."

When Gloria felt better she said to me:

"I wasn't in love with Román, Andrea.... *Chica,* I see everything you think in your face. You think I didn't despise Román...."

The truth is I didn't think anything. My mind was too exhausted. With Gloria's hands in mine, and listening to her conversation, I forgot about her.

"I was the one who made Román kill himself. I denounced him to the police and that's why he committed suicide.... They were supposed to come for him that morning...."

I didn't believe anything Gloria told me. It was more believable to imagine that Román had been the ghost of a dead man. A man who had died years earlier and now had finally returned to his hell.... Remembering his music, that despairing music I liked hearing so much and that in the end gave me an exact impression of extinction, of disappearing into death, I sometimes felt moved.

My grandmother came to me from time to time, her eyes opened wide, to whisper I don't know what mysterious consolations. Illuminated by a faith that could not weaken, she prayed constantly, convinced that at the final instant divine grace had touched the sick heart of her son.

"The Virgin told me so, my child. Last night she came to me in a halo of heavenly grace and she told me. . . ."

The mental disturbance evident in her words seemed comforting to me, and I caressed her and agreed.

Juan was out of the house for a long time, possibly more than two days. He had to accompany Román's body to the mortuary and perhaps, later, to its final, remote resting place.

When one day, or one night, I finally saw him at home, I thought we'd gone through the worst times. But we hadn't yet heard him cry. Never, no matter how many years I live, will I forget his desperate sobbing. I understood that Román was right when he said Juan belonged to him. Now that he had died, Juan's grief was unashamed, maddening, like that of a woman for her lover, like that of a young mother at the death of her first child.

I don't know how many hours I went without sleeping, my eyes open and very dry, collecting all the griefs that swarmed, as alive as worms, in the entrails of the house. When at last I fell into bed, I don't know how many hours I was asleep. But I slept as I'd never slept in my life. As if I, too, were going to close my eyes forever.

When I realized again that I was alive, I had the feeling I'd just climbed up from the bottom of a very deep well and had retained the cavernous sense of echoes in the darkness.

My room was in half-light. The house was so silent it gave me a strange, sepulchral sensation. It was a kind of silence I'd never heard on Calle de Aribau.

When I fell asleep I recalled the house filled with people and voices. Now it seemed as if no one was there. It seemed as if all its inhabitants had abandoned it. I looked into the kitchen and saw two bubbling stew pots sitting on the fire. The tiles looked swept and there was a slow, soft, homey tranquillity that seemed incongruous there. In the back, in the gallery, Gloria, dressed in black, was washing a child's outfit. My eyes were puffy and I had a headache. She smiled at me.

"Do you know how long you slept, Andrea?" she said, coming toward me. "You slept two whole days." Then she asked me: "Aren't you hungry?"

She filled a glass with milk and gave it to me. The warm milk seemed wonderful, and I drank it greedily.

"Antonia left this morning with Trueno," Gloria announced.

"Ah!"

That explained her tranquil presence in the kitchen.

"She left before dawn this morning, while Juan was sleeping. Juan didn't want to let her take the dog, *chica*. And you know that Trueno was her love. . . . The two of them ran away together."

Gloria gave a silly laugh and then she winked at me.

"Your aunts arrived last night. . . ." Now she was making fun of me.

"Angustias?" I asked.

"No, the other ones—you don't know them. The two who are married, with their husbands. They want to see you, but get dressed first, *chica*, that's my advice."

I had to put on my only summer dress, badly tinted black and smelling of home dye. Then I reluctantly went to the back of the house, where that bedroom was located. I could hear a murmur of voices before I went in, as if they were praying there.

I stopped in the doorway, because everything hurt my eyes then: light and shadow. The room was almost dark and smelled of cloth flowers. Large shapes of well-fed humanity stood out in the darkness, giving off bodily odors squeezed out by the summer. I heard a woman's voice:

"You spoiled him. Remember how you spoiled him, Mamá. This was the result. . . ."

"You were always unfair, Mamá. You always preferred your boys. Do you realize you're to blame for this?"

"You never loved us girls, Mamá. You looked down on us. You humiliated us. We always heard you complaining about your daughters, but they haven't done anything but please you; this, this is how your sons pay you back, the sons you spoiled. . . ."

"Señora, you'll have a lot to answer for to God because of that soul you've sent to hell."

I couldn't believe my ears. And I couldn't believe the strange sights before my eyes. Gradually the faces were being outlined, hooked or flattened, like one of Goya's Caprices. These people in mourning seemed to be celebrating a strange witches' sabbath.

"Children, I loved all of you!"

I couldn't see the old woman from there, but I imagined her sunk in her wretched armchair. There was a long silence and at last I heard another tremulous sigh.

"Oh, Lord!"

"You just have to look at the poverty in this house. They've robbed you, they've stripped you bare, and you're blind to whatever they do. You never wanted to help us when we asked you to. Now we've been cheated out of our inheritance. . . . And if that wasn't enough, a suicide in the family . . ."

"I helped the ones who were more unfortunate. . . . The ones who needed me more."

"And by doing that you've sunk them deeper into poverty. But don't you realize the result? If at least they'd been happy, even if we girls were robbed; but now you see, what's happened here proves we're right!"

"And that miserable Juan who's listening to us: married to a slut, not knowing how to do anything useful, starving to death!"

(I was looking at Juan. Hoping for one of Juan's rages. He seemed not to hear. He looked past the windowpanes at the strip of light on the street.)

"Juan, my child," said my grandmother. "Tell me if they're right. Tell me if you believe it's true. . . ."

Juan turned around, crazed.

"Yes, Mamá, they're right. . . . Damn you! And damn all of them!"

Then the entire room stirred with a flapping of wings, with croaking. Hysterical shrieks.

XXIV

I remember that I didn't really believe in the physical fact of Román's death until much later. Until the summer was turning gold and red in September, it seemed to me that upstairs, in his room, Román still had to be lying down, smoking cigarettes without stopping, or caressing the ears of Trueno, the sleek black dog the maid had carried off like a lover running away with his beloved.

Sometimes, when I was sitting on the floor in my room, hot like the rest of the house, half dressed in order to catch any bit of coolness, and listening to the creaking wood, creaking as if the light that turned red in the cracks of the windows was sizzling as it burned . . . On anguished afternoons like that, I began to remember Román's violin and its warm moan. If I looked in the mirror in front of me, that parade of forms reflected there . . . the brown-colored chairs, the greenish-gray paper on the walls, a monstrous corner of the bed, a part of my own body sitting in the Moorish manner on the tile floor under that symphony and oppressed by the heat . . . At these times I began to suspect from which corners he had transposed his music to the violin. And I no longer thought the man was so bad when he knew how to capture his own sobs and compress them into a beauty as dense as old gold.... Then I was overcome by nostalgia for Román, a desire for his presence that I'd never felt when he was alive. An awful yearning for his hands on the violin or the stained keys of the old piano.

One day I went upstairs to the little room in the garret. One day when I couldn't stand the weight of this feeling, I saw that everything had been stripped, miserably. The books and shelves had disappeared. The divan, without its mattress, was leaning upright against the wall, its feet in the air. Not a single charming trinket, of all those Román had kept there, had survived him. The violin cupboard was open and empty. The heat was unbearable. The small window that opened to the flat roof let in a stream of fiery sun. It became too strange not to hear the crystalline tick-tock tick-tock of the clocks....

Then I knew, beyond any doubt, that Román had died and that his body was decomposing and rotting somewhere, under the sun that was mercilessly punishing his former lair, so wretched now, its former soul dismantled.

Then the nightmares began that my weakness made constant and horrifying. I began to think about Román wrapped in his shroud, those nervous hands that knew how to catch the harmony and physicality of things destroyed. Those hands that life made hard and flexible at the same time, their color dark and yellowish because of tobacco stains, could say so much simply by moving upward. They knew how to express the precise eloquence of a moment. Those skilled hands—the hands of a thief, curious and greedy—appeared to me at first as crudely puffy, soft, swollen. Then, transformed into two clusters of fleshless bones.

These horrifying visions pursued me that late summer with monotonous cruelty. During the suffocating twilights, the long nights heavy with languid weight, my terrified heart received images that my reason was not strong enough to banish.

To drive away the ghosts, I went out a great deal. I wandered the city, uselessly wearing myself out. I wore my black dress that the dye had shrunk and that kept getting bigger on me. I wandered instinctively, embarrassed by my shabby clothing, avoiding the expensive, well-tended neighborhoods in the city. I came to know the suburbs with their sadness of poorly made, dusty things. The old streets attracted me more.

One twilight near the Cathedral I heard the slow tolling of a bell that made the city older. I looked up at the sky, turning a softer, bluer color with the first stars, and I had an impression of almost mystical beauty. A desire to die there, off to the side, looking up, under the great sweetness of the night that was beginning to fall. And my chest ached with hunger and unconfessable desires when I breathed. It was as if I were smelling the scent of death and finding it good for the first time, after it had caused terror in me. . . . When a strong wind began to blow, I was still there, leaning against a wall, benumbed and half ecstatic. From the old balcony of a dilapidated house a sheet appeared, and when it was shaken it took me out of my daze. My head wasn't right that day. The white cloth seemed like a huge shroud to me, and I started to run. . . . I was half crazed when I reached the house on Calle de Aribau.

This was how I began to sense the presence of death in the house when almost two months had passed since the tragedy.

At first life had seemed completely unchanged. The same shouts threw everything into an uproar. Juan kept hitting Gloria. Perhaps now he was in the habit of hitting her for any reason at all and maybe his brutality had intensified. . . . The difference, however, was not very great in my eyes. The heat was suffocating all of us, and yet my grandmother, growing more and more wrinkled, trembled with cold. But there wasn't much difference between this grandmother and the earlier one. She didn't even seem sadder. I still received her smile and her gifts, and on the mornings when Gloria called to the *drapaire,* she went on praying to the Virgin in her bedroom.

I remember that one day Gloria sold the piano. The sale was more lucrative than the ones she usually made and my nostrils soon noted that she allowed herself the luxury that day of putting meat in the food. Now that Antonia wasn't there to pry into the stews and make them filthy by her mere presence, Gloria seemed to be trying to improve things.

I was dressing to go out when I heard a great disturbance in the kitchen. In a rage, Juan was throwing all the stew pots that only a moment ago had aroused my gluttony, and kicking Gloria, who was writhing on the floor.

"You wretch! You sold Román's piano! Román's piano, you wretch! You filthy sow!"

My grandmother was trembling, as usual, holding the baby's face against her so he wouldn't see his father like that.

Juan's mouth was foaming and his eyes were the kind you tend to see only in madhouses. When he grew tired of kicking, he raised his hands to his chest, like a person who's choking, and then he was possessed again by irrational fury with the pine chairs, the table, the pots and pans. . . . Gloria, half dead, got away, and we all walked out, leaving him alone with his shouting. When he calmed down—according to what I was told—he sat holding his head, crying silently.

The next day Gloria came slowly into my room, whispering as she talked to me about bringing in a doctor and putting Juan in an asylum.

"I think that's good," I said (but I was sure the idea would never go beyond being a plan).

She was sitting at one end of the room. She looked at me and said:

"Andrea, you don't know how frightened I am."

Her face was as inexpressive as always, but tears of terror filled her eyes.

"I don't deserve this, Andrea, because I'm a very good girl. . . ."

She was quiet for a moment and seemed lost in thought. She went over to the mirror.

"And pretty . . . Aren't I pretty?"

Forgetting her anguish, she touched her body with a certain complacency. She turned to me.

"Are you laughing?"

She sighed. She immediately became frightened again.

"No woman would suffer what I suffer, Andrea. . . . Since Román's death, Juan doesn't want me to sleep. He says I'm an animal that doesn't do anything but sleep, while his brother howls with sorrow. Said just like that, *chica*, it's funny. . . . But if it's said to you at midnight, in bed! . . . No, Andrea, it isn't funny to wake up half strangled, with a man's hands around your neck. He says I'm a pig, that all I do is sleep day and night. How can I not sleep during the day if I can't sleep at night? . . . I come back from my sister's house very late and sometimes I find him waiting for me in the street. One day he showed me a big razor that he said he carried so if I was half an hour late he could slit my throat. . . . You think he wouldn't dare to do it, but with a crazy man, who knows! . . . He says Román comes to him every night and tells him to kill me. . . . What would you do, Andrea? You'd run away, wouldn't you?"

She didn't wait for me to answer.

"And how can you run away when he has a razor and legs to follow you to the ends of the earth? Oh, *chica*, you don't know what it means to be scared! . . . To go to bed when it's almost dawn, your whole body exhausted, the way I go to bed, beside a man who's crazy. . . .

"I'm in bed, waiting for the moment when he falls asleep to let my head sink into the pillow and finally get some rest. And I see that he never sleeps. I feel his open eyes beside me. He throws off all the covers and lies on his back, his big ribs heaving. Every minute he asks: 'Are you asleep?'

"And I have to talk to him so he'll calm down. Finally I can't stand it anymore, sleep comes in like a black sorrow behind my eyes and I let go, exhausted. . . . Right away I feel his breathing close to me, his body touching mine. And I have to be alert, sweating with fear, because his hands move very softly around my neck and then they move around again. . . .

"And if he was always bad, *chica,* I could hate him and it would be better. But sometimes he caresses me, begs my pardon, and begins to cry like a little boy. . . . And what can I do? I start to cry, too, and I feel regret, too . . . because we all have our regrets, even me, believe me. . . . And I caress him, too. . . . Then, in the morning, if I remind him of those moments, he wants to kill me. . . . Look!"

She quickly took off her blouse and showed me a large, bloody welt on her back.

I was looking at the terrible scar when we realized there was another person in the room. When I turned around I saw my grandmother angrily shaking her wrinkled head.

Ah, my grandmother's anger. The only anger I remember seeing in her. . . . She was holding a letter that had just been handed to her. And she shook it indignantly.

"You're both bad! Bad!" she said. "What are you two plotting there, you little villains? An asylum! . . . For a good man, who dresses and feeds his son and walks him at night so his wife can sleep! . . . You're crazy! The two of you and I will be locked up together before they touch a hair on his head!"

With a vengeful gesture, she threw the letter to the floor and left, shaking her head, whining and talking to herself.

The letter on the floor was for me. Ena had written to me from Madrid. It would change the direction of my life.

XXV

I finished packing my suitcase and tied it tightly with the cord to secure the broken locks. I was tired. Gloria told me that supper was on the table. She had invited me to eat with them on that last night. That morning she had leaned toward my ear:

"I sold all the mirrors with candelabra. I didn't know they'd pay so much money for that old, ugly junk, *chica.* . . ."

That night there was an abundance of bread. And white fish. Juan seemed to be in a good mood. The baby prattled in his high chair, and I realized to my amazement that he had grown a great deal during the year. The familiar lamp was reflected in the dark windowpanes to the balcony. My grandmother said:

"Naughty girl! Be sure you come back soon to see us. . . ."

Gloria placed her small hand over mine, resting on the tablecloth.

"Yes, come back soon, Andrea—you know I love you. . . ."

Juan intervened:

"Don't pester Andrea. She's doing the right thing, leaving. At last she has an opportunity to work and do something. . . . So far you can't say she hasn't been lazy."

We finished supper. I didn't know what to say to them. Gloria piled up the dirty dishes in the sink and then went to put on lipstick, and her coat.

"All right, give me a hug, *chica,* in case I don't see you. . . . Because you're leaving very early, aren't you?"

"At seven."

I embraced her and, strangely, I felt that I loved her. Then I watched her go out.

Juan was in the middle of the foyer, not saying a word, without my struggles to place the suitcase next to the street door. I wanted to make the least noise and cause the least bother possible when I left. My uncle put his hand on my shoulder with an awkward amiability and looked at me like that, separated by the length of his arm.

"Well, niece, I hope things go well for you. In any case, you'll see how living in a house of strangers isn't the same as being with your family, but it's a good idea for you to have your eyes opened. For you to learn what life is like. . . ."

I went into Angustias's room for the last time. It was hot and the window was open; the familiar reflection of the streetlight extended over the floor tiles in sad, yellowish streams.

I didn't want to think anymore about what surrounded me, and I got into bed. Ena's letter had opened up for me, and this time in a real way, the horizons of my salvation.

. . . There's work for you in my father's office, Andrea. It will allow you to live independently and attend classes at the university as well. For the moment you'll live here, but later you can choose your own place, since it's not a question of keeping you sequestered. Mamá is having a very good time getting your room ready. I can't sleep I'm so happy.

It was a very long letter in which she told me about all her concerns and hopes. She told me Jaime was also coming to live in Madrid that winter. He'd finally decided to finish his studies, and after that they'd be married.

I couldn't sleep. I found it idiotic to be feeling the same eager expectation that a year earlier had made me jump out of bed in the village every half hour, afraid I'd miss the six o'clock train, but I couldn't help it. I didn't have the same illusions now, but the departure moved me as if it were a liberation. Ena's father, who had come to Barcelona for a few days, would pick me up the next morning and I'd go back to Madrid with him. We'd travel in his car.

I was already dressed when the driver knocked discreetly at the door. The entire house seemed silent and asleep in the grayish light coming in through the balconies. I didn't have the courage to peer into my grandmother's room. I didn't want to wake her.

I went down the stairs slowly. I felt a strong emotion. I remembered the terrible expectation, the longing for life, when I had climbed them for the first time. I was leaving now without having known any of the things I had confusedly hoped for: life in its plenitude, joy, deep interests, love. I was taking nothing from the house on Calle de Aribau. At least, that's what I thought then.

Standing beside the long black car, Ena's father was waiting for me. He extended his hands in cordial welcome. He turned to the driver to give him some instruction or other. Then he said to me:

"We'll eat lunch in Zaragoza, but first we'll have a good breakfast." He smiled broadly. "You'll enjoy the trip, Andrea. You'll see. . . ."

The morning air was stimulating. The ground seemed damp with night dew. Before I climbed into the car, I looked up at the house where I had lived for a year. The first rays of the sun were hitting its windows. A few moments later, Calle de Aribau and all of Barcelona were behind me.

ABOUT THE AUTHOR

Born in Barcelona and raised in the Canary Islands,
CARMEN LAFORET (1921–2004) had a profound impact on Spanish literature. Her debut novel, *Nada*, was
awarded the first Premio Nadal in 1944. She is also the
author of a collection of short stories and five other
novels, including *Al doblar la esquina* (Around the Block)
and *La mujer nueva* (The New Woman), which won the
National Prize for Literature in 1955.

A NOTE ON THE TYPE

The principal text of this Modern Library edition
was set in a digitized version of Janson, a typeface that
dates from about 1690 and was cut by Nicholas Kis,
a Hungarian working in Amsterdam. The original matrices have
survived and are held by the Stempel foundry in Germany.
Hermann Zapf redesigned some of the weights and sizes for
Stempel, basing his revisions on the original design.